Spring Offensive

Allison & Busby Limited
11 Wardour Mews
London W1F 8AN
allisonandbusby.com

First published in Great Britain by Allison & Busby in 2024.

Copyright © 2024 by Edward Marston

First Edition

ISBN 978-0-7490-3165-7

Typeset in 12/17 pt Adobe Garamond Pro by
Allison & Busby Ltd.

By choosing this product, you help take care of the world's forests.
Learn more: www.fsc.org.

Printed and bound by
CPI Group (UK) Ltd, Croydon, CR0 4YY

a&b

Spring Offensive

Edward Marston

CHAPTER ONE

March, 1918

Summoned to the commissioner's office, Superintendent Claude Chatfield knew that something serious had happened. After hurrying along the corridor, he knocked on the door and opened it to find that Sir Edward Henry was looking at some notes he had jotted down on a pad. His face was ashen.

'Bad news, Sir Edward?' he asked.

'No,' replied the other. 'It's disastrous news. I've just spoken to someone at the War Office. The German offensive has finally happened.'

'It has been expected.'

'Yes, but not on this scale.' He read from his notepad. 'A million shells have been fired at British lines on the Western Front. The Fifth Army has sustained horrendous losses. Thousands of British soldiers have been killed or wounded and, humiliatingly, twenty thousand have been taken prisoner.'

'How on earth has that happened?' asked Chatfield in alarm.

'German stormtrooper units have moved at speed and made significant advances. General Ludendorff must be rubbing his hands with glee.'

'This is grim news indeed.'

'He's a cunning old devil,' said the commissioner, putting the notepad down on his desk. 'Instead of one attack, he launched four.'

Sir Edward was a slim, wiry man in his sixties with a small moustache. As usual, he was wearing an impeccably tailored three-piece suit. Chatfield, by contrast, was younger, clean-shaven and hollow-cheeked. His neatly barbered hair sported a centre parting.

'They've changed their tactics,' Chatfield observed. 'Until now, trench warfare has been the order of the day. Armies have been largely stationary – not any more. The Germans have obviously deployed their stormtroopers with deadly effect. The units move quickly and strike when least expected.'

'If only our reinforcements had arrived from America!'

'They may come too late, Sir Edward.'

'Don't let us be pessimistic,' said the other, pulling himself up to his full height. 'Remember that we have a brave army with equally brave Allies. I still believe in ultimate victory.'

'And so do I.'

'Let's put the war to one side for a moment, shall we?' suggested the commissioner. 'Let's consider our own situation. We, too, have suffered losses, albeit on a much smaller scale. Thousands of our officers have resigned to join the army, so we have a depleted force left behind. Every man we have is vital.' He remembered someone. 'What's the news about Detective Sergeant Keedy? Has he been released from hospital yet?'

'He's due to leave any day – once the problem has been resolved.'

'Problem?'

'It's not clear where he should go, Sir Edward. If it was up to Keedy, he would come straight back to Scotland Yard to resume his duties. But that is impossible. He needs a period of rest.

During the siege in which we were involved, he was shot in the stomach from short range. The damage was extensive. The wounds will take time to heal. He must be cared for.'

'That shouldn't be problematic, should it?'

'It shouldn't,' said Chatfield, wearily, 'but it is.'

'Really?'

'There's been an unholy row about where he will convalesce.'

'That's the last thing he needs.'

'I agree, Sir Edward.'

'Then why are they wasting time arguing about it?'

'I've no idea,' said Chatfield. 'For some reason, the bickering goes on. They are still unable to reach a decision acceptable to all parties.'

There were three of them in the room at the hospital. Joe Keedy, wearing pyjamas, dressing gown and slippers, was sitting in a chair. Alice Marmion, his fiancée, was seated beside him, one hand on his arm. Having come straight from work, she was wearing the uniform of the Women's Police Force. Standing in front of them was Keedy's elder brother, Dennis, a tall, well-built, impressive man in a thick black overcoat. He spoke quietly but firmly.

'We must bring this argument to an end,' he declared. 'There is only one option open to you, Joe, and that is to return to the family home to be looked after by Mother and Father.'

'That's out of the question,' said Keedy, dismissively.

'Our parents would take good care of you.'

'It's kind of them to offer, Dennis, but I'm staying here in London.'

'Did Mother's entreaties mean nothing to you?'

'Of course, they did,' replied Keedy. 'I was touched that they

9

made the effort to come and see me. But I could never go back home. Apart from anything else, they'd try to persuade me to leave a job that I love.'

'Joe is very proud to be part of the Metropolitan Police Force,' said Alice.

'He should be equally proud of working with me in the family business,' argued Dennis. 'Being a funeral director is a responsible job. I still don't understand why you turned your back on a career alongside me, Joe.'

'I wanted excitement, Dennis,' said Keedy.

'Getting yourself shot is not my idea of excitement.'

'That's unfair,' said Alice, hotly. 'It was brave of Joe to go into that house during the siege.'

'Brave but foolish.'

'I'm not complaining about what happened,' said Keedy, stoutly.

'Well, I am,' said Dennis, raising his voice. 'I'd prefer a live brother to a dead hero.'

Before he could speak, Keedy felt a warning squeeze on his arm. Alice was trying to calm him down because she believed that nothing could be achieved by a pointless argument with his brother. Eager to be involved in Keedy's convalescence, she could not do that if he went back to the family home in Nottingham. His injury had reminded them of the dangers he faced, and it had persuaded them to bring the date of their wedding forward. It was now a matter of weeks away rather than months before they were married. Alice was keen to nurse him in readiness for the event.

'There is simply no alternative,' said Dennis, reasonably.

'Yes, there is,' she claimed. 'Joe could move in with my parents. My mother would be there to look after him during the day and I would pop in regularly when I was not on duty.'

'Think of how it would look, Alice.'

'I don't give a damn how it looks,' said Keedy. 'People should mind their own business.'

'What about the vicar?'

'It's nothing to do with him, Dennis.'

'Have you told him that you'd be under the same roof as Alice?'

'Well, no . . .'

'I live on the other side of London,' she pointed out, 'and I'll be spending most nights at my flat. I'd only sleep at home now and then.'

'I still think it would be unwise,' said Dennis. 'And I know that our vicar in Nottingham would disapprove strongly.'

'Thank God he's not going to marry us then!' retorted Keedy.

'It's your duty to come back home, Joe.'

'I'm staying here in London.'

'Try it for a week. That's all I ask.'

'I've made my decision, Dennis, and I'm sticking to it.'

'Can't we at least find a compromise?' asked his brother. 'I came all this way to plead with you, Joe. Don't send me back home with upsetting news for our parents. It will hurt them terribly.'

'I'm sorry but it can't be helped. I need to stay here.'

'I agree,' said Alice.

After glaring at each of them in turn, Dennis grabbed his hat off the table and stalked out of the room, leaving the door wide open. Alice got up to close the door.

Keedy grinned. 'I think we deserve a kiss.'

CHAPTER TWO

The fire started in the dead of night. It ate hungrily through the interior of the empty shop then spread to the houses either side of it. Terrified occupants leapt from their beds and ran out into the street. They hammered on the doors of neighbouring houses to wake people up. Panic spread quickly. The noise brought even more people dashing out through their front doors, horrified to see the flames. There was pandemonium. It was not long before the deafening clang of fire engines filled the air. Nobody heard the burglar alarm that was ringing away in a road nearby.

Two uniformed policemen were walking side by side on their beat when they became aware of the commotion. Breaking into a run, they turned a corner and saw two men in the gloom, leaving a bank at speed. The policemen tackled the robbers and tried to arrest them, but they came off worst. One of them was stabbed and the other was clubbed viciously to the ground. The bank robbers jumped into a waiting car and were whisked off at speed. The policemen lay on the pavement in pools of their own blood.

* * *

Harvey Marmion was summoned by the insistent ring of the telephone. Sensing an emergency, he scrambled out of bed and tried to wipe the sleep out of his eyes as he padded downstairs. When he picked up the receiver, he heard the voice of Claude Chatfield barking at him.

'There's a police car on the way to pick you up,' he said.

'Where am I going?' asked Marmion.

'It's somewhere near Paddington Station. I'll meet you there.'

'What's happened, sir?'

'There's been a bank robbery. Two policemen were on duty nearby and sought to arrest the burglars. One of our officers was stabbed to death and the other is still in a coma.'

'What were their names?'

'Does it matter?'

'It matters a great deal to me,' said Marmion with concern. 'Sam Collard has a beat near Paddington Station, and I know for a fact that he's working nights. He's a close friend of mine.'

'Then I've got bad news for you, Inspector. I'm afraid that Collard was the murder victim.'

The phone went dead. Marmion was too stunned to replace the receiver.

Prompt action by the fire brigade meant that the blaze at the houses either side of the empty shop was quickly brought under control. No other premises were affected. The families who had been forced to flee their homes were allowed back inside them, only to discover that the arrival of the fire engines had been a mixed blessing. In dousing the fire, the water had caused a lot of damage to their properties, smashing windows, soaking their walls, and drenching their furniture. Neighbours were quick to offer them help. When the flames were finally under control, the fire brigade started to clear up the mess in the empty shop, trying to work out how the fire had started in the first place.

Preoccupied with their own crises, nobody in the street realised that a murder had taken place less than a hundred yards away.

When the police car took him to the scene of the crime, Marmion found that Claude Chatfield was already there. The superintendent was trying to calm down the bank manager, Douglas Boucher, a short, red-faced, pompous individual with piggy eyes. Marmion was introduced to Boucher, but he was more interested in the fate of his friend.

'What happened to Sam Collard?' he asked.

'An ambulance took the body off to the nearest hospital,' said Chatfield. 'Constable Lee was also taken. Collard was pronounced dead at the scene. Lee is in a coma but is expected to recover.'

'I'd like to take on the job of speaking to Collard's wife,' volunteered Marmion. 'It's dreadful news to pass on, but I feel that it's my duty.'

'I understand,' said Chatfield. 'You are obviously the best person for the task.'

'What about my bank?' wailed Boucher. 'That's the major crime here.'

'I disagree, sir.'

'So do I,' added Marmion. 'One police officer was killed, and another was wounded. And they met their fates when they were trying to arrest some men who robbed your bank. You should be grateful that they acted so bravely.'

'Well, yes,' said Boucher, 'I admire their courage, of course, but the fact remains that a substantial amount of money was stolen. I was fast asleep when the news was brought to me. Imagine how I felt when I got here and realised what had happened.'

Chatfield was blunt. 'Inspector Marmion and I were also dragged out of our beds in the middle of the night, sir,' he said. 'So don't expect sympathy from us on that account. You should be trying to work out exactly what did occur here.'

'Isn't it obvious? The bank has been robbed.'

'Yet, when you arrived, there was no burglar alarm ringing.'

'No,' said Boucher. 'It had been switched off.'

'How did the robbers manage to do that?' asked Marmion. 'Burglar alarms, for obvious reasons, are usually very difficult to tamper with. When they entered the premises, it would have gone off immediately. How on earth did they silence it?'

'It's a question that only the people who installed the system could answer,' said Boucher. 'I'll contact them as soon as their office opens.'

Marmion shook his head. 'I doubt if the alarm was at fault, sir,' he said. 'May I ask if any of your employees have left the bank recently?'

Boucher was indignant. 'You're surely not suggesting that one of my clerks was involved.'

'I'd like an answer to my question, please.'

'Everyone who worked for me was thoroughly vetted beforehand.'

'We've dealt with bank robberies before,' said Chatfield.

'Yes,' added Marmion, 'and an employee has been involved in every instance.'

'Well, that's certainly not the case here,' insisted Boucher. 'I can vouch for every single person that I employ.'

'What about those who no longer work at your bank?' asked Chatfield. 'Can you vouch for them as well?'

Boucher fell silent.

* * *

15

After her visit to the hospital the previous evening, Alice Marmion had spent the night at the family home. She and her mother were now having an early breakfast so that Alice could get off to work in time. Ellen Marmion reached for the teapot.

'Not for me, thank you,' said Alice, raising a hand.

'It's cold outside. You need something to keep you warm.'

'I've already got it. All I need to do is to remember Joe's brother and my whole body is on fire. I'm surprised that steam doesn't come out of my ears.'

'Was Dennis that bad?'

'Well, you've met him. He's very bossy. Dennis thinks that he's always right.'

'It was very rude of him to stalk off like that.'

'We were grateful that he left,' said Alice. 'It meant that Joe and I had some time together.'

'That's the best medicine Joe could have.' They shared a laugh. 'I hope that the sound of the police car didn't wake you up in the middle of the night.'

'I slept through it, Mummy.'

'I wish that I could. I always know when your father is no longer in bed.'

'I daresay that it will be the same when Joe and I are married. When Daddy is contacted during the night in the future, he'll wait for the police car then drive to our house to pick Joe up. Isn't that a lovely thing to say?' she added with a giggle. 'Our house, I mean. It's only a matter of weeks to go and we'll be moving into a place of our own.'

'It will be a lovely moment, Alice.'

'The whole occasion will be wonderful.'

'I'm not so sure about that,' said Ellen. 'Your father and I will be as delighted as you and Joe, but Dennis will be there as well. He'll be glowering away, I daresay.'

'We had to ask him and his wife. He's family.'

'I know and he has a right to be at his brother's wedding – though Joe was determined not to have Dennis as his Best Man.'

'That would have been a disaster – in every sense.'

Ellen stifled a laugh. 'I hate to say this,' she admitted, 'but Dennis does have a point. If Joe does move in here, the word will soon spread. You and he will be under the same roof most evenings. People have suspicious minds.'

'Ignore them, Mummy.'

'I've been trying to think of a way out of this situation.'

'There isn't one. Coming here is the only option for Joe.'

Ellen was pensive. 'I wonder . . .'

Nora Collard was in the scullery of their little house, humming to herself as she prepared her husband's breakfast. She knew the routine by heart. Whenever he was on a night shift, he would arrive home tired and hungry. All that he wanted was a hearty breakfast before he went off to bed. Nora had already taken up a cup of tea to her elderly mother. With that chore out of the way, she waited for the return of her husband, wondering why he was so late that morning. There was a gentle knock on the door. Had Sam forgotten his key yet again? She resolved to tease him about it. Walking down the passageway, she rehearsed what she was going to say by way of reprimand. Nora then unlocked the door and opened it wide.

The words died on her lips. Instead of her husband, she was looking at the familiar sight of Harvey Marmion. Fear hit her like a punch in the stomach. Her jaw dropped and she turned white. Marmion stepped forward to catch her as she fell. He then carried her gently into the house.

CHAPTER THREE

Because her bus had been held up in traffic, Alice Marmion was ten minutes late for work. When she went into the main room, she discovered that the inspector had decided to make an example of her in front of the other policewomen. Inspector Thelma Gale was sarcastic.

'Ah, here she is at last,' she said. 'She has finally decided to favour us with her presence.'

'My bus was late, Inspector,' explained Alice.

'Then you should have caught an earlier one, shouldn't you? You should have used what little common sense you possess. Everyone is in the same boat,' she added, gesturing to the ranks of uniformed policewomen. 'The difference is that we all got here on time whereas you failed to do so. I expected better of you, I must say.'

'I'm sorry. It was not my fault.'

'I believe that it was.'

'Alice is the most punctual person in this room,' said Iris Goodliffe, coming to the defence of her best friend. 'It's unfair to criticise her.'

'Did I ask you to speak?' said the inspector, turning on her with a malevolent glare.

'No, Inspector.'

'Then please shut up.'

'But I think you're being unfair.'

'Your opinion counts for nothing. We are here to serve the public and we can only do that if we catch the bus that will get us here on time. Now then,' she continued, reaching for a pad, 'these are your instructions for today.'

Inspector Gale started to reel off names and assignments. Alice gave her friend a grateful smile. Iris winked at her in return. They had both learnt to stand up to the woman whose vicious tongue had earned her the nickname of Gale Force. The inspector's strictures no longer hurt them. Both friends knew how to take them in their stride. When they were given their orders for the day, they left the room immediately. Once outside the building, Iris was as excitable as ever.

'There's less than twenty-eight days to go, Alice,' she said, excitedly. 'Then you're going to change from Miss Marmion to Mrs Keedy. You and Joe will tie the knot at long last.'

Alice beamed and they walked off happily on their beat.

Marmion spent a long time at the house, offering what comfort he could to Nora Collard. A note of resignation finally came into her voice.

'I knew this could happen one day.'

'Sam was a first-rate policeman. Always remember that. He just happened to be in the wrong place at the wrong time. Other officers might have been more cautious but not your husband. Despite the danger, Sam simply had to respond. Unfortunately, his courage cost him his life.'

'Thank you for coming to tell me.'

'It was the least I could do, Nora. We were friends at school,

Sam and me. I've got some wonderful memories of him.'

'He could say the same about you.'

'I'll have to go, I'm afraid, but I hate leaving you like this. Is there someone who could come in and sit with you?'

'Rita Dowling. She's my best friend. She lives at number ten.'

'I'll ask her to come here as quickly as she can.'

'Thank you, Harvey.'

He looked upwards. 'What about your mother?' he asked. 'Would you like me to go upstairs and break the news gently to her?'

'That's my job,' said Nora, firmly.

'Then I'll be off.'

She hugged him impulsively and it was minutes before she released him. When she stood back, tears were coursing down her cheeks. She dabbed at them with a handkerchief.

'Give my love to Ellen,' she said.

'You'll be able to do that in person. When I tell her the sad news, Ellen will certainly want to call on you as soon as possible.'

When the superintendent sent for him, Clifford Burge responded quickly. He was a thickset man in his thirties with a mop of dark hair. In the wake of Keedy's absence, he had been made an acting detective sergeant and was determined to show that he deserved the temporary promotion. Burge was surprised to see how weary Claude Chatfield looked. The superintendent explained that he had been up most of the night.

'A bank near Paddington Station was robbed in the early hours,' he said. 'They got away with a sizeable haul, I daresay, but not before they killed one of the constables on duty in the area and knocked his partner unconscious. Both were taken to

20

the nearest hospital. Inspector Marmion went there to get full details of the survivor's condition. He was then going on to break the sad tidings to the widow of the murder victim.'

'What was his name, sir?'

'Constable Samuel Collard.'

'I've heard Inspector Marmion mention that name.'

'They were close friends. Anyway,' said Chatfield, 'there's been a development. About the same time as the bank was being robbed, the fire brigade was attending a blaze in a street that was not very far from the bank. I want to know if it was a coincidence.'

'I'll ring the Paddington fire brigade and find out, sir.'

'Get the exact time when they were told of the fire and ask how quickly they were able to reach it. That information could be crucial.'

'I'll get it straight away, sir.'

Glad to be involved in a new case, Burge left the room at speed. Chatfield crossed to the mirror on his wall and peered at himself. It was like staring at his death mask. He shuddered.

Marmion had kept his word. He went straight to a house opposite and told Rita Dowling what had happened. The neighbour responded immediately. Grabbing her coat, she put it on then more or less scurried across the road and let herself into the Collard house. Marmion, meanwhile, asked his driver to take him to the nearest police station. He rang home from there and passed on the news to his wife. Ellen was both shocked and upset. She and Nora Collard were good friends. Within minutes, she promised, she would be on a bus that would take her to the grieving widow.

Having been driven back to Scotland Yard, the inspector

went straight to Chatfield's office to give his report. The superintendent listened carefully.

'Constable Lee is still in a coma,' said Marmion, sadly. 'Whoever hit him almost cracked his skull open. But he is still alive, thank God.'

'What about Collard?'

'They told me that he must have died almost instantly.'

'From a knife wound?' said Chatfield. 'Where exactly was he stabbed?'

'It was through the heart, sir.'

'Did they have any idea what sort of knife it might be?'

'It wasn't a knife at all, Superintendent. I spoke to the surgeon who examined him.'

'And?'

'He is an expert on wounds involving a blade.' Marmion took a deep breath. 'In the surgeon's opinion, Sam Collard was killed by a bayonet.'

Ellen Marmion was luckier than her daughter. While Alice's bus had been delayed, the one that her mother caught had a clear run. Less than twenty minutes after leaving the house, she was getting off the vehicle at the bus stop in the street where the Collard family lived. Ellen walked quickly to their home and knocked on the door. It was opened by a tearful Nora Collard. Seeing her friend there, she flung herself into Ellen's arms. After a lengthy embrace, she pulled away and invited her visitor into the house. Having met her many times before, Ellen needed no introduction to the motherly Rita Dowling. She and Ellen hugged each other.

'I'll put the kettle on,' said Rita, heading for the scullery.

'Thank you,' replied Nora. She took Ellen into the living

room. 'It's so good of you to come. The news about Sam came as a bombshell,' she admitted. 'I was so grateful that your husband delivered it. Harvey was kind and considerate. If a stranger had come instead, the blow would have been unbearable. Your husband was so gentle.'

'He had his own grief to cope with,' said Ellen. 'When he rang me, Harvey was close to tears. He told me how painful it was to lose one of his best friends. As young men, he and Sam had been inseparable. They joined the police force together.'

'I know. They were like brothers.'

'One thing I can promise you, Nora. This case will have top priority. Harvey will not rest until he's found and arrested the man who did this. It will be like a mission for him.'

'That's very comforting,' said the other woman, 'but it won't bring Sam back to life.'

'I know that.'

Nora glanced upstairs. 'But I'm so grateful to see you,' she said. 'I don't know what to do about mother. I'm not sure if I should tell her the truth or . . . wait a bit.'

'She's bound to notice that Sam is not here.'

'Rita thinks that I should leave it for a few days and pretend that nothing has happened.'

'I don't agree, Nora. You can't deceive your mother. I know that she's disabled but her mind is still clear. If you tell her a lie, she might never forgive you. Apart from anything else, she'll see that you are so upset. You can't hide the truth from her.'

'You're right,' agreed the other. 'When the tea is made, I'll take a cup up to her.' She bit her lip. 'Oh, I'm sorry to be in such a state, Ellen. I just can't think straight. But you're right. Mother deserves the truth. She knows that Sam's life was always at risk when he was on duty. I'll tell her what happened.'

Holding back tears, Nora gave her a grateful hug then went off into the scullery.

When he went back to the superintendent's office, Clifford Burge found that Marmion was still there. He asked him for more details about the events in Paddington. Claude Chatfield stepped in.

'First things first,' he said to Burge. 'What did you discover?'

'I rang the fire brigade, and they told me that the blaze in Whitmore Street had probably been a case of arson. An empty shop was set alight. They found evidence of petrol cans that were used.'

'What time did someone raise the alarm?'

'It was at 3 a.m. precisely.'

'Bang on the hour?' asked Marmion.

'That's what it says in their log-book, sir.'

'What time did the robbers gain entry to the bank?'

'I'll bet that it was shortly afterwards,' decided Chatfield.

'I agree,' said Marmion. 'They waited until they heard the fire engines racing to Whitmore Street, then they broke into the bank. When the burglar alarm went off, its noise was largely muffled by the clang of the fire engines. The burglars must have disabled the alarm before the clamour in the nearby street died down.'

'Then the fire was started deliberately as a diversion,' said Burge. 'All the interest was focused on Whitmore Street.'

'Meanwhile, the burglars were inside the bank, helping themselves to a sizeable amount of money. I'm certain that they had help from a former employee,' insisted Marmion. 'How else would they know where the burglar alarm was and how they could switch it off so quickly?'

'Mr Boucher refused to accept that someone he employed was involved in the raid,' said Chatfield. 'Let's hope that he soon comes to his senses.'

'I'll get back there immediately, sir.'

'Take Burge with you, Inspector, and acquaint him with the full details.'

'He's already aware of the most important detail,' said Marmion. 'We're dealing with some very clever people. In starting that fire, they committed one crime to disguise another. Clearly, they are armed and dangerous.' He turned to Burge. 'Who actually got in touch with the fire brigade?'

'A man arrived there, almost breathless from running,' said Burge.

'Did he give his name?'

'Yes, sir, it was Arthur Davies. He said that he lived opposite the blaze and had been woken up by the sound of uproar in the street.'

'We must speak to him first,' said Chatfield.

'Well, we won't find him living in Whitmore Street,' suggested Marmion. 'Possibly he's in league with the bank robbers. He might even be the man who stabbed Sam Collard to death. That's one more reason why we must hunt him down.'

'How many of them were there?' wondered Chatfield.

'Three, at least. Two of them broke into the bank and the third was probably waiting nearby in a car. Sam Collard and Harry Lee were experienced constables. They were brave enough to tackle two suspects, but they'd think twice about tackling three or four. What they didn't expect was that the two men were armed – one with a cosh and the other with a bayonet.'

'Two weapons that can be used silently,' noted Burge. 'Gunfire would have given them away.'

'All that our officers had were truncheons,' complained Marmion.

'They'd been trained to use them,' Chatfield reminded him. 'They're perfectly effective for most arrests. In this case, unfortunately, they were not.'

'We should heed the warning, sir. If we get close to these men, we need to carry guns.'

'I'll think about it, Inspector.'

'It's an obvious precaution.'

'We'll have superior numbers.'

'I'd be safer with the feel of a firearm in my hand.'

Chatfield sighed. 'That's what Sergeant Keedy thought and look what happened to him.'

Joe Keedy had been throbbing with anticipation all morning. He was finally being released from hospital. After he had been shot at close quarters during a siege, he had been taken to a military hospital and given excellent care. He had been transferred from there to Edmonton Military Hospital, a place where he was given a cordial welcome because he and Marmion had once solved the murder of one of their surgeons. When he started to recover, he was moved to an ordinary hospital because he was very conscious of taking up a bed that should be occupied by a wounded soldier. There was another reason why he was moved. One of the criminals involved in the siege had stalked him at the first military hospital. Thankfully, that man and his accomplices were now in custody.

It was a relief to be back in his own clothes again. As soon as he was dressed, Keedy had gone from bed to bed, thanking each one of the patients and wishing them the best of luck. By treating him as a hero, they had helped to lift his spirits. Although he would miss them, he was glad to leave, going back into a normal life with the prospect of marriage to Alice Marmion only weeks away. Now that he was back on his feet, he was able to visit other wards to thank the members of staff who had looked after him so well. When that duty was done, he went slowly downstairs with a porter carrying his suitcase. As he settled into a chair, he was smiling broadly. He was about to return to normal life at last. All that he had to do was to wait until his future mother-in-law arrived in a taxi that would whisk them all the way back to the Marmion residence.

Yet she never came. It worried him. After thirty nervous minutes, he was manufacturing excuses. The taxi was running late. Ellen had some shopping to do first. They were having trouble parking in the hospital car park. When almost an hour had elapsed, the excuses were replaced by deep anxieties. Keedy began to wonder if something was amiss. At the last moment, had problems arisen? Might he not be escaping hospital, after all?

When somebody came hurrying into the waiting room, Keedy paid no attention to him. It was only when the man walked straight up to him that he recognised Raymond Marmion, brother of his future father-in-law. As usual, Raymond, a tall, sturdy man with a reassuring smile, was wearing the uniform of the Salvation Army.

'Hello, Joe,' he said, extending a hand. 'Good to see you again.'

'It's nice to see you again, Raymond.' They shook hands. 'Are you visiting a patient?'

'Yes, but he's an ex-patient now and his name is Joseph Keedy.'

'Ah, I see,' said Keedy, relaxing at last. 'You've come to take me back to your brother's house, haven't you?'

'Not exactly. Hasn't Ellen been in touch?'

'I'm afraid not.'

'She and Alice had a long talk about where you should go when discharged. Although Alice was keen for you to go to her parents' house, Ellen had doubts. In the end, she rang me.'

Keedy was baffled. 'Why?'

'My wife and I are going to provide you with accommodation for a while,' said Raymond. 'It will silence the gossipmongers who disapprove of the fact that you and Alice would be so . . . well, close to each other before you were actually married.'

'I don't pay any attention to prudes!'

'Your future mother-in-law does and, I suspect, so does my brother. I was happy to provide a solution. You're coming to us, Joe. Nobody can complain when they hear that you're being cared for by the Salvation Army.' Raymond grinned. 'I don't suppose you're fit enough to play a big bass drum, are you? The band go marching on a Sunday.'

Keedy's heart sank.

CHAPTER FOUR

When they got to the bank, there was a subdued air about the place. Tellers were largely silent, heads bowed as if at a funeral. Customers were dutifully quiet, all too conscious of the fact that the bank had been robbed during the night and that a policeman had been murdered on the pavement outside. Marmion and Burge had to wait until the manager was free. Only when the deputy manager emerged from the office could the detectives take his place. After giving them a token welcome, Douglas Boucher waved them to a seat apiece then settled into his own chair behind a large desk. Marmion introduced his companion, but Burge was only given the merest nod of the manager's head. Boucher was in a combative mood.

'I told you that I was right,' he announced. 'Fryer agreed with me.'

'Fryer?' echoed Marmion.

'Stuart Fryer, the deputy manager. You must have seen him leave my office when you arrived. Excellent man, been with me for years. Fryer is a blessing in a crisis like this.'

'I'm sure that he is, sir.'

'We went through the list of people employed at this bank.

Every one of them is above suspicion. Loyalty is my watchword. I only take on people who will be unswervingly loyal to me and to this bank. We maintain the highest standards.'

'That's to your credit.'

'As for employees who have moved on,' said Boucher, glancing at a piece of paper in front of him, 'they are three in number.'

'Could we have their names, please?' asked Burge, taking out his notebook.

'Of course. The first one is Walter Greenlow. Ill health forced him to retire two years ago.'

Marmion nodded. 'Then we can exclude him, I fancy.'

'The second man is Martin Beale,' said the manager. 'I'm ashamed to say that he deserted us and went to a rival bank.'

'For what reason, sir? More money? Promotion?'

'Well, it was not because of dissatisfaction with us. He told me that he felt in need of a change. Much as he enjoyed his time here, he said, he felt the appeal of pastures new.'

'Do you have his address?' asked Burge.

'Yes, of course.' After giving the details, he glanced at his list. 'The third person who left was the one who surprised me most. Neil Paterson came from a banking family. He loved the work and was always the first to volunteer for overtime.'

'What happened to him?' asked Marmion.

'He left us abruptly.'

'Was no reason given?'

'His wife missed Scotland, I gather. I assume he needed to go north of the border with her.'

'Might we have his address, please – and that of Walter Greenlow?'

After providing the information requested, Boucher sat back in his chair.

'Let me warn you that all three men were trusted employees. Indeed, Paterson was considered for the position of deputy manager when it became vacant. I chose Stuart Fryer because of his greater experience.'

'What happened to the previous deputy manager?'

'He contracted a serious illness and died only months after he'd resigned.'

'That leaves us with three possible suspects, then.'

'You'll be wasting your time if you imagine that any one of them could possibly betray me and the bank in which each of them was employed for so long.'

'Your warning has been duly noted, sir.'

'Then let me have a turn at asking the questions. What have you learnt so far?'

'I've been reminded how dangerous it is for policemen to be on the night shift when desperate criminals are at large. By confronting two bank robbers, one of our men was killed and the other was knocked senseless. When I saw him at the hospital, his face was a mass of bruises.'

'I'm sorry to hear that,' said Boucher, quietly.

'As for the bank robbers, we have made some headway. Robbing your bank was only one of the crimes they committed during the night. We now know that they set fire to an empty shop not far away then broke into your bank at a time when the deafening noise of the fire engines blocked out any other sound. Once inside the building,' Marmion continued, 'they quickly switched off the burglar alarm. Who taught them how to do that?'

'Heaven knows!'

'Did any of the men whose names you have given us have responsibility for security here?'

'Yes,' admitted Boucher.

'Which one?'

'Neil Paterson . . . but he's above suspicion.'

'We'd still like to question him, sir,' said Marmion, firmly. 'You'll be surprised how many people who are "above suspicion" end up in a police cell.'

Joe Keedy was used to sudden changes of circumstances. Work in the Metropolitan Police Force had taught him how to adapt quickly to them, but he was not able to do so in this case. Much as he liked Raymond Marmion, he was not sure that he would enjoy being looked after in a Salvation Army hostel. To begin with, he would be among strangers, homeless men picked up off the streets, most of them with physical or mental problems. As they drove there in a van, Raymond assured him that he and his wife were looking forward to being his temporary guardians. Keedy was unable to discern the slightest pleasure in the new arrangements, and he was still unnerved by the fact that he was given no advance warning of them.

'How are you feeling now?' asked Raymond.

'Glad to be out of hospital at last.'

'I heard that they treated you well.'

'Very well,' said Keedy, 'but I was still happy to leave. I'm dying to get back to work.'

'You may have to wait for a while, Joe, until you're good and ready.'

'I feel fine, honestly.'

'Then why were you walking so gingerly when we left the hospital? It's obvious that you're not fully fit. I noticed that you winced at one point.'

'I get these occasional twinges, that's all.'

'They're reminders that you have a little way to go.'

Keedy nodded. 'I suppose so.'

When the van turned a corner, the hostel came into sight. Having been there before, Keedy knew very well what the inside of the building looked like. To his surprise, however, they drove past the hostel and stopped outside a house two blocks away. Raymond brought the vehicle to a halt.

'This is where you'll be staying, Joe,' he said. 'In our house.'

Keedy was relieved. He was also pleased to see the front door opening so that Lily Marmion could come hurrying out. She was a sprightly middle-aged woman who had kept her figure and whose face seemed to glow with kindness. When she reached the van, she flung open the door.

'Hello, Joe,' she said. 'Welcome to your new home!'

It had been a busy day for Alice Marmion. She and Iris Goodliffe had been involved in a series of incidents as they walked on their beat. They had intervened in a heated argument between two stallholders in a market, helped an old lady to her feet when she tripped up and hit the pavement, gave directions to various drivers with orders to deliver, stopped a man from urinating in an alleyway, and subdued a large, angry dog who was barking at anyone who passed. Their real success had been in catching a shoplifter. As they walked side by side along a street, the figure of a small boy emerged at speed from a shop, closely followed by an angry woman. Since there was no chance of her catching him, all that the shopkeeper could do was to hurl abuse at the young thief.

Alice and Iris leapt into action. Taking to their heels, they went after the boy. It was a long chase. Iris tried hard to keep up with Alice, but it was a forlorn hope. The latter was lighter, faster and more determined than her. She was helped by the fact that the boy cannoned into a man and bounced a yard backwards. Setting off again, he tried to outrun her, but it was impossible. Alice was quickly gaining on him. As a last resort, he suddenly turned down a lane, but she would not be shaken off. After putting in a final spurt, she grabbed him by the shoulders and held him tight as he struggled to get free.

'Stop right there!' she ordered.

'You can't touch me,' he retorted. 'You're not a real policeman.'

'Oh, yes I am.'

'I done nothing wrong.'

'Yes, you did. You stole that packet of biscuits.'

'I was hungry.'

'Then you should have paid for them.'

'Got no money.'

'Stealing is wrong. Don't you know that? And why aren't you at school? Are you playing truant?' The boy's face fell. 'Right,' she said, tightening her grip on him.

'Where are you taking me?'

'Back to that shop. You can hand over the biscuits, then apologise to the shopkeeper.'

He was fearful. 'Are you arresting me?'

'We'll see.'

'I'm sorry,' said Iris, gulping for air as she reached them. 'I couldn't keep up with you.'

'It doesn't matter, Iris. I caught him.'

'Well done!'

'He's coming back to that shop with us.'

The boy looked up hopefully. 'Can I have a biscuit before I give the rest of them back?'

* * *

34

After learning that many thousands of pounds had been stolen from the bank, Marmion and Burge went in search of the first name on their list of suspects. The police car took them to an address less than half a mile away. Walter Greenlow lived in a quiet street with two rows of terraced houses facing each other. The properties were small but well-maintained, and there was an air of pride about the street. Unlike so many others in the capital, it had been spared bomb damage during the raids by the German air force. The detectives got out of the car and knocked on the door of a house. There was a noise from within, but it was the best part of a minute before an old man finally reached the door and opened it. Resting on his walking stick, he blinked at them.

'Mr Greenlow?' asked Marmion.

'That's me,' he replied. 'Who are you?'

'We are detectives from Scotland Yard. I am Inspector Marmion, and this is Sergeant Burge.'

'Then why are you bothering me?'

'The bank where you used to work has been robbed.'

'I never worked in a bank,' said the old man, offended at the notion. 'I had a proper job in the docks.' He put his walking stick aside so that he could display both palms. They were pitted with tiny scars. 'You don't get hands like these working behind a counter.'

'You are Walter Greenlow, aren't you?' asked Marmion.

'No,' grunted the other. 'I'm Alf Greenlow. Wally is my son.'

'Is there any chance of speaking to him, sir?'

'Not unless you've got a very loud voice.'

'What do you mean?'

'He's in the churchyard three blocks away,' said the old man, reclaiming his walking stick then using it to indicate a direction. 'St Margaret's is that way. You'll find Wally there.'

Burge was disappointed. 'Is he dead?'

The old man chortled. 'I bloody well hope not,' he said.

'What do you mean, Mr Greenlow?'

'Wally does the cooking here – most of it, anyway. This is a Lena day, see? My son always goes to the churchyard on a Lena day to be with her.'

'Is that his mother?'

'No, it's his wife.'

'Thank you, sir. We'll go and find him.'

'Wally doesn't like to be disturbed in the churchyard,' warned the old man.

'We need his help.'

They turned away and got back into the police car. Within a minute it was pulling up outside the parish church of St Margaret, a small, almost picturesque building that had been on the site for over three hundred years. The detectives found the churchyard at the rear. It was cluttered with gravestones standing at differing heights and angles due to random settlement of the earth. A man in a raincoat was seated on a bench, staring at the grave in front of him. Having removed his hat, he was holding it in both hands.

When they got closer, they noticed that his eyes were closed, and his lips were moving.

'Who is he talking to?' whispered Burge.

'How should I know?' replied Marmion. 'Himself? His dead wife? God?'

'He's a lot better dressed than his father.'

'That's the difference between a banker and a docker, Cliff.'

'What do we do, sir?'

'Wait patiently and hope that he soon finishes.'

They walked down the path and stopped a few yards away,

staring at a man in his mid-forties who looked perfectly fit and healthy. It was difficult to believe that he was the son of Alf Greenlow. Ears pricked, Burge stepped in closer to see if he could hear what the man was saying. Without looking at him, Greenlow issued a warning.

'Don't come close,' he warned. 'I've almost finished.'

Feeling embarrassed, Burge took a few steps backwards. Within a minute, Greenlow opened his eyes and put on his hat. He looked from one man to the other.

'You're from the police, aren't you?' he said.

'How do you know?' asked Marmion.

'There was a robbery at the bank. I knew someone would come looking for me.'

'Who told you about the robbery?'

'Nothing much happens around here that I don't get to hear about.'

Marmion introduced Burge and himself then he sat down on the bench.

'We called at your house and spoke to your father.'

'Did he show you his hands?' asked Greenlow.

'He did, as a matter of fact.'

'He's proud of what he did in the docks, but I wanted something different. Something that didn't leave me looking like Dad. That's why I studied so hard. Lena Daly would never have given me a second look if I came home dirty every day. But she did notice me when I got a job as a bank clerk. I was respectable, see? Lena liked that. We began to go out together.'

'When did your wife die, sir?' asked Marmion, gently.

'She's still alive to me,' murmured Greenlow. 'Forget Lena. Ask me about the bank, if you must. That's why you're here, isn't it?'

'Yes, it is.'

'You must have met Mr Boucher.' They nodded. 'What did you make of him?'

'Well . . .'

'Be honest, Inspector. I won't tell him.'

'Let's just say that I'd hate to work for him,' said Marmion.

'And so would I,' added Burge.

'He isn't too bad when you get to know him,' said Greenlow. 'There are worse bank managers.'

'How did you get a job in a bank in the first place?' asked Marmion.

'That was down to Uncle Jonah. He's the brains in our family. He worked in a bank and taught me all I needed to know. Uncle Jonah got me taken on as a sort of errand boy at the place where he worked. I'm a quick learner and good at sums. That helped,' said Greenlow. 'I was eventually tried out as a clerk and had well over thirty good years in the bank. Then my chest let me down,' he went on, 'and I was coughing all the time. That's no good if you're serving customers. I had to retire. Funny, isn't it? I worked indoors all my life and ended up as an invalid. My father, who spent his working life outdoors, is as fit as a flea at eighty-six.'

'I need to ask you about some of your colleagues at the bank.'

'Go ahead, Inspector. You'll get honest answers from me.'

Joe Keedy was pleasantly surprised at the efforts they had made on his behalf. Overlooking the little garden, his bedroom was spotless. Apart from the single bed, it contained a dresser, a tallboy, an armchair with a small table beside it, and a mirror. There was also a bookcase but one glance at the titles on it told Keedy that he would not be doing much reading. On the bedside table was a copy of the Holy Bible, another volume he was unlikely to open.

Lily Marmion, who had taken him up to his room, was keen to make it clear that he had complete freedom of movement in the house.

'You don't have to stay up here, Joe,' she explained. 'Come downstairs whenever you wish. Raymond and I are not here during the day. We'll be at the hostel. You're welcome to call in there.'

'Thank you, Lily.'

'What did they tell you at the hospital?'

'To get as much rest as I can,' he replied. 'I've done far too much of that already. I want to get out and about.'

'Don't overdo it.' She beamed. 'Oh, I'm so glad that we were able to help you. Make yourself at home.'

'Thanks, Lily.'

'I daresay that Alice will call on you this evening.'

'That will be a real treat.'

'Well,' she said, 'I'll let you settle in. If you want a cup of tea, feel free to make your own. We usually have an evening meal around seven o'clock.'

'It will be wonderful to sit at a table again. In hospital, every meal was served on a tray.'

'Those days have gone. You're back in the real world again.'

Keedy grinned. 'And I couldn't be happier.' Wincing slightly, he put a hand to his stomach. 'They warned me not to get too excited. I've got to behave myself.'

When they asked him about Martin Beale, Greenlow talked fondly about his friend. He had learnt a lot from his colleague and been disappointed when Beale moved to another bank. They had kept in touch but saw very little of each other now.

'What about Neil Paterson?' asked Burge.

'Oh, he was very different to Martin,' replied Greenlow. 'He kept himself to himself. I worked beside Neil for years, yet I never really got to know him. He was a very private man. Then, out of the blue, he announced that he was leaving and wouldn't say exactly where he was going.'

'That's rather odd behaviour,' said Marmion.

'Neil was an odd person.'

'Was he good at his job?'

'He was very good – and he knew it. I've got this theory, see,' said Greenlow. 'Neil was being groomed for the job of deputy manager. Then – without warning – the manager appointed Stuart Fryer instead. That really hurt Neil. He hated Fryer. I think that's why he resigned.'

'Does he still work in a bank?'

'Who knows? He wouldn't say.'

'When he was working with you, he was in charge of security, wasn't he?'

'That's right, Inspector.'

'In that case, he would have known how to turn off the burglar alarm.'

'Yes,' said Greenlow, 'and he was very upset when Stuart Fryer was appointed deputy manager and took control of security at the bank. That was a real blow to Neil.'

'Would you describe him as vengeful?'

'Not really – I don't think he had the guts.'

'What about Martin Beale?'

'He had no reason to want revenge. Mr Boucher treated him well and Martin left because he went after a promotion.' Greenlow shook his head. 'I'm sorry but you're looking in the wrong direction. Martin and Neil had their faults, but they were as honest as the day is long. If you want to arrest someone who helped the bank robbers, you'll have to search elsewhere.'

As they waited for the bus that would take them to the address, Alice Marmion was critical of her mother.

'You might have warned Joe in advance, Mummy,' she said.

'I thought it would be a lovely surprise.'

'He was expecting to move in with you and Daddy.'

'Well,' sighed Ellen, 'maybe that wouldn't have been such a good idea, after all.'

'In other words, you let Joe's brother talk you out of it.'

'No, Alice. I found a compromise.'

'But you didn't bother to tell Joe about it,' said her daughter, harshly.

'There's no need to be so angry. I solved a problem, didn't I?'

'But you didn't. You surrendered to Dennis.'

'Well, he did have a point.' Ellen put her hand on her arm. 'Look, I'm sorry. Perhaps I should have mentioned the idea to you beforehand. Your father agreed. Joe has always got on very well with Raymond and Lily. He enjoys their company.'

'I feel that we're imposing on them.'

'But they were delighted to look after him for a while. It's part of his convalescence.'

'I see it from Joe's point of view. He's looking forward to coming to you and he's whisked off miles away. What will he do all day, stuck in a Salvation Army hostel?'

'He'll be staying with them at their house.'

'Oh, I see,' said Alice. 'That's different.'

'I'm sure that Joe will like it there.'

'He'd have preferred living with you.'

41

'Think what people would have said.'

'I don't care two hoots, Mummy. It's none of their business.'

'They're our neighbours, Alice. I know they seem narrow-minded to you, but we've known them for years and got on with them very well.'

'That's true, I suppose,' conceded Alice.

'Also, they read newspapers. They'll have seen the way that Joe was hailed as a hero for daring to tackle those men in the siege. He's been recommended for a medal.'

The bus arrived and ended their conversation. During the ride, Alice was largely silent. When they eventually got off the vehicle, they headed towards the house belonging to Raymond and Lily Marmion. Ellen could see that her daughter was still very upset about the way that the decision about Keedy's temporary home had been made.

'Let's not argue in front of him,' said Ellen.

'Of course not, Mummy. We don't want Joe to see us bickering. When we go in the house, we'll present a united front. Will that suit you?'

Ellen linked arms with her and smiled. 'It will suit me very well.'

When Marmion and Burge got back to Scotland Yard, they went straight to Claude Chatfield's office. The superintendent was glad to see them. They sat down in front of his desk.

'I've just had a phone call from my third newspaper editor,' said Chatfield. 'All three of them are putting pressure on us to solve the crime.'

'They'll have to wait,' said Marmion.

'Have you brought me no good news at all?'

'I'm afraid not, sir. But if they want something to write about, tell them to find a photo of Sam Collard and put that in their papers. He's typical of every copper who walks the beat – brave men who face the possibility of attack or even death, as in Sam's case, every time they walk through the streets of London. He deserves praise for what he did,' argued Marmion. 'Passing on the news of his death to his wife was heart-breaking.'

'It was good of you to take on that task,' said Chatfield.

'I felt that I had to, sir.'

'I'm sure that Mrs Collard appreciates that.'

'Our first visit,' said Burge, opening his notebook, 'was to the bank itself. We had a long chat with the manager, Mr Boucher, who refused to believe that any employee of his would help the bank robbers.'

'Have any of them been sacked in recent years?' asked Chatfield.

'No, sir, but three people have left the bank to go elsewhere.'

'Did you track any of them down?'

'Yes,' said Marmion. 'We spoke to a former bank clerk named Walter Greenlow. Ill health forced him to retire. We met him talking to his wife in a churchyard.'

Chatfield shrugged. 'Nothing unusual in that, is there?'

'Yes, there is, sir. Mrs Greenlow died years ago.' Amused by the look of surprise on Chatfield's face, he nodded to Burge. 'This is what he told us.'

Referring to his notebook, Burge read out details of their conversation with Greenlow, ending with the man's warning that neither of the other former employees at the bank – Martin Beale and Neil Paterson – was a credible suspect. The detectives needed to look elsewhere.

'I hope that you ignore that advice,' said Chatfield, briskly.

'We certainly will, sir,' Marmion assured him. 'We know

43

where Beale works but we've been unable to trace Paterson so far. He certainly isn't employed by a bank in London.'

'Didn't Greenlow know his address?'

'Yes, he did and was happy to give it to us. When we got there, we were told that Paterson had left the house months ago, giving no forwarding address.'

'That sounds fishy to me.'

'And to me, sir. Paterson was an expert on the bank's security. If anyone knew how to get into the building and disable the burglar alarm, it was Neil Paterson. I'm telling you this in confidence,' said Marmion. 'Please don't pass on his name to the newspapers.'

'You should know me better than that,' said Chatfield. 'If he is a party to the crime, the last thing we want him to know is that we're on his tail.'

When they had delivered their report, Marmion and Burge got up to leave.

Chatfield was curious. 'Any news about Sergeant Keedy?'

'He came out of hospital this morning, sir.'

'I daresay he's delighted about that.'

'He thinks that he's fit enough to return to work.'

'That's not what his doctor told me.'

'He needs rest, sir. The problem is that he loves action. When I see him this evening,' said Marmion, 'I guarantee that Joe Keedy will badger me for every detail about this case. Obviously, I won't tell him anything.'

It was amazing how quickly he had adapted to his new home. Liberated at last from a hospital bed, he could now do what he wanted at a pace that he himself set. Keedy had never thought that he would share a home with two people who put on the uniform of the Salvation Army every morning. While he didn't agree with all that they stood for, he had the greatest admiration for the work they had done for the war effort, sending teams abroad to offer support and distribute food to the soldiers. More recently, they had taken an interest in what was described as 'unruly girls' – young females who had gone astray in a variety of ways. Keedy was impressed by the Salvation Army's dedication to its principles.

He was in the living room when the first guests arrived. Lily opened the front door to let them in. Alice ran straight over to Keedy but, conscious of his wound, she did not embrace him as warmly as she wished to do.

'I've missed you so much, Joe,' she said.

'And I've missed you,' he replied. 'It's wonderful to be able to hold you properly again at last.'

'Let's hope you never have to go back to hospital.'

Alice stood aside so that her mother could move in to kiss Keedy, then study him.

'You look as good as new, Joe,' she said.

'I feel it,' he said with a grin. 'Now, what case is Harv working on? I want all the details.'

'Well, you won't get them from Mummy or from me,' warned Alice. 'You're still a patient, remember. You must devote all your time to getting better.'

'I can't just sit here and twiddle my thumbs.'

'Read a book. Keep your mind occupied.'

'Yes, Nurse Marmion,' he teased.

'Oh, it's so kind of you to take Joe in at short notice,' said Alice turning to Raymond and Lily. 'I can't thank you enough.'

'He's always welcome here,' said Lily.

'Yes,' added Raymond. 'Especially if he can join the band on Sundays.'

CHAPTER FIVE

Harvey Marmion had learnt long ago that a murder investigation demanded total commitment. It never fitted easily into any time pattern. He would put in endless hours of work, but, when he finally got home, his brain would still be grappling furiously with the problems in the case. Because it had involved the death of a policeman who had been a close friend of his, he had a special reason to catch the man responsible for the latest murder. An image of Sam Collard's distraught wife was always at the back of his mind.

Having left Scotland Yard, he had gone alone to the home of Martin Beale, one of the men who had left the bank in recent years. Beale turned out to be a quiet, balding man in his fifties with eyes that gleamed with intelligence behind his spectacles. The contrast with Walter Greenlow was complete. Indeed, it was difficult to believe that the two men had once worked side by side in a bank. When Beale had returned home that evening, he found Marmion waiting for him and showed no surprise.

'I had a feeling someone would contact me,' he said, exchanging a handshake with the inspector. 'When a bank is robbed, I'm afraid that everyone who has ever worked there is a suspect. Can I offer you a cup of tea, Inspector?'

'Your wife has already done so, sir. I declined the offer.'

'Then let's get down to it, shall we? Take a seat and ask me whatever you wish.'

'Thank you, sir,' said Marmion, lowering himself onto a chair.

There was a confidence about Beale that triggered a warning in the detective's brain. The man had taken the sudden arrival of a detective in his house with remarkable calm. He looked like a man who would have rehearsed all the answers beforehand. As he opened his notebook, Marmion wondered how he could wipe the quiet smile off Beale's face.

'When did you first learn of the bank robbery?' he asked.

'As soon as I arrived at work,' replied the man. 'Word travels fast in the world of banking.'

'What was your reaction to the news?'

'I was upset, naturally. I have good friends still working there.'

'Did you know that a policeman had been killed when he tried to arrest the robbers?'

'No, I didn't, Inspector,' said the other with genuine surprise, 'and I'm very sorry to hear it. Was he shot?'

'He was stabbed through the heart by a bayonet.'

Beale grimaced. 'That's terrible!'

'London is a dangerous city after dark, sir.'

'It's the reason my wife and I rarely venture out at night.'

'Why did you choose to leave the bank?'

'The offer was irresistible,' said Beale. 'I now have more authority, a bigger office and, of course, a larger income. I would have been a fool to turn it down.'

'Might there have been another reason why you left?'

'What do you mean?'

'I've met Mr Boucher. He didn't strike me as the easiest man to work under.'

There was a pause. 'We got along,' said Beale, crisply.

'And I daresay that you "got along" with colleagues like Walter Greenlow and Neil Paterson as well.'

'Why do you pick them out?'

'Like you, they left the bank to go elsewhere.'

'Walter was a strange man,' said Beale, 'and he got even stranger when his wife died. I liked Neil a lot more. He was the kind of chap with whom you could have a drink and talk politics.'

'Let's go back to Greenlow. He was indebted to you, wasn't he?'

'Is that what he told you?'

'He looked up to you because you were older and more experienced than him and, over the years, you offered him some good advice.'

'Walter was keen to learn everything he could about banking. He borrowed some books off me.'

'Was he always so self-conscious about his limited education?'

'He made up for it, Inspector. He became a keen student. I admire him for that.'

'Let's move on to Paterson,' said Marmion. 'He used to be responsible for security at the bank. At least, that's what Mr Boucher told us.'

'Neil had a number of responsibilities.'

'Did he discharge them well?'

'Extremely well.'

'He was in line to be deputy manager, I understand.'

'Yes, he was. Neil was clearly the best man for the job.'

'Then why didn't he get it?'

Beale sniffed. 'Mr Boucher opted for Stuart Fryer instead.'

'Do you have any idea why?'

'No, I don't. What I can tell you is that Neil was deeply upset. Within weeks, he handed in his notice and left the bank.'

'Where did he go?'

'I wish I knew. I'd like to have kept in touch with him.'

'What sort a man was he?'

'Neil was a trifle dour, but you expect that of a Scot. He worked hard at his job and – if you went to the pub with him – he'd tell you that what he wanted most was an independent Scotland.'

'I don't agree with that notion.'

'Neither did I. We had some lively discussions about it.'

'Please think twice before you answer my next question,' said Marmion, watching him closely. 'Could you believe that he might – just might – be involved in the bank robbery?'

Beale's laugh was derisive. 'That's a ridiculous idea, Inspector.'

'I disagree, sir.'

'Why?'

'It's clear from the way that they got into the bank and switched off the alarm, that they'd been helped by someone who used to work there. Was it you, perhaps?'

Beale met his gaze without flinching.

Raymond, Lily and Ellen were chatting in the kitchen so that Alice and Keedy could have a little time alone. The pair took full advantage of it. He not only kissed her and stroked her arm, Keedy pulled her close to him. He winced and eased her away.

'What's the trouble?' she asked.

'This surgery of mine. Whenever I try to forget it, I have a nasty reminder that I'm still not fully fit. I'm sorry, Alice.'

'It was partly my fault.'

'Don't be silly. You're not to blame.'

'Then why do I feel so guilty?' She moved away from him on the sofa. 'How long will it be before you're completely recovered?'

'A matter of weeks, they said. But that's only the physical side of it.'

'I don't follow.'

'They told me there might be mental scars as well.'

'Does it prey on your mind?'

'Not when I'm awake. I forget all about it then. The problem comes when I go to sleep.'

'Do you still have dreams about it?' she asked, a soothing hand on his shoulder.

'They're more like nightmares.'

'I'm so sorry, Joe.'

'Don't apologise. You're the antidote to those terrible dreams. When I'm sleeping next to you, Alice, there'll be no nightmares.'

She lowered her voice. 'Are you quite sure that . . . ?'

'Yes, of course,' he told her. 'I get stronger by the day – and the wedding is still weeks away.'

Clifford Burge was basking in his role as acting detective sergeant. It gave him more authority, the right to commandeer a police car and – the real benefit – a chance to work alongside Inspector Marmion. He learnt something new from him every day. Burge had now been given the task of going to the former home of Neil Paterson to speak to more of his neighbours and ask if they were still in contact with him. When he got there, however, he realised that he had drawn a blank. People were keen to help him, but nobody had the slightest idea where Paterson was now.

Reginald Naylor acted as their spokesperson. He was a retired estate agent whose life consisted for the most part of taking his dog for a walk twice a day, helping his wife to do the shopping and popping his head into the estate agency to see if they were managing without him. Clearly a man with time on his hands, Naylor, a tall, elegant, straight-backed man with an educated voice, was delighted to say his piece.

'I knew Neil as well as anybody,' he boasted.

'Then why didn't he confide in you, sir?' asked Burge.

'As a rule, he did. He told me that he was going to work in a bank in Scotland, but he didn't say exactly where it was. When my wife spoke to Flora – that was Neil's wife – she got a different story. According to her, they were moving because they wanted to be closer to her family.'

'Do you think that Mr Paterson was deliberately lying?'

'Well, he certainly wasn't telling the whole truth.'

'You said a moment ago that you knew him as well as anybody.'

'I did – at least, I thought so. We had long chats sometimes.'

'What's your guess about his present whereabouts?'

Naylor narrowed his eyelids. 'I don't think he works in a bank any more.'

'Then where does he work and how does he support his family?'

'I hope you can find that out for us.'

Burge was disappointed. During the car ride back to Scotland Yard, he pieced together the few facts that he knew about Paterson. Having held an important job in the bank, he was clearly an intelligent man. Friendly with his colleagues, he did not, however, confide in any of them. Nor did he tell any of his neighbours where he was moving on to. Paterson and his wife had just announced their departure, waved their goodbyes, and disappeared. The family who bought their house were not given a forwarding address. It was odd behaviour from the banker.

By the time he reached his destination, Burge was coming around to the view that Paterson was a likely suspect regarding the bank robbery. Having been overlooked for the job of deputy manager, he had resigned from his job and vanished into thin air. What possible reason did he have to do that?

Burge had hoped to discuss his findings with the inspector, but Marmion had left Scotland Yard and was reportedly on his way to visit his future son-in-law. Any discussion about the case would have to wait until the following day. Burge accepted that. He was keenly aware that the inspector had been standing nearby when Keedy was shot during the siege. Even though the sergeant had volunteered to enter the building first, Marmion was bound to feel a sense of responsibility for what had happened. Now that Keedy had been finally released from hospital, it was an occasion that both men would savour.

It was a muted celebration. Marmion had arrived at the house with a flagon of beer and a bottle of port. While he and Keedy drank the beer, Ellen and Alice each sipped a glass of port. Raymond and Lily were confirmed teetotallers, so they politely refused the offer of a drink. Their work routinely involved collecting drunks from shop doorways at night and taking them back to the hostel until they sobered up. Yet they had no objection to the alcohol being consumed in their house. In their view, it was right to toast Keedy's heroism during the siege and to mark his final release from hospital.

The women, inevitably, drifted into the kitchen to get

refreshments and to discuss the forthcoming marriage. As soon as the men were alone, Keedy demanded to hear about the case on which Marmion was working.

'I'm off duty now, Joe,' said the other.

'You told me that we're never off duty,' Keedy reminded him.

'That's true, but I don't want to bore Raymond with details of an investigation.'

'Don't worry about me,' said his brother. 'I'd find it interesting.'

'Very well . . .'

Marmion had a long sup of beer before giving them the salient details of his latest case. His listeners waited until he had finished before making any comment.

'I hadn't realised how distressing it was for you, Harvey,' said Raymond. 'You lost a close friend during the robbery. No wonder you're so determined to catch his killer.'

'What about the other policeman?' asked Keedy.

'Constable Harry Lee was knocked out by one of the robbers,' said Marmion. 'He's come out of his coma but is unable to remember many details about what happened. The fact that Sam Collard was killed has really shaken him.'

Raymond nodded. 'That's understandable.'

'What did they tell you at the bank?' pressed Keedy.

Marmion gave him a precis of their visit to the bank and their conversation with the manager. He also talked about the three former employees whose names they had been given.

'We've spoken to Walter Greenlow,' he told them. 'He's a rather sad old character who can't adjust to the fact that his wife has died. I don't believe that he is in any way involved in the crime.'

'What about Beale?' said Keedy.

'I had a long talk with him.'

'And?'

'He's rather too fond of himself, Joe.'

'Do you think he might have assisted the robbers?'

'It's a possibility, I suppose.'

'That leaves this man, Paterson.'

'Cliff Burge went off to find him. By the time I had to leave Scotland Yard,' said Marmion, 'he still hadn't reported back. What interested me is that Paterson used to have responsibility for security at the bank. It's not only an important job, it meant an increase in his pay.'

Raymond's face puckered. 'I don't follow, Harvey.'

'When a new deputy manager was appointed, he took over that responsibility.'

'Ah, I see.'

'At a stroke, Neil Paterson, who'd been in line for promotion, had not only failed to secure it, he had also, in effect, been demoted and docked the extra money he earned by being in charge of security. That's why I'm not surprised that, in due course, he resigned.'

'In other words,' said Keedy, 'Paterson is your man.'

'It's starting to look that way.'

'How can you be certain?' asked Raymond.

'That depends on what Cliff finds out.'

'What if none of these three suspects is guilty?'

'It's a possibility we must consider.'

'What happens then?'

Marmion took a deep breath. 'We have a problem . . .'

Alone together in the kitchen, the three women were deep in conversation about the forthcoming wedding. Since they belonged to an older generation, Ellen and Lily recalled experiences that Alice found almost laughably out of date – but she had the sense not to say so. Economy was the theme of her wedding. Germany never let them forget for one moment that there was a war on. Heavy bombing from the air continued and there was peril below the water in the shape of enemy submarines. So many merchant ships had been torpedoed that food supplies intended for British shelves were limited. Severe rationing had had to be brought in. That was bound to have a marked effect on the wedding reception.

'At least we can all feel safe in the church,' said Lily.

'What do you mean?' asked Alice.

'Well, we'll have half the Women's Police Force on duty.'

'They'll certainly be on duty, Auntie Lily, but not at the wedding itself.'

'I assumed that you'd invite all your friends.'

'Gale Force would never allow that.'

Lily was mystified. 'Who?'

'It's their nickname for Inspector Gale,' explained Ellen, 'and it's very cruel.'

Alice pulled a face. 'You don't have to work for her, Mummy.'

'I did speak to her once and found her very pleasant.'

'Then she was on her best behaviour. Iris Goodliffe, my best friend, is coming,' said Alice, 'and so are a few others. But they are the only ones able to get the time off.'

'What about this Inspector Gale?' asked Lily. 'Will she be there?'

'Not if I can help it!'

'I think you're being very harsh, Alice,' said her mother.

'Try working under her and you'd soon change your mind.'

'I've never seen you so hostile,' said Lily.

'I'm sorry,' apologised Alice, calming down. 'You caught me on a raw nerve. Let's talk about someone else, shall we?'

Ellen nodded in agreement. 'That's a good idea.'

'What about Paul?' asked Lily. 'I don't suppose that he will be there, will he?'

Alice traded a look of despair with her mother. 'No,' she said, turning to her aunt. 'Paul won't be coming. To be honest, I'm grateful for that.'

'So am I,' agreed Ellen.

'The truth is that we don't even know where Paul is.'

'Or even if he's still alive.'

'It will be strange not having my brother there,' said Alice, 'but that's the way it is, I'm afraid.'

'Do you still have no idea of his whereabouts?' asked Lily.

'No, we don't.'

'We just hope that he's alive and well,' sighed Ellen.

Alice nodded in agreement. 'Paul is always in our thoughts.'

Marmion arrived at work the following day to find a telephone message awaiting him. It was from Stuart Fryer, the deputy manager, asking him to make contact at once. When he rang the man, Marmion became quietly excited. There had been a development.

'Where are we going?' asked Burge, climbing into the police car beside him.

'The bank.'

'Why?'

'They've discovered something,' replied Marmion.

'Is that good or bad?'

'Wait and see.'

The driver maintained as fast a speed as possible, dodging

cars, vans, buses and horse-drawn vehicles. When he eventually pulled up outside the bank, there was an immediate response. A door in the building opened and Fryer came out to greet the detectives. They had seen him before but had not been properly introduced to him. Fryer shook hands with each of them in turn. He was a tall, slender man in his forties, wearing a dark suit. What both detectives noticed was his unusually pale skin.

'Thank you for coming so quickly, Inspector,' he said.

'I could hear the urgency in your voice,' replied Marmion.

'The idea had never occurred to me until I went to bed last night. When it did, it kept me awake for most of the night. That's why I got here so early – to test my theory.'

'What theory is that?' asked Burge.

'Perhaps they didn't gain entry by the side door on the ground floor.'

'How else could they have possibly got into the bank?'

'Follow me, Sergeant.'

He led them into the building and up a flight of stairs. Most of the bank's activities were on the ground floor. The first floor consisted of a series of offices of varying sizes. Fryer led them to a room at the end of the corridor. Taking out a key, he inserted it into the lock.

'Now for my discovery,' he said with a quiet smile.

Opening the door, he stepped into a room with a trapdoor in the centre of the ceiling. Reaching for the ladder propped up against a wall, he moved it against the edge of the trapdoor above their heads and clipped it in place.

'Follow me,' he said.

After climbing the steps, he moved a bolt aside, pushed up the trapdoor and switched on the light. He then went up nimbly into the attic and waited for them. Marmion climbed the steps with some difficulty and looked around him.

'You've got a huge space up here, Mr Fryer,' he observed.

'That's what I kept thinking about,' said the other. 'It has a significant defect over every other part of the bank.'

'What defect is that?' asked Burge, climbing the ladder to join the two men.

'It has no burglar alarm. If anyone gained entry to the attic, nobody would be any the wiser. And I believe that someone did get in here.' He picked up a brown paper bag with crumbs in it. 'After he got in by means of the door to the roof, I fancy that he sat down and ate his supper.'

'I'm beginning to see what you mean,' said Marmion. 'Instead of getting in here by means of that side door out in the street, one of them got into the attic by night and, at precisely the time that house was on fire, went down into the bank and disabled the alarm.'

'It would have taken thirty seconds at most,' said Fryer.

'As soon as the alarm was out of action,' said Burge, 'he opened the side door to let his accomplice in. They somehow got into one of the safes and helped themselves to some money!'

'You have to admire the way they planned it.'

'I do, Mr Fryer,' said Marmion. 'What I don't admire is the way that they attacked the two policemen who caught them leaving the building. It's the reason I'll do whatever it takes to get the robbers in custody.'

'That goes for me as well,' added Burge.

'I understand your feelings,' said Fryer. 'In your place I'd feel the same. Clearly, they were professionals. Most bank robbers would have forced their way in and grabbed what they could before making a run for it. These men were experts. They worked everything out in advance – even to the point of enlisting the aid of the fire brigade. While a disaster was occupying the attention of people only streets away, two men got away with many thousands of pounds in crisp banknotes.'

'We'll catch them,' insisted Marmion, 'long before they can spend much of their haul.'

'You agree with my theory, then?' asked Fryer.

'Yes, I do, sir. You've made a real contribution to our investigation.'

'Be careful, Inspector. These men are clever. They'll stop at nothing.'

'Neither will we, sir,' said Marmion.

Joe Keedy decided to take advantage of his new freedom. The sun was shining and there was a cooling breeze. During his time in hospital, he had forced himself to have regular exercise even if it was of the most limited kind. No restrictions existed now. After leaving the house, he headed for the nearby park and enjoyed the simple pleasure of listening to the birds. Now that he had got used to his new home, he realised how perfect it was for him. Raymond and Lily were wonderful hosts, and his accommodation was ideal. The welcoming party for him on the previous evening had made him feel certain that he was back in the real world again.

His body craved exercise, but his mind required a challenge. It was the reason he had pressed Marmion for details of his latest case. Though he had been given only a broad outline, there was enough to excite his interest. Since a policeman had been cruelly murdered in the wake of the bank robbery, Keedy had felt the urge to wreak revenge on his behalf. That was why he had promised to squeeze every detail of the case out of his future father-in-law.

But it was Alice who soon filled his mind. With their marriage only weeks away, Keedy knew that he had to brace himself for a big change in his life. He'd seen many police colleagues surrender the joys of being a bachelor for the constraints of marriage. Some had settled into the new life with ease, but others had chafed against its limitations. He was full of hope and confidence, but they were tinged with doubt. While the hospital surgeon had assured him that he would be able to lead a normal life in due course, Keedy did not feel that he had reached that point yet. Desperate not to disappoint Alice on their wedding night, he was praying that, when the time came, all would be well.

Until then, he vowed, he would have regular exercise that pushed him to the limit. By way of proving his commitment, he lengthened his stride and increased his speed.

He felt truly alive at last and, more importantly, he had a new sense of purpose.

While they were given their assignment for the day, Iris Goodliffe had to suppress her urge to bombard Alice with questions. The moment that the two of them left the building, however, she had the first one ready.

'How did you get on last night?' she asked.

'It was . . . very nice, Iris.'

'Very nice,' she repeated with a hollow laugh. 'For the first time in weeks, you see your future husband outside a hospital and all you can tell me is that it was "very nice". I know you better than that, Alice Marmion. And I'm certain that Joe Keedy would have been dying to see you when he was at liberty, so to speak. Something must have happened.'

'We did have a moment together,' admitted Alice.

'Well, I hope you took full advantage of it.'

'We . . . got very close, if that's what you mean.'

Iris grinned. 'How close?' she asked.

'That's none of your business.'

'In that case, it was very close.'

'My parents were in the kitchen with Uncle Raymond and Auntie Lily. In other words, they were less than ten feet away. We had to keep our voices down.'

'And what did Joe say to you?'

'We just enjoyed the simple pleasure of being alone together at last without a nurse hovering or someone pushing a hospital trolley past us. Joe told me that it would be the first night for ages when he could switch the light off whenever he chose instead of waiting for someone else to do it.'

'How does he get on with your uncle and aunt?'

'Very well. He couldn't be happier that he's staying with them.'

'What will that big brother of his say?'

'In his own peculiar way,' said Alice, 'I think he'd feel satisfied. Joe and I are being kept apart. It's all that Dennis wanted.'

'He had no right to force you apart.'

'The problem has been solved now. That's the main thing.'

'How was Joe?'

'He looked wonderful, Iris – a picture of health. My only complaint is that he thinks he's back on duty. As soon as Daddy joined us, Joe was desperate to talk to him about this latest case.'

'That bank robbery, you mean?'

'Yes – it was in all the newspapers today.'

'Joe is on sick leave. He should let other people solve the crime.'

'That's exactly what I told him,' said Alice, 'and he even pretended to agree. But I know Joe Keedy of old. He simply must be involved. It's in his blood, Iris.'

When they had delivered their report to him, Claude Chatfield was interested in the turn of events.

'What do you think of Mr Fryer's theory?' he asked.

'I'm ready to accept it without question,' replied Marmion. 'He's clearly put a lot of thought into it. All that the manager can do is to throw his hands in the air and wail about the stolen money, but his deputy is doing something practical.'

'I agree,' said Burge. 'Thanks to him, we now know exactly how the bank was entered.'

They were in the superintendent's office, seated side by side. Chatfield remained on his feet, trying to absorb the latest information and work out how to pass it on to the commissioner.

Marmion was cautious. 'It might be best if we keep this latest discovery from the press,' he advised. 'We don't want them swarming around the bank and asking to be allowed up on to the roof. They're under our feet enough, as it is.'

'I agree,' said Chatfield. 'Right – what exactly do we know about the robbers?'

'They're cunning,' replied Burge, 'and quite ruthless.'

'I'd go further than that,' added Marmion. 'This crime was planned with military precision. These men have been in the army. Who else would carry a bayonet but a former soldier? One of them climbed in through the roof and waited in the attic until the agreed time. Once he heard the fire engines setting out, he clambered down through the trapdoor and ran off to disable the burglar alarm. Once that was done, he let his accomplice into the building and the pair of them somehow opened a safe and helped themselves to its contents.'

Chatfield nodded. 'Thousands of pounds of it!'

'They had a car standing by,' Marmion continued, 'but, before they could reach it, they were challenged by two policemen. One was killed, the other was knocked senseless. Sam Collard and Harry Lee were not mugs. They were experienced coppers who'd been in dozens of awkward situations. Yet they were quite unable to make an arrest. The bank robbers escaped. There were reports of a car speeding away from the area.'

'Organise house-to-house enquiries near the bank,' instructed the superintendent. 'Someone must have seen or heard something.'

'What they heard were cries of despair from the street where a house was on fire,' noted Burge.

'The bank robbers made sure that attention was focused on that,' said Marmion.

'You said a moment ago,' recalled Chatfield, 'that these men were former soldiers.'

'I'm certain of it, sir.'

'In which army did they serve – British or German?'

CHAPTER SIX

Many people found newspapers far too depressing to read. They always seemed to be full of bad news. The war was now in its fifth year and the end was nowhere in sight. Losses on both sides were horrendous. New weapons with even more deadly effect were being developed. Politicians kept chattering away but made no visible progress towards a peace process that would allow the Allies to bring hostilities to an end, and to walk away with their heads held high. Instead of spreading hope of a lasting peace, the government was instead talking about legislation that would increase the maximum age of conscription to fifty. Another generation of British men might soon be forced into uniform and sent in due course to the Front, leaving anxious families in their wake.

Sir Edward Henry was duly shocked by the latest development.

'Raising the age of conscription to fifty,' he said, glancing at the newspaper headline. 'It's a terrifying thought!'

'The younger generation has sustained appalling losses, Sir Edward,' said Chatfield. 'They have to be replaced somehow.'

'But where will it end, Superintendent? At fifty? At sixty?

Is the government contemplating regiments of men in their seventies?'

'I don't believe that we will be pushed to that extreme.'

'I sincerely hope not.'

They were in the commissioner's office. Claude Chatfield had come with a report about the bank robbery, but Sir Edward Henry's mind was still fixed on the war. The commissioner searched for comfort.

'I'm certain that the Germans are suffering just as badly. They've lost untold thousands of soldiers – and there have been casualties among their sailors and pilots as well.'

'Indeed, there have.'

'I'd love to be free of air raids on the capital,' said the commissioner. 'After all this time, they still terrify the population of London.'

'Yet we've learnt to react quickly to any damage caused,' argued Chatfield. 'That's to our credit.'

'London is a city of bomb sites. Whole districts are in ruins.'

'Far be it from me to criticise you, Sir Edward, but . . . I think that you exaggerate.'

'I daresay that I do,' admitted the other with a chuckle. 'It's a failing of mine. I do apologise. Let's put the war aside for a while and concentrate on the important task of policing London.'

'I've brought news of that bank robbery.'

The older man's eyes glinted. 'An arrest, by any chance?'

'Not yet, I fear, but there has been a measure of progress. We now have a clearer idea of exactly how the robbery was planned.'

Chatfield went on to describe the theory advanced by the deputy manager of the bank. It had been endorsed by Marmion, who had discussed the matter in depth with Stuart Fryer. Both had climbed into the attic at the bank with Burge. Sir Edward was fascinated by the new information.

'This fellow, Fryer, sounds like an intelligent man.'

'Marmion rates him highly, sir.'

'And what deductions has the inspector drawn from this new information?'

'He believes that the bank robbers are former soldiers.'

The commissioner was startled. 'Really?'

'Everything was planned meticulously,' said Chatfield. 'They got exactly what they wanted from the raid then fled into the night.'

'Not before they'd killed one policeman and severely wounded another.'

'Quite so.'

'Does Marmion believe that these men were German soldiers?'

'No,' said Chatfield. 'The inspector thinks that German soldiers would have stolen more money and created far more damage. At the very least, they'd have left a bomb inside the building. Think of the chaos that would have caused when it went off.'

'I shudder at the thought!'

'Marmion believes that they are British deserters, men who fled the battlefield with a view to using the skills they'd learnt in the army for criminal purposes.'

'Do they have no sense of loyalty?' demanded the commissioner.

'It seems not.'

'Is there any way of tracing these cowards?'

'I've asked the War Office to supply us with a comprehensive list of deserters,' said Chatfield. 'Marmion believes that it may be that one of them is from the area where the bank is situated. As a result, he would know that the place was vulnerable.'

'I hope that you've given the inspector sufficient men to handle this case.'

'Marmion can have as many as he wishes,' said Chatfield. 'Unfortunately, the person he most wishes to have beside him is not available.

'Detective Sergeant Keedy?'

'He's been released from hospital and is staying with the inspector's brother.'

Sir Edward raised an eyebrow. 'Is that the one in the Salvation Army?'

'Yes, it is – Raymond Marmion.'

Joe Keedy enjoyed a leisurely breakfast at his new home. Lily Marmion was an excellent cook and made the best of their limited supply of groceries. She was happy to see their guest so relaxed.

'You seem to have settled in very well, Joe,' she observed.

'Thanks are due to you and Raymond. You've made me feel at home.'

'I'm sorry that my husband couldn't join us for breakfast. There was trouble at the hostel. Raymond went over there to sort it out.'

'I admire his dedication.'

'It's a way of life we both chose.'

'You and Raymond are always so bright and cheerful.'

'We don't always feel that way,' admitted Lily with a laugh. 'What are your plans for today?'

'I'd like to start with a long, bracing walk.'

'You've certainly got the weather for it. It's lovely out there.'

'To be honest, Lily,' he confessed, 'I feel such a cheat.'

'What do you mean?'

'Well, I'm fit enough to be discharged from hospital and should go straight back to work. Instead of that, I'm imposing on you and behaving as if I'm on holiday.'

'You're convalescing, Joe.'

'My body may be doing that, but my mind is buzzing. I yearn for action. I'd love to be involved in catching the villains behind this bank robbery.'

'You need to be completely fit first.'

Before he could reply, Keedy heard the front door being unlocked. Moments later, Raymond Marmion came into the room. He exchanged greetings with their visitor.

'You've got so much colour in your cheeks today,' said Raymond.

'I feel ready for anything,' said Keedy.

'In that case, we'll have you in the band on Sunday.'

'Ah, I'm afraid not. Alice is dragging me off to All Saints' Church. We're going to hear the banns being read for the second time. I missed last week's service because I was in hospital. Alice went alone.'

'She'll enjoy having you beside her, Joe,' said Lily.

'I'm a bit uneasy about it, to be honest.'

'Why?' asked Raymond. 'It should be a proud moment for you.'

'I'll be shaking in my shoes,' confessed Keedy. 'When the vicar publishes the banns of marriage, he goes on to say that, if anyone knows cause or just impediment why these two persons should not be joined together in Holy Matrimony, they are to declare it.'

'I don't see any problem there.'

'I do, Raymond. What if someone from my past jumps to her feet and says that the wedding should not take place?'

'I can't believe that that will happen,' said Lily, smiling.

'There's one certain way to make sure that it doesn't,' added her husband. 'Instead of going to the church, join us on our march. When you're beating that drum nice and loud, nobody would dare to spoil your fun.'

Burge and Marmion were in the latter's office. The inspector sifted through the list of army deserters with mixed feelings. He was reminded that his son, Paul, was on a list of missing persons circulated to every police force in the realm. During the Battle of the Somme, Paul had been wounded, blinded, and sent back to a military hospital in England. Though he had fully recovered his sight, he had displayed worrying symptoms. Chief among them were his erratic behaviour at home and his callous treatment of young women. When Paul had left home without any warning to his family, Marmion was unable to decide why their son had taken such extreme action. It left him feeling that they had somehow let him down. The search for Paul had been constant but to no avail. They could not even be sure if he was still alive.

As he went slowly through the names of the deserters, Marmion realised that each one represented a personal tragedy. Some had fled their regiments in fear, others had rejected a life that kept them stuck in trenches and under constant bombardment, while a smaller number sneered at the notion of national service and sneaked back to the comparative safety of their homeland.

'I hadn't realised there were so many of them,' admitted Burge, looking over Marmion's shoulder. 'Have we got all those cowards on the loose?'

'No, we haven't,' said Marmion. 'Some of these men are probably dead. Desperate to get back here, they had to take enormous risks. They've stolen boats and faced the terror of trying to cross the Channel. The white cliffs of Dover may look surprisingly close from France but reaching them is by no means a foregone conclusion. It's unlikely that the deserters are all trained sailors. Imagine what the crossing must be like in bad weather.'

'I'd rather not, sir.'

'What I can't find in this list is anyone whose home address is in the Paddington area. I'd hoped for someone who knew that bank well and saw it as a target.'

'Perhaps they just picked it by chance,' said Burge.

'I think that's unlikely.'

'So how did they get the information they needed about that bank?'

'They had it from someone who used to work there.'

'We've already talked to Walter Greenlow, and you spoke to Martin Beale.'

'That leaves Neil Paterson, the man who disappeared without trace. Why didn't he tell any of his friends where he and his wife were moving to? It's odd.'

'For some reason, they wanted to cover their tracks.'

'What possible reason could that be?'

'I need you to find out, Cliff. My guess is that they went back to Scotland.'

'That's what Reginald Naylor believed,' said Burge. 'Paterson was always talking about "going home" one day, it seems. And he was a confirmed Scottish Nationalist.'

'It doesn't make him a bank robber,' warned Marmion.

'Maybe not, sir, but he has to be a possible suspect in this case.'

'That's why I'm sending you to Scotland to find him. I'll have to clear it with Chat but I'm sure that he'll endorse my decision.'

Burge was stunned. 'I'm going to Scotland?'

'Don't look so shocked,' said Marmion with a laugh. 'They're as British as you and me up there. Look how many of them volunteered to join the army when the war broke out. You'll be among friends.'

'We have no idea where Paterson is, sir.'

'You'll find him, if you look hard enough.'

'I wouldn't know where to start.'

'Glasgow,' declared Marmion. 'It's the beating heart of Scotland. The city is full of iron foundries, steelworks, shipyards and engineering shops. Since the war started, Glasgow has been churning out essential artillery, munitions and, of course, battleships. It's the main reason why Scotland is called the workshop of the world.'

'That's true.'

'And didn't that fellow Naylor tell you that Paterson's wife hailed from Glasgow?'

'Yes,' said Burge, 'he did.'

'Then that's the most likely place they'd go. Don't you agree?'

It was impossible to walk the streets of London without being reminded that there was a war on. Signs of bomb damage were everywhere and there were endless examples of wounded soldiers as well. Alice and Iris saw several of them on their beat – men who had lost limbs on the battlefield or been blinded for life. Some had hideous facial scars, others needed crutches to help them limp along or someone to push them in wheelchairs. When they turned a corner, they saw a man in his early twenties, seated on a piece of sacking and using his one remaining hand to hold

71

a pipe to his mouth. They paused to listen to a halting version of 'It's a Long Way to Tipperary' then Alice dropped some coins into the cap beside the man. He acknowledged the gift with a grateful smile.

'I don't have any money on me,' explained Iris, 'or I'd have left something for him.'

'I feel so sorry for young men like that.'

'So do I, Alice.'

'What sort of future can they have?'

'I dread to think.' As they resumed their walk, Iris heaved a sigh. 'When we see someone like that, you must always think of Paul.'

'His situation is different,' said Alice. 'It's not his body that's wounded, it's his mind.'

'Are you sure that he's still alive?'

'Yes, of course.'

'How do you know?'

Alice shrugged. 'We just do, Iris.'

'But you haven't heard a single word from him since he ran away.'

'That's true and it's very . . . upsetting. Paul chose to turn his back on the family.'

'How could he do that?' asked Iris. 'It's unnatural.'

'We've had to . . . adjust to it. I don't have a brother any more.'

'It's so sad, Alice.'

'We try not to dwell on it. We just hope that he is alive and well and living a different sort of life somewhere.'

'Won't you feel a pang on your wedding day?' asked Iris.

'I'll be far too excited. I've waited a long time to marry Joe and – after what happened during that siege – I'm determined to enjoy every moment of it. I almost lost him, remember. Joe was not only shot in the stomach, he was stalked afterwards by the man who had fired at him.'

'Thank goodness your father was able to arrest that person!'

'It's the best wedding present we could have.'

They walked on in silence for a few minutes then Iris remembered something.

'Has Joe seen what you've done to the house?' she asked.

'Not yet.'

'He's going to have a wonderful surprise.'

'I hope so, Iris. Mummy and I have spent hours working there. We made a huge difference to the place. It's a real home now.'

'I'd love to be there when Joe sees it for the first time.'

'I'm sorry,' said Alice, 'but that's a treat I've been promising myself for a very long time. I want to see his sheer amazement when I take him there.'

In the short time that Keedy had been at the house, he'd come to admire even more the work that Raymond and Lily did for the Salvation Army. They were tireless. Apart from helping to look after the people in their hostel, they had lots of other commitments. It meant that Keedy was left alone for long periods. One bonus was that he had free access to the large bookcase in the living room. Many of the titles were related to the work of the Salvation Army, but there were also novels, anthologies of short stories, travel books and a handbook on carpentry. The last book was the one he chose first. Keedy was deep into the third chapter when Raymond returned to the house.

'That's what I like to see,' he said. 'A man who loves reading.'

'It's something I rarely get time to do, Raymond. Detective

work consists largely of writing in my notepad. That's the only reading I manage to do.'

'Which book have you chosen?'

'It's a handbook on carpentry,' said Keedy, holding it up. 'It's going to come in useful when we move into our new house.'

'Then feel free to take it with you. Not that you need it, mind you. I'd always put you down as a real handyman.'

'That's what I thought I was. This book tells me there's still a lot to learn.'

'What else have you been doing?'

'I've been for a couple of long walks, and I've been working on the jigsaw.'

Raymond was puzzled. 'We don't have a jigsaw.'

'I'm talking about the one in my mind. Each investigation throws up a different set of pieces. Fitting them together is a real challenge.'

'You've been thinking about this bank robbery, haven't you?'

'It fascinates me. That's why I pumped your brother for the details.'

'You're supposed to be recuperating, Joe.'

'What better way to do it than by helping to solve a crime?'

'You could learn more about the finer points of carpentry,' suggested Raymond. 'It may not give you the same excitement as a bank robbery, but you'll be learning something that will come in useful when you and Alice move into your house.'

'Oh, I hope to be back at work before that happens.'

'Don't rush it. You need to be fully recovered.'

'I soon will be.'

'Remember what that doctor at the hospital told you. Rest means rest.'

'That's only my body,' said Keedy. 'My mind is the problem.

I want to get it back in working order. It's the reason I need a daring crime to solve.'

'Fair enough,' conceded Raymond. 'You know best, I suppose.'

'I do. Mind you,' added Keedy with a grin, 'I was tempted by your invitation to join the band. I've always wanted to show off by marching through the streets and banging a big drum.'

Marmion was so accustomed to having his requests turned down by the superintendent that he braced himself before entering the office. After knocking on the door, he obeyed the order from within and stepped into the office. Chatfield was behind the desk, flipping his way through a sheaf of papers. He looked up.'

'Is there a problem, Inspector?' he asked.

'I hope not, sir.'

'Well?'

'I firmly believe that someone must go to Scotland in search of Neil Paterson. He's a crucial figure in this investigation and must be tracked down.'

'I agree wholeheartedly. When do you leave?'

Marmion needed a moment to overcome his surprise. 'Actually,' he said, 'I was intending to send Sergeant Burge.'

'A good decision. Get him on the next train to Edinburgh.'

'We believe that Paterson and his wife are more likely to be in Glasgow.'

'Then send Burge there at once.' He opened a drawer and took out a metal cash box. 'He may have to stay a night or two. I'll take care of his expenses.'

'Thank you, sir.'

'Don't look so surprised, man!'

'I was expecting you to be . . . well, difficult.'

'I'm never difficult,' replied Chatfield, indignantly. 'I resent the suggestion.'

'Then I take it back immediately, sir.'

'Give Burge his orders then send him in here to pick up his expenses.'

'I'll do so at once.'

'Oh, one more thing.'

'Yes, sir?'

Chatfield spread his arms wide. 'I'm not that much of an ogre, am I?'

Stifling a reply, Marmion left the room quickly.

Nora Collard had spent hours preparing herself for the shock. The body of her husband had already been identified by policemen who knew him as a friend and colleague, but his wife insisted on seeing the corpse. Ellen Marmion had offered to go with her, but Nora chose her friend and neighbour, Rita Dowling. A police car picked them up and drove them to the morgue. Rita took a firm hold of her friend then helped her into the building. A man in a white coat spoke to them in a hushed voice but they heard little of what he said. The women were too busy screwing up their courage for what was bound to be a harrowing few minutes.

Led by the man, they went into a room where the temperature was suddenly cooler. The body of Sam Collard lay under a sheet on a table. The man gave them a couple of minutes to ready themselves. Straightening her back, Nora gave him a nod. He removed the sheet far enough to expose the head and shoulders. Rita could not bear to look at her former neighbour, but Nora's eyes never left the face of the man with whom she had lived so happily for so many years. Memories flooded back and made her shudder with despair. As she turned away, the sheet was lowered over the body again. Supported by her friend, Nora left the room with the feeling that she had done her duty and taken a long, sad, silent farewell.

When they stepped out of the morgue, Rita was still supporting her.

'How do you feel, Nora?' she asked.

'I'm fine now,' murmured the widow. 'The worst is over.'

As he waited at the railway station, Clifford Burge had time to reflect on the sudden change in his life. The injury that had put Joe Keedy in hospital had been a boon to his deputy. Plucked out of a whole battery of detective constables, he had been upgraded to the status of an acting detective sergeant. It meant that he was being entrusted with the important task of visiting Scotland in search of a man deemed to be a key witness in the bank robbery – if not an accomplice of the deserters. Summoned to Chatfield's office, Burge had been given expenses then he had been driven in a police car to his flat so that he could pack a small suitcase. He now had a train ticket in his pocket and a desire to justify the faith put in him by senior colleagues.

It was only when he was seated in the compartment of a train that he realised the enormity of his task. He had no idea whatsoever of the whereabouts of Neil Paterson and his wife. Glasgow was a big city and a complete enigma to him. How on earth should he start? He spent a fruitless hour or more going through the possibilities. It was only when he was steaming through the north of England in a train that the answer finally dawned on him.

What would Joe Keedy do in his position?

* * *

He had still not adjusted to the fact that he was a free man at last. After weeks in hospital, Keedy had been at the mercy of regular routines. It had been comforting at first and had clearly contributed to his recovery. But that life was behind him now. Though he was staying with friends, he had no wish to impose on them. Reading the handbook of carpentry had reminded him that he and Alice now owned a house that needed all manner of repairs. The least he could do was to list every one of them and devise a plan to tackle them in turn. Raymond and Lily were, as usual, busy that afternoon. Not wishing to alarm them, he left a note to say that he had decided to go to his future home for a short while. He promised to make his way back to them that evening.

Getting to the house posed a problem. Keedy routinely made use of a police car to ferry him around London. None was available when he was off duty. He therefore had to resort to public transport. On his way to the park, he had noticed a bus stop only a hundred yards or so from the house. After putting on his raincoat, he stepped out into the gloom of late afternoon. When he reached the bus stop, he found an elderly couple standing there, arm in arm. Keedy told them where he wished to go, hoping that they could give him at least some idea of how to get there. They were only too glad to help him.

'Of course,' warned the man, 'it's going to be tricky. You'll need two different buses.'

'Three,' corrected his wife.

'He asked me, not you.'

'I'm just trying to help, Cyril.'

'Where will the first bus take me?' asked Keedy.

'All the way to the depot,' said the man. 'Get off there and catch a number twenty-nine.'

'Number thirty would be better,' argued his wife. 'Then he could change when he gets to the cemetery. A bus from there would get him where he wants to go.'

The man gave a reluctant nod. 'I think you're right, Mabel.'

'I often am.'

Keedy had to listen to a few minutes of marital jousting before they were ready to confirm his route. When the first of his three buses came towards them, he thanked them for their help. The woman's advice had been sound. Almost half an hour later, he was dropped off within easy walking distance of the house. Keedy's spirits lifted. In a matter of weeks, he would finally be alone with his wife in their first home. The thought made him feel that an exciting new life awaited him.

In the short term, however, there was a serious problem. When he approached the house, he saw that there was a light on in the front bedroom. Keedy was alarmed. Who had been foolish enough to leave it on? There was no point in wasting electricity when the house was empty. He quickened his step. As he got closer, he saw something that alerted him to danger. The curtains were being drawn in the bedroom. Someone was inside the house. He felt a surge of anger.

When he reached the front door, he found that it was securely locked. How had the person inside gained entry? Was he dealing with a burglar, taking advantage of the fact that the property was unoccupied? Keedy was far too angry to care about his personal safety. He had arrested burglars before, and they had always carried a weapon of sorts. In the past, he had overpowered an intruder, but he had no handcuffs with him now. He had to temper his anger with caution.

What he did possess was the element of surprise. He took out the spare key that he had brought and inserted it gently in the lock, opening the door soundlessly and slipping inside the house. Keedy closed the door behind him then walked to the stairs. Noises from above told him that the intruder was moving around. He went silently up the stairs and crept over to the door of the front bedroom. He took a deep breath. After summoning up his strength, he flung the door open and yelled at the top of his voice.

'You are trespassing on private property and I'm putting you under arrest!'

When he recognised the visitor, he was both relieved and delighted.

'What, in heaven's name, are you doing here, Alice?'

'To be honest,' she admitted, 'I'm frightened to death.'

He put his arms around her. 'I'm so sorry. I thought you were a burglar.'

'I only came to tidy the place up before you saw what we'd done.'

'You did all this?' he said, looking in amazement at the new wallpaper and the freshly painted woodwork. 'I was expecting to decorate in here myself.'

'Mummy and I saved you the trouble. We've worked here for weeks.' She smiled up at him. 'You're not really going to arrest me, are you?'

CHAPTER SEVEN

Clifford Burge had not realised how long a journey it was to reach Glasgow. Hours went past, but whenever the train came into another station he realised that they were still well short of the Scottish border. To keep his mind occupied, he read through every detail about the bank robbery he had recorded in his notebook. He was intrigued by the characters they had met during their investigation. Douglas Boucher had been the first, a self-important man who treated the bank robbery as a personal attack on him and who hated the way that the crime was reported in the newspapers. Walter Greenlow had been next, a strange, lonely individual who had retired from the bank to build his life around his dead wife. Burge was bound to admire a self-made man who had educated himself to a point where he could go to work in a suit, instead of in the filthy dungarees that his father had routinely worn as a docker.

Though he had never met Martin Beale in person, Burge had been given a detailed description of the man by the inspector. Marmion had found him bright, self-satisfied and without any real sympathy for his former colleagues at the bank. Beale had, however, spoken warmly of Neil Paterson, a more amenable work colleague than Greenlow would have been. None of the three men, Burge decided, had been entirely happy working under the manager. Paterson had the stronger reason to dislike him, having been rejected for the post of deputy manager and forced to watch Stuart Fryer being rewarded with the promotion. Was that the main reason why Paterson had given his notice and left the bank? Or did he have a stronger motive to do so?

Of all the people he had so far encountered, Burge had found the deputy manager the most impressive. Stuart Fryer had looked closely at the details of the robbery and worked out that one of the men involved had got inside the building at night. He had been extremely helpful to the detectives, making them look at the crime from a different angle. In appointing Fryer as deputy manager, Burge reasoned, the manager had chosen the right man. Had Paterson simply fled London in a fit of pique, or might he have been involved in some way with the robbery? Might that explain his sudden flight?

Before the train had departed, Burge had bought a morning paper. The bank robbery was still featured on the front page, but the reporter had few of the details that had been uncovered by the police. All that they could offer was fevered speculation. There was no mention of Neil Paterson.

Flipping his notebook shut, Burge stowed it away in an inside pocket. He then realised that the train was slowing down. What he could see through the window was a blanket of darkness, but huge shapes soon began to flash by. The train thundered into a station and came to a juddering halt. Burge lowered a window and spoke to a porter.

'How long before we get to Scotland?' he asked.

The man grinned. 'Oh, you've hours to go yet, sir. Try to get some sleep.'

Keedy had found the tour of the house quite astounding. Jobs that he had set aside for himself had already been done. Attention had been lavished on every room. With the help of her mother, Alice had expended every minute of free time on improving their new home so that it was completely ready for occupation. When he had seen the whole house, Keedy took her back upstairs to the main bedroom and clasped her in his arms.

'What a clever woman I'm going to marry,' he said.

'It wasn't only for your benefit, Joe. I wanted the place comfortable for myself.'

'It's more than comfortable – it's perfect!'

'There are still one or two last things to do.'

'Forget them, Alice. They're my responsibility now. I feel strong enough to take on anything.'

'Remember what you were told,' she warned. 'Don't do too much too soon.'

'Your example has made me want to pick up a paintbrush right now.'

'Any painting must be done in daylight.'

'How on earth did you and your mother find time for what you did?'

'It was a mission we set ourselves.'

'I'm so grateful – and so lucky to find you here this evening.'

Alice gave an involuntary shiver. 'You terrified me, Joe. You threatened to arrest me.'

'That was because I thought you were a burglar.'

'Do I look like a burglar?' she demanded.

'No,' he said, holding her at arm's length so that he could appraise her. 'You look like the woman I want to spend the rest of my life with.' He hugged her again. 'Hey, I've just thought of something.'

'What is it?'

'We've never been alone in our own bedroom before.'

She was uneasy. 'I'm not sure that we should be here now.'

'This moment is something I've dreamt about.'

'Don't get carried away,' she said, detaching herself from him.

'But we must celebrate what you've done to the house, Alice.'

'Mummy did just as much as me.'

'Luckily,' he said with a grin, 'she's not here, is she? But you are.'

Alice backed away. 'I don't like that naughty look in your eye, Joe Keedy.'

'Yes, you do. In fact, you love it.'

Lunging forward, he got his arms around her and pulled her close. Keedy then kissed her on the lips. After offering token resistance, Alice welcomed the embrace and kissed him in return. As their hearts began to beat, they were drawn closer and closer in every way. It was at that point that a horn sounded in the street outside. They ignored it at first, but it became too insistent. Moving to the window, Keedy pulled back the curtain. His face fell.

'It's your Uncle Raymond,' he gasped. 'I recognise that van of his.'

Given the intense pressure that he was under, the chances of seeing her husband relatively early that evening were very slim.

84

Resigning herself to a long wait, Ellen Marmion reached for the latest library book she had borrowed and began to read it. She was soon lost in the story of a doomed romance between a female secretary at the War Office and a British agent operating behind enemy lines. She did not get very far in the story. The moment she finished the first chapter, she heard a key being inserted in the front door lock. Marmion was back.

'What a lovely surprise!' she said, rushing into the hall to give him a welcome kiss. 'I didn't expect you this early.'

'I'm famished,' he told her, taking off his hat and raincoat before hanging them up. 'You cook a much better meal than anyone else.'

She pretended to bridle. 'Is that all I am – a good cook?'

'Of course not, Ellen.'

He put an arm around her and took her into the living room. They sat together on the sofa.

'Has something happened?' she asked, hopefully.

'Not really,' he confessed. 'I've sent Cliff Burge off to Scotland to find someone who used to work at the bank, and I've had a couple of fraught conversations on the phone with Mr Boucher.'

'The bank manager?'

'He's like everyone else who has been robbed. He expects an immediate arrest. A lot of thought went into that robbery. Once they'd worked out how to get their hands on the money, the criminals had planned how to avoid arrest.'

'Do you still think they had help from someone who once worked there?'

'All the signs point that way, love.'

'Do you have any idea where they might be?'

'Instinct tells me that they're not in London,' he said. 'They'll have driven off to a place that was picked beforehand.

Everything has been planned down to the last detail. That's why I know that they must be deserters. They were trained by the British army.'

'Not to rob a bank, surely.'

'If they're on the run, Ellen, they need money – and a lot of it. Thousands of pounds can buy them all the camouflage they want.'

'Be careful, won't you,' she said, quietly.

'I always am, Ellen.'

'After what happened to Sam Collard . . .'

'Yes, I know. It's made me think twice before I try to make an arrest.'

'I do wish that you had Joe beside you.'

'I've got him,' said Marmion. 'He's my armchair assistant. I've given him the relevant details of the case so that he can try to solve the crime with us.'

'Joe is still an invalid, remember. He needs rest.'

'Nothing will stop him offering an opinion. That's why I've confided in him.'

'Does the superintendent know that?'

Marmion laughed. 'I'm not that stupid, love.'

'What if he finds out?'

'Look. I've got Chat on my side this time so I'm careful to keep it that way. He's approved of everything I've done – including my decision to send Cliff Burge off to Scotland.'

'What happens when Joe goes back to work?'

'I'll be heartily relieved.'

'Where will that leave his replacement?'

'In due course, Cliff will go back to being a detective constable. Before that, he'll have earned a lot of praise for the way he's worked on this case. Chat will take note of that. Cliff Burge is the kind of man who thinks on his feet,' said Marmion. 'He deserves a promotion.'

'Would you recommend him?'

'I certainly would – especially if he discovers that the person he's after really did recruit the men who robbed that bank.'

He had no idea how long he had slept. What roused Burge was the fact that the train had stopped in another station. All the passengers in his compartment got out. Burge looked blearily through the window, but he could not make out the name of the station. An old man soon clambered into his compartment. Burge shook himself fully awake.

'How long before we reach Scotland?' he asked.

'You're in it,' replied the old man, chortling. 'You crossed the border ten minutes ago.'

Lily Marmion had been delighted when her husband had driven Keedy and Alice back to the house. When she heard that Keedy had tried to arrest his future wife, Lily burst out laughing.

'It's lucky that Raymond came along when he did,' she said.

'Yes,' Raymond added. 'When I realised where you'd gone, I knew that you'd be coming back after dark in two or three buses. I could drive to the house in half the time it would take the buses. That's why I came over there.'

'Thank heavens you did, Uncle Raymond!' said Alice.

'Yes,' agreed Keedy. 'We couldn't believe our luck.'

All four of them were enjoying an evening meal together. The ride back in the van had saved the visitors a great deal of time and discomfort. While Alice and Keedy kept thanking Raymond for coming to their rescue, each of them was wondering what might have happened if he had not turned up at that moment. It was the reason that the couple tried to avoid each other's eyes.

'I was staggered by what Alice had done,' said Keedy.

'Don't forget Mummy,' she reminded him. 'She worked beside me.'

'The house has been transformed. Between them, Alice and her mother have done all the jobs that I had on my list. It's magical.'

'We wanted it to be a surprise, Joe.'

'That's exactly what it was,' he said. 'It never crossed my mind that you'd been to the house.'

'We had to do something while you were in hospital.'

'And I saw the results for myself,' said Raymond. 'You and your mother have got a real talent, Alice. If you ever get fed up with the police force, you can start up in business.'

'No, thank you.' she said. 'By the time that we'd finished, we were both really fed up with decorating. We used to spend ages trying to get the paint off our hands.'

'Are you going to have a house-warming party?' asked Lily.

'Of course,' said Keedy. 'Once we've settled in properly, we'll invite everybody there.'

Alice was worried. 'Does that include your brother?'

'No, it doesn't. Dennis would be out of place at a party.'

'We had to invite him and his wife to the wedding.'

Keedy pulled a face. 'We all have our cross to bear.'

'Let's not get into religion,' warned Raymond with a grin. 'That can be dangerous.'

'It's lovely that you could be here this evening, Alice,' said Lily. 'We weren't expecting you.'

'I'd promised myself I'd try to mend a skirting board in the bedroom. You can imagine how terrified I was when someone yelled out that he was going to arrest me.'

Keedy chuckled. 'Force of habit.'

'Well,' said Raymond, 'now that you're here, Alice, don't worry about having to go back to your flat by means of buses. My trusty van will get you there much quicker.'

'Thank you, Uncle Raymond.'

'And I'll be sitting in the back of the van,' said Keedy, happily, 'just to make sure that you get there safe and sound.'

Ellen Marmion knew better than to disturb her husband when he was lost in contemplation. She recognised the signs. After eating a meal together, they had moved to the living room. They had chatted for a few minutes then Marmion had reached for the evening newspaper. Once he was engrossed in reading it, his wife picked up her library book. She was acutely aware of the moment he put the newspaper aside and took out his notebook to check certain details. Once he had done that, he sat back to organise his thoughts. He was now totally beyond her reach.

They sat there in silence for the best part of an hour. While Marmion went over the details of the investigation, Ellen was caught up in the fractured romance in her novel. When her husband spoke, she was jolted back into reality.

'I'm sorry, love,' he said.

'For what?'

'Drifting off like that.'

'You had things to sort out in your head,' she told him. 'I know that look on your face.'

'It must have seemed rude to you.'

'Not at all. The only jolt I had was when you started talking again.'

'This case is getting more complex by the day,' he explained.

'I'm wondering if I've made mistakes. For instance, was I right to discuss it with Joe?'

'Of course, you were.'

'Technically, he's on sick leave.'

'That's because his body needs time to recover. His mind is still healthy. Joe needs something to keep his brain ticking over.'

'I wonder . . .'

'Besides, you've already replaced him.'

'Nobody could replace Joe Keedy,' he said, firmly. 'He has a knack of coming up with good suggestions and occasional brainwaves. Cliff Burge is as keen as mustard but he's still learning as he goes along. That's another thing on my mind. Was I right to send him off to Scotland?'

'Somebody had to go.'

'We need to trace one of the men who used to work in that bank.'

'Do you think he could be involved in the robbery?'

'It's not impossible,' said Marmion. 'Then again, I might have sent Cliff off on a wild goose chase. But I did try my best to help him.'

'In what way?'

'When he gets to Glasgow, he'll find a pleasant surprise awaiting him.'

The misery of an interminable train journey to Scotland had left Burge feeling depressed. This was not helped by the fact that Glasgow was awash with heavy rain. Getting to police headquarters was a nightmare, involving, among other things, a fierce row with a taxi driver. When he finally walked into the building, he was tired, hungry, irritable and bedraggled. The duty sergeant eyed him with disdain. Burge approached the desk and took out his warrant card.

'My name is Clifford Burge, and I'm an acting detective sergeant at Scotland Yard. I've come in connection with a bank robbery in London.'

'Ah, yes,' replied the other with a nod, 'we heard about that. We do have newspapers up here, you know.' He picked up a sheet of paper and glanced at it. 'I've a note here to tell me that you were expected.' He offered a hand. 'Welcome to Glasgow!'

Burge shook his hand and felt the power of the man's grip. The duty sergeant was a big, swarthy, bearded man in his fifties with bristling eyebrows. Because the sergeant had a strong Glaswegian accent, Burge had difficulty understanding every word that was spoken.

'I'm Sergeant Robbie,' said the man. 'That's Ben Robbie. We'll help you all we can.'

'Thank you – but how did you know that I was coming?'

Robbie indicated the sheet of paper. 'According to this, a Detective Inspector Marmion rang from Scotland Yard to say that you were on your way. Forewarned is forearmed. It meant that we were able to book you into the nearest hotel for the night. It's no prize-winner as a hotel, but it's only five minutes away and they'll take good care of you.'

'That's a relief.'

'How long do you plan to stay?'

'As long as it takes,' said Burge.

'Then you'll be here for a week at least. Do you have any idea how many Neil Patersons we have in the city? It's a very common name. And you've another problem to cope with.'

'What is it?'

'If the man you want has committed a crime, he might have

91

had the sense to change his name. That will make your search even more difficult. I don't envy you.'

Burge was deflated.

When they reached her flat, Keedy insisted on getting out of the van to walk Alice to the front door. After a farewell kiss, she let herself into the building. Keedy climbed back into the van and sat beside Raymond Marmion. They drove off in the opposite direction.

'That was very kind of you,' said Keedy.

'I couldn't let my niece make her own way back here.'

'It was wonderful seeing you turn up at our house.'

'Really?' said Raymond with a smile. 'I had the feeling that I was . . . in the way.'

'Yes and no,' replied Keedy. 'Could I ask you a personal question?'

'Of course. Ask anything you wish.'

'Did you see much of Lily before you were married?'

'Yes, I did. We worked alongside each other.'

'Alice and I have never had that pleasure. Meetings between us have been quite rare. You've no idea how many times we've had to cancel a night out because something has come up at Scotland Yard.'

'It's different now. When you were in hospital, Alice visited every day.'

'She did and I was always delighted to see her – even though it was in a ward filled with other patients. Alice and I never had any privacy.'

'You'll have all the privacy you wish when you get married.'

'I doubt it,' said Keedy. 'As soon as I'm back at work, I'll be tied up in the latest investigation. Alice knows that. She understands how difficult it is to live with a detective. Think of all the times when her father has had to leave the house in the middle of the night to attend a crime scene.'

'Lily and I have faced the same problem,' said Raymond. 'We get called out at night regularly. That's something you accept if you join the Salvation Army. In our case, of course, there was an advantage.'

'I don't see any advantage in a sleepless night.'

'We worked through the night together, Joe. That took the edge off the discomfort. If someone was in need, we responded at once. It helped Lily and me to grow even closer.'

'Joining the Salvation Army must have been a big step for you.'

'Not at all,' said Raymond. 'It's what I always wanted to do. It's my vocation.'

Marmion arrived early at Scotland Yard next morning to find a report awaiting him. It had been sent from the Paddington fire brigade. On the night in question, the alarm had been raised at exactly three o'clock. News of the fire had been brought by a man named Arthur Davies and it had prompted action from the fire brigade. Two vehicles were dispatched immediately with bells clanging away.

Before he could finish the report, Marmion was interrupted by Claude Chatfield.

'Good morning, sir,' he said. 'You've come at just the right time.'

'Why is that?'

'I've heard from the fire brigade.'

'What do they tell us?'

'The man who raised the alarm had given them a false name,'

said Marmion, reading from the report. 'As I suspected, he was not Arthur Davies. In fact, nobody with that name lives in the area. The fire brigade believe that he might have started the blaze that he then reported.'

'Is there any description of him?'

'Yes, there is, sir. He was a stocky man in his twenties with a dark complexion. He had a flat face and needed a shave. Davies – or whatever his real name is – was wearing a crumpled old suit. According to the report, he was panic-stricken.'

'I daresay that it was just for show.'

'They believe that he might have started the blaze with petrol cans.'

'That was your guess as well.'

'When they'd got the fire under control,' said Marmion, 'they looked around for Davies, but he'd disappeared. I bet that he'd run off to the bank.'

'The report confirms what you'd guessed, Inspector.'

'Something jumps out at me.'

'What is it?'

'If the man calling himself Arthur Davies was in his twenties and physically fit, why wasn't he in the army?'

'You had the answer to that – he must have been a deserter.'

'And so were his associates,' said Marmion, looking up. 'The question I ask is this. Which one of those bank robbers stabbed Sam Collard to death?'

'Could it be this fellow, Davies?'

'We'll have to wait and see, sir. One thing is clear, however. These men will stop at nothing. The sooner we put them behind bars, the better.'

CHAPTER EIGHT

The Spurrier Hotel turned out to be small, cluttered and noisy but Clifford Burge ignored its shortcomings because of its compensating virtues. It was clean, decent and served an excellent breakfast. Its proximity to police headquarters made it ideal for his purposes. When he returned there next morning, he found that there was feverish activity. Uniformed policemen were dashing to and fro. Sergeant Ben Robbie was no longer on duty. His place behind the desk had been taken by Sergeant Nairn Redpath, a tall, angular man in his fifties with a weathered face.

'Ah,' he said, eyebrows aloft. 'Ben Robbie warned me to expect you.'

'I'm Acting Detective Sergeant Burge.'

'That's what I was told. You're looking for bank robbers.'

'Actually,' said Burge, politely, 'I'm in search of someone who may have helped them.'

'Then I wish you good luck. You'll need help, so the place to start is in Hector's office.'

'Hector?'

'Detective Sergeant Hector Reed. He knows Glasgow like the back of his hand.'

'Where would I find him?'

'His office is on the first floor,' said Redpath, pointing to the staircase. 'It's at the far end of the corridor. It was Hector who took the phone call from Inspector Marmion.'

'Good – he'll have some idea what this is all about.'

Burge moved away from the desk and walked towards the staircase. Coming down it was a uniformed constable in his late fifties. His hair was already peppered with grey. Burge had seen very few younger policemen there. Like the Metropolitan Police Force, the Glasgow Constabulary had lost untold numbers of young men to the army. Older policemen now dominated.

When he located the office belonging to Hector Reed, he rapped on the door then opened it. He was confronted by the sight of a middle-aged man, standing on a chair to retrieve a file from the top of a large bookcase.

'Don't say anything,' warned Reed, 'or I'll fall. I've no sense of balance.'

Stepping uneasily to the ground, he put the file on the desk then took a first look at his visitor. Reed was a well-built man in his forties with a gnarled face and deep-set eyes.

'You must be Sergeant Burge,' he decided.

'That's me.'

'What do you like to be called?'

'Cliff.'

'Then we'll settle for that. I'm Hector, by the way.

'It's good to meet you, Hector.'

'Shut the door, Cliff, and take a seat.'

After doing what he was told, Burge was able to study the man. To begin with, Reed had only a trace of a Scottish accent. He sounded as if he had been brought up in England and had clearly had a good education. Reading his mind, the man smiled.

'Believe it or not,' he said, 'I was born in Glasgow and spent part of my childhood here. My father moved us to Durham because he'd always liked the city. That's where I grew up. But I always had a sneaking affection for Glasgow.'

'How long have you been in the police?'

'Getting on for twenty-five years. What about you?'

'It seems like half a century.'

They laughed. Reed sat down and reached for a sheet of paper.

'This is your starting point,' he said, handing the sheet to Burge.

'Who are these people?' asked the other, staring at a list of names.

'They're men named Neil Paterson and they've all been in trouble with the law.'

'You don't understand. The man we're after has no criminal record as far as we know.'

'Inspector Marmion seemed to think he might have been involved in a bank robbery.'

'It's a possibility that I've been sent to clarify,' said Burge. 'We are certain that the robbers had help from a former employee at the bank. It might well be Neil Paterson.'

'In that case, we can forget this list. Because your man has no criminal record, it will make him very difficult to find. Any idea in which part of Glasgow he lives?'

'I'm afraid not, Hector.'

'Then what is he doing here?'

'His wife was born in the city.'

'What was her maiden name?'

'I haven't a clue,' admitted Burge.

'That's a pity. If he really was somehow involved in that bank

97

robbery, he'd want to cover his tracks. Changing his name would be his first move. He might well have reverted to his wife's family name, but you haven't any idea what that was.'

'I'm afraid not.'

'Then let's try a different approach. If he moved here, he might have found a job in the same profession. Let's see if any of our banks have taken on a Neil Paterson, shall we?'

'Good idea.'

'Right,' said Reed, getting to his feet, 'let's get busy, shall we? It might be easier if you left the talking to me. Agreed?'

Burge felt a surge of gratitude. 'Yes, please, Sergeant Reed!'

'Hector,' reminded the other.

'Of course – I'm sorry, Hector.'

Alice Marmion had been careful not to disclose much information to Iris Goodliffe about her private life. When the other woman pressed her for detail, Alice was usually evasive. This time, however, the truth had burst out of her before she could check herself. Iris was wide-eyed.

'You were alone together in an empty house?' she gasped.

'It's not empty. Every room is furnished.'

'Do you mean that there was a bed there?'

'There's one in all three bedrooms.'

'But Joe caught you in the main bedroom.'

'He frightened the living daylights out of me,' said Alice. 'I had no idea how anyone could have got into the house.'

The two friends were on their beat together, walking side by side at a steady pace. Iris brought them to a sudden halt so that she could face her friend.

'You must have known that Joe had a key,' she said.

'Yes, of course – but I didn't realise it was him. When he

barked a command, it didn't sound anything like Joe.' Alice put a hand to her heart. 'Honestly, I was so relieved that it was him.'

Iris giggled. 'What happened then?'

'He apologised for frightening me. He thought I was a burglar.'

'But you weren't. You were his future wife.'

'I was shaking like a leaf,' confessed Alice.

'Then he must have taken you in his arms to comfort you.'

'Well, yes . . .'

'Don't stop now,' complained Iris. 'What did Joe do?'

'That's our business,' said Alice, afraid that she had already said too much.

'But the two of you were alone together in the bedroom where you'd sleep as husband and wife. You must have felt, well . . . tempted. I know that I would have been,' sighed Iris. 'Not that I'd ever have such luck.'

'Let's talk about something else, shall we?' suggested Alice.

'Don't be silly. We've just reached the interesting bit.'

'What happened was . . . a private matter.'

'You can tell me, surely.'

Alice was firm. 'Frankly, I can't, so please stop badgering me for details. All I can tell you is that Uncle Raymond had driven to the house in his van to pick Joe up. When he saw the light in the bedroom, he tooted his horn.'

'Then he spoilt everything. You and Joe must have been so annoyed.'

'To be honest, we were relieved. Getting Uncle Raymond's house by bus would have been a nightmare. We were delighted to have a lift.'

'If I'd been in that bedroom,' said Iris, 'I'd have cursed him.'

'Why?'

'I'd feel . . . cheated.'

'We were just grateful. I'd been looking forward to the moment when Joe saw what we'd done to the house. He was amazed at the way that Mummy and I had worked there whenever we had a spare moment. In that sense,' said Alice, 'it was a very special moment. We suddenly saw what our life was going to be like.'

'Weren't you both drawn together?'

'Stop prying.'

'But I'm your best friend, Alice.'

'Then you should have the sense to stop pestering me. I've told you all that I intend to tell you, so please let's leave it there.' Iris gave a reluctant nod. 'Is that a promise?'

'No,' muttered Iris.

Marmion's first port of call that morning was to the bank. It was not yet open to the public, but he was admitted and shown to the manager's office. Boucher rose from his seat with a hopeful smile.

'Have you brought good news, Inspector?'

'I'm afraid not, sir.'

Boucher sagged. 'Oh, dear.'

'This is a major investigation,' said Marmion. 'It will take time and require great patience.'

'Surely you've gathered sufficient information by now?'

'All that we're certain of is that the robbery was carefully planned by men who were ready to kill if they were interrupted. Thanks to your deputy, we now know exactly how the robbers gained access to the bank.'

'Fryer took me up to the roof to show me,' said Boucher. 'I couldn't believe that anyone could climb up the drainpipe in the dark.'

'Well, they obviously did, sir. They somehow unlocked the door to the attic and settled in there until it was time to climb down to disable the burglar alarm. What the fire brigade didn't know,' said Marmion, 'was that they were innocent accessories to the crime, distracting attention from the bank and putting out a blaze in the street nearby.'

Boucher was peevish. 'Why on earth did they choose my bank?'

'That takes us back to former employees here.'

'I still can't bring myself to believe that anyone who worked here was implicated.'

'I'd bet money on it, Mr Boucher.'

'Please keep me informed at every stage.'

'That was the purpose of my visit,' said Marmion. 'The search has moved to Glasgow. I've sent someone up to Scotland in search of Neil Paterson.'

'But he had no reason to be part of a robbery here.'

'Isn't it possible that he was angry at seeing someone else being promoted to the position of deputy manager?'

'Stuart Fryer was the best choice.'

'That's not what we've been told, sir.'

'He and I are two of a kind – conscientious and committed.'

'Paterson may have felt that he was unfairly overlooked.'

'Neil had his virtues, I agree, but he also had his weaknesses.'

'What was the main one?'

'Well,' said Boucher, pondering, 'I suppose the truth is that I never found him completely dependable. Stuart Fryer, however, is rock solid. Paterson was . . . unreliable.'

'Martin Beale spoke well of him.'

'They were good friends.'

'Beale struck me as a good judge of character.'

Boucher's cheeks reddened. 'Are you saying that I am not?'

Marmion decided to remain silent.

In the normal course of his life, Clifford Burge made only occasional visits to a bank. Yet he had just been into six of Glasgow's banks with Hector Reed. All six visits had been disappointing. None of the banks had employed a man named Neil Paterson. As they left the last of the six, Burge voiced his unease.

'We're getting nowhere, Hector.'

'You have to be patient.'

'Instead of driving around like this, we could be back in your office, contacting bank managers by means of a phone.'

'I agree,' said Reed, 'we could do just that. But I wanted you to see a bit of Glasgow so that you had some idea of the problems we face.'

'It's been interesting to see the city, but I wonder if we should take a different approach.'

'What do you mean?'

'Well, if Neil Paterson is here, it's because of his wife. Her name is Flora and her family still live in Glasgow. Can you see what I'm thinking?'

'Yes, I can,' said Reed. 'The likelihood is that they were married here.'

'In that case, there must be a record of the event. Visiting churches might be more profitable than talking to yet another irritable bank manager.'

'That's true. Let's go back to the office and get a list of them.'

They climbed into the waiting police car and were driven off. Reed was curious.

'How long have you been a detective?' he asked.

'Over three years,' replied Burge. 'We were having great trouble from gangs of youths in the East End. I was born and brought up there, so they sent me to investigate. It's one of the most terrible consequences of the war. Kids have nobody to control them. Their fathers are in the army and their mothers, as like as not, work in a munitions factory. The kids form gangs and guard their territory with ferocity. You wouldn't believe the weapons they carry.'

'Oh, yes, I would,' said Reed with feeling. 'We have gangs of our own. Some of them are vicious. We simply don't have the manpower to control them – and the little devils know it.'

'We have twenty thousand special constables in London, but the majority are older men. What chance do they have of catching thieves who can run like the wind? The little buggers taunt us.'

'It's the same here, Cliff.'

'At least I helped to put two gangs out of action. I sometimes wonder if I shouldn't have waited and let them kill each other.'

'I had the same feeling about the Redskins, one of Glasgow's worst gangs. There were moments when we feared a complete breakdown of law and order.'

'It's a product of war. Children are left to run wild.'

'We've obviously had similar experiences, Cliff. Gangs are on the rampage.'

'It's the same all over the country, I'm afraid.'

Reed grinned. 'At least they haven't reached the stage of robbing banks.'

'No,' agreed Burge. 'That's a job for professionals.'

The abandoned farmhouse was within a few miles of High Wycombe. Although it was in a state of disrepair, it was ideal for their purposes. The house ran to three bedrooms, a living room, a large kitchen, and a cellar. There was a courtyard and some stables. Most importantly, there was a sizeable barn in which to hide their car. Two of them sat beside the grate in the kitchen, feeding logs into the fire. One of them was a stocky man in his twenties with a dark complexion. He kept twitching nervously, as if he feared instant discovery.

'What's keeping him?' he asked.

'Relax,' said his companion. 'He'll soon be back.'

'Terry should have been here by now.'

'He'll be back in his own time.'

'What if he's been caught by the police?'

'No chance of that happening!' said the taller man with a scar on his cheek. 'Terry knows better than to give himself away. Trust him, Sid. That's what I do.'

There was a prolonged silence. Sidney Mills stared into the flames as he reviewed what had happened. It had left him frightened. They were now marked men. It worried him.

'You shouldn't have killed that copper,' he said.

'What was I supposed to do – let him arrest me?'

'You murdered him in cold blood, Max.'

'Yes, I did,' admitted the other, 'but we had to get away.'

'Terry only knocked the other copper out. That was enough to let us escape.'

'He did it his way – I chose mine.'

'But it means that we now have a death sentence hanging over us.'

His friend sneered. 'So what? The police will never catch us.'

'I'm not so sure, Max.'

'Don't you dare tell me that you're losing your nerve,' warned the other. 'You had the balls to join me and Terry when we deserted the army. What's happened to them?'

'I don't know. I just feel . . . uneasy.'

'You're hungry, Sid. You need a good meal inside you. Terry will soon be back with enough provisions for a week. That'll put a smile on your ugly mug.'

His friend was rueful. 'I'm worried by what it said in that newspaper.'

'Then stop reading them.'

'There's a manhunt for us – and it's led by that famous detective.'

'Forget him. Inspector Marmion doesn't have the slightest idea where we are.'

'He'll be out there right now – searching for clues.'

'Shut up!' ordered Gadney, standing up and cuffing him with the back of his hand. 'I'm fed up with your whingeing. Terry and I broke into the bank. That was the dangerous bit. All you had to do was to raise the alarm at the fire station, then wait outside the bank in the car.'

'I didn't know you were going to stab someone to death.'

'Neither did I, you idiot. I just reacted to the sight of a copper, that's all. It was the same reason Terry knocked out that other man.'

'We'll have the whole of the Metropolitan Police Force after us.'

'Then where is it?' demanded Max Gadney, going to the door, and throwing it open. 'Can you hear any sirens? Can you see any baying dogs? No,' he added, slamming the door shut. 'All you can hear is silence because we have the ideal hiding place.'

'Yes, Max. You're right. I'm sorry if I get a bit edgy now and then.'

'Just keep your trap shut. That's a warning. Got it?'

'I've got it.'

Mills tried to smile but it froze on his face when he heard the approach of a car. He looked anxiously towards the door.

'Don't you recognise the sound?' said Gadney. 'Relax, will you? That's our car. At least, it has been since we stole it. Terry is back. Do something useful and help him unload the grub.' As the other man rose to his feet, Max grabbed him by the throat. 'Behave yourself, Sid,' he snarled. 'Or we may have no further use for you.'

Mills could see the molten anger in his eyes. It was no idle threat.

When the commissioner called on Claude Chatfield, he was in a more buoyant mood. German advances had been checked and the offensive was starting to lose its thrust. Sir Edward Henry waved the newspaper in his hand.

'Two pieces of good news,' he said. 'Our army is fighting back, and the bank robbery is no longer on the front page.'

'That's a relief,' sighed Chatfield. 'I prefer it if our major investigations are tucked away in the inside pages. Too much scrutiny of our work is a handicap.'

'It's something we must endure, Superintendent. Newspapers have their rights.'

'And far too many of them, if you ask me.'

'Any developments?'

'Yes, Sir Edward,' said the other. 'Marmion feels certain that Neil Paterson is involved somehow. As a result, he's sent Acting Detective Sergeant Burge off to Glasgow in search of a trail.'

'How is Burge coping?'

'Extremely well, I'm told.'

'I like the man. He has a good future ahead of him.'

'I'd still rather have Sergeant Keedy working on the case.'

'I agree,' said the commissioner. 'He and Marmion bring out the best in each other.'

'However, Burge does have his virtues. And he's ready to work all hours.'

'Has he sent any report from Glasgow?'

'Not as yet.'

'Let me know as soon as he does. Marmion wouldn't have sent him to Scotland without a very good reason.'

'He believes that Paterson is our prime suspect.'

'That's reassuring. His instincts are razor sharp.'

'I felt that Marmion should have gone himself, but he argues that there's far too much for him to do here in London. He's probably right.'

'He usually is.'

Chatfield winced at the note of approval in the commissioner's voice. He felt that Marmion often got praise for things that he, the superintendent, had suggested. It was the same situation with the press. Newspapers tended to congratulate Marmion and ignore the man who controlled the inspector's assignments. It was manifestly unjust.

'What's the latest news about Keedy?' asked the older man.

'He's out of hospital and keen to get back into action.'

'What have the doctors said?'

'Keedy has been warned to be realistic. The consultant told him that he needed ten days at least before he even thought of going back to work – a fortnight, ideally.'

'If I know him, he'll be eager to return to action.'

'I want him fully fit, Sir Edward.'

The commissioner smiled. 'I'm sure that's what we'll soon get.'

* * *

After working at the hostel, Raymond Marmion slipped back to the house to see how their guest was getting on. When he let himself in, he saw that Keedy was in the kitchen, staring at a series of small pieces of paper scattered on the table. Raymond watched him for a few moments, noting the look of concentration on his face. Suddenly aware that he was under surveillance, Keedy looked up.

'Oh,' he said. 'Hello, Raymond. I didn't hear you come in.'

'Don't let me disturb you.'

'That's okay – I've more or less finished.'

'What exactly are you doing?' asked Raymond, crossing over to him.

'I'm trying to solve a crime. As you can see, each piece of paper has a name written on it. This one here, for instance,' he said, pointing, 'is Mr Boucher, the bank manager. The person next to him is Mr Fryer, the deputy manager.'

'Why is his name in capitals while his boss's name is in lower case?'

'Look at the other names in capitals – Fryer and Paterson.'

'I don't follow.'

'They're both suspects.'

Raymond was astounded. 'The deputy manager is a suspect?'

'Let's just say that he needs to be looked at closely.'

'But my brother was praising him for working out how the robbers got into the bank.'

'Bear something else in mind. Fryer was best placed to help them.'

'What possible motive could he have?'

'Nobody is immune to the lure of money,' said Keedy. 'I'm not saying that Fryer really did help the robbers, I just feel that we must watch him carefully.'

'Are you going to tell Harvey about this?'

'Of course – it was his idea that I should play this little game. Who knows?' he asked, looking up. 'I may be able to save your brother a huge amount of time.'

After a few wasted visits to churches, they decided to return to police headquarters and resort to the telephone. Burge was happy to let Hector Reed contact a sequence of vicarages.

'Good day to you,' said Reed into the receiver. 'It's Detective Sergeant Reed here from the Glasgow Constabulary. I wonder if you could help me, please?' He laughed. 'No, no, St Mark's is not in any trouble. My interest is in marriages that have taken place in your church.'

'I'm happy to help you, Sergeant,' said an elderly voice.

'You sound as if you've been at St Mark's a long time.'

'Indeed, I have but I like to think that I have a few more years in me.'

'So do I, Reverend. I take it that you have officiated at several marriages.'

'It's one of the joys of my calling.'

'How good is your memory?'

'My brain is in reasonable order.'

'That's reassuring,' said Reed. 'Can I take you back twenty years or so?'

'You can take me back as far as you wish, Sergeant.'

'Do you remember marrying a Neil Paterson to a young woman named Flora something?'

'I'm afraid not.'

'Are you quite sure?'

'I'm certain of it. The thing I remember most clearly are services of holy matrimony. I do recall a Michael Paterson, but he married a charming young lady called Grace Hayward.'

'Then I'm sorry to have bothered you . . . Goodbye.'

'Goodbye . . .'

Reed put down the telephone and rolled his eyes. 'This could be a marathon.'

'We'll take it in turns,' volunteered Burge. 'That way, the burden is shared.'

'It still feels heavy . . .'

In a very busy day, Marmion had somehow managed to fit in a visit to the hospital to see Constable Harry Lee. His hope was that the man who had been knocked unconscious in the wake of the bank robbery might have remembered something of use to the police investigation. When Marmion found the patient, Lee was sitting up in bed with his head swathed in bandages. What little was visible of his face was covered with ugly bruises. He was still in a daze. Marmion touched his arm gently.

'Hello, Harry,' he said. 'It's me again.'

'Oh, it's good to see you, Inspector,' said Lee, stirring.

'I wanted to ask if they were looking after you.'

'I've got no complaints.'

'Do you remember what I said last time I was here?'

'Yes, you asked me to do my best to remember what happened.'

'Any detail, however small, could be of value to us.'

'I know, Inspector, but my mind keeps wandering. Then there's Sam's family. What happened to him preys on me. The shock will have knocked his wife for six.'

'It did, Harry. I had the job of telling Nora what . . . had happened. Sam Collard was a special friend. I want the man who killed him – and I want the one who attacked you as well. They both deserve to be hanged.'

110

'I'd pull the lever myself,' said Lee, rancorously.

'Think back, please. You've told me a little of what happened but I'm hoping that something new has popped into your mind. Can you describe the man?'

'He was brutal, Inspector. I'm surprised he didn't kill me.'

'Did you get your truncheon out?'

'Of course, but I had no chance to use it. He whacked me across the hand and made me drop my weapon. Next moment, he knocks off my helmet and starts hitting me hard on the head. It was agony. All I remember is falling to the ground. They found dark bruises all over my body so he must have kicked me as well.'

'What sort of build did he have?'

'He was big and heavy.'

'What about the other one?'

'Never had time to look. But there was one thing,' said Lee, straining hard to pluck a piece of information from his weary brain. 'I heard my attacker call a name.'

'What was it?'

'He urged his friend to kill Sam.'

'And what was the friend's name?'

Lee frowned as he struggled to recall it. Marmion was sympathetic.

'Take your time,' he said. 'I can wait as long as I need to.'

'Thank you, sir . . .'

Lee seemed to go off into a trance. He closed his eyes and Marmion feared that he had dropped off to sleep. Eventually, however, the name surfaced.

'Max,' said Lee. 'That was the other man's name – Max.'

CHAPTER NINE

Max Gadney took a bite out of his pie and chewed vigorously. After swallowing the food, he gave a nod of approval.

'This is good,' he said. 'Well done, Terry!'

'Yes,' added Mills, 'I was starving.'

'I did what Max suggested,' said Hillier. 'I parked the car a couple of hundred yards away from the market. I'm sorry there's not much choice. To buy most things, you need a ration book. Before I walked in there, I took one arm out of its sleeve so that I looked as if I'd lost it in the war. That got me a bit of sympathy. It also stopped people asking me why someone of my age wasn't in the army.'

'It's because we didn't like it,' said Gadney. 'That's why we deserted.'

'Best decision we ever made, Max.'

'We made a run for it, and we got away.'

'But the police and the army are on our tail,' warned Mills, anxiously. 'We're always going to be looking over our shoulder.'

'That's better than being stuck in a trench, waiting for another attack by the Huns,' said Gadney. 'The thing I hated most was those bleeding rats. They were everywhere.'

'I hated that officer even more,' said Hillier, curling a lip. 'He just kept on yelling at us, day after day. If we'd stayed in the army any longer, I'd have had to kill him.'

'That life is behind us, Terry.'

'Thank goodness!'

'We owe it all to you, Max,' said Mills. 'You came up with a plan and we stuck to it. That's why we escaped the army and ended up as free men.'

They were seated around the fire in the kitchen, enjoying their meal. Since they had managed to sneak away from the Western Front, they had put up with all sorts of privations. Crossing the Channel at night in a stolen boat had been a real trial, but they had somehow managed it. The experience had brought them closer together. Terence Hillier, the youngest of them, was a big, burly man with the look of a boxer about him. He was quite fearless.

'When do we split the money?' he asked.

'When I choose,' warned Gadney. 'Until then, it stays with me.'

'Can't I have my share now?' said Mills.

'No, Sid, you can't. You'd only do something stupid.'

'You promised, Max.'

'I promised that you'd get your share, but only when the time is right. Don't forget that there's someone else who needs to be paid as well. Without him, we'd never have dreamt of robbing a bank. He gave us all the information we needed.'

'I did my share,' bleated Mills.

'Yes, you sat in a car and waited.'

'I stole the car in the first place.'

'There wasn't much risk involved,' argued Hillier. 'It was Max who climbed into the bank and who switched off the burglar alarm. When he let me in, we opened that safe and grabbed what we could. If those coppers hadn't turned up, we'd have got away easily.'

'But we didn't,' complained Mills. 'We left one of them dead and the other unconscious. That's why the police force started a manhunt.'

'Stop going on about it!' yelled Gadney. 'What's done is done. Forget about it and just think about our escape. It's no good having that money if there's no chance to spend it. And we can't stay here indefinitely. We need to keep on the move.'

'What about him?'

'Who?'

'That friend of yours,' said Mills. 'It was his idea, after all.'

'Leave him to me, Sid.'

'Can he be trusted?'

'Of course he can be trusted, you fool,' said Gadney. 'He's got the sense to keep his mouth shut and wait until it's safe to share out the money.'

'When will that be?'

'I'll let you know.'

Mills was curious. 'You still haven't told me how much money he'll expect to have.'

'And I'm not going to,' said Gadney.

'Why won't you tell us his name?'

'He made it possible for us to rob a bank,' snapped Gadney. 'What more do you need to know?'

Joe Keedy looked at the pieces of paper spread out on the table and wondered about possible connections between them. Unable to name any of the three suspects, he put a large question mark on the paper denoting each of them. He then wondered if Stuart Fryer, the deputy manager, really had been their accessory. It had seemed a ludicrous idea at first but, the more he thought about it, the more convincing it sounded. After staring at the pieces of paper for several minutes, he gathered them up and shuffled them like a pack of cards. Keedy spread them on the table yet again.

'Still at it, are you?' asked Raymond Marmion, coming into the room.

'Oh, yes. I'll get the right answer in the end.'

'Is this how you always solve major crimes? Playing with pieces of paper, I mean.'

'No,' said Keedy, laughing, 'of course not. An investigation is much more scientific. We stick closely to established facts and slowly add to them as new evidence emerges.'

'Why did you single out the deputy manager?'

'I just had this feeling.'

'But you've never even met the man.'

'I know – whereas your brother has met him and was very impressed. I suppose I thought that he was in the ideal place to mastermind the robbery.'

'What connection could he possibly have with such dangerous men?'

'Good question, Raymond.'

'They killed one policeman and knocked the other senseless. Can you imagine Stuart Fryer condoning such vicious behaviour?'

'No, I can't,' admitted Keedy. 'Yet the deputy manager keeps popping up in my mind for some reason. Is he related to one of the robbers? Is that the link with them?'

'I believe that those men were acting independently.'

'Then how did they know how to disable the burglar alarm? More to the point, how did they know how to open the safe containing the money? They must have had inside help. It stands to reason.'

'I agree. That's why my brother is looking at the suspects who no longer work at the bank.'

'I wish him well.'

'Has he named one of the three as a prime suspect?'

'He's far too careful to do that, Raymond. He likes to keep his options open. I, on the other hand, have been far too quick to name a fourth suspect. As a result, I was led astray.' He picked up the piece of paper with Fryer's name on it and scrunched it into a ball. 'I've taken him off my list of suspects. I can now focus all my attention on the three former employees of the bank who were able to give the robbers all the information they needed. In a time of crisis like the one we have now, we all need that. If one of those three men really did help the robbers, then he's in for a share of many thousands of pounds. That's one hell of a temptation.'

Clifford Burge was learning a lot about religion in Scotland. He discovered that there were two major Presbyterian Churches – the established Church of Scotland and the United Free Church. He also discovered that many places of worship were more likely to be known as kirks. There was also a cluster of Roman Catholic churches in Glasgow. When it was his turn to make the telephone calls from Hector Reed's office, he found himself in contact with one of them.

'Is that the vicarage of St Alban's Church?' he asked, politely.

'Yes, it is. Father Drummond speaking . . .'

'My name is Detective Sergeant Burge and I've been sent to Glasgow from Scotland Yard in search of a man named Neil Paterson.'

'We have rather a lot of Neil Patersons,' said Drummond. 'What is so special about the man you are searching for?'

'He may well be connected with a bank robbery in London.'

'Dear me! That sounds serious.'

'In the course of the robbery, a policeman was stabbed to death.'

'That's dreadful,' said the priest. 'Are you telling me that a Neil Paterson was the killer?'

'No, I'm not, but we do feel that he may – just may – have helped the robbers.'

'In what way?'

'That remains to be seen.'

'Why have you telephoned me?'

'We are contacting places of worship in the hope that we can find where Neil Paterson was married. All that we know about his wife is that her Christian name was Flora. The ceremony would have taken place between fifteen and twenty years ago.'

'Heavens!' exclaimed Father Drummond. 'I have difficulty remembering what happened last week, let alone what happened in this church so long ago. Are you telling me that Paterson and this woman may were married here?'

'It's a possibility.'

'Is mine the first church you contacted?'

'No,' said Burge, wearily. 'We've been in touch with several.'

'Then you clearly have a good reason for pursuing this individual. Bear with me, Sergeant. I'll need to do a spot of burrowing in our records. The bride's name was Flora, you say?'

'That's correct.'

'If you give me your number, I'll ring back in due course.'

'Thank you very much, Father Drummond.'

He read out the number on the telephone then replaced the receiver. He turned to Reed.

'He's gone to consult the records.'

'They all did that,' said the other, 'but not one of them gave us the names we needed.' He heaved a sigh. 'I've got the uneasy feeling that we're completely in the dark.'

'Never give up – remember Inspector Marmion's motto. Persistence pays dividends.'

Reed spread his arms. 'Then where the hell are they?'

Marmion had spent the entire day working hard but he had very little to show for it. It was well over twenty-four hours since he had sent Burge off to Glasgow, yet he had not heard a single word from him. Activity in the Paddington area had been disappointing. Though Marmion had deployed several men to make house-to-house calls in streets close to the bank, nothing of use had surfaced. All that people remembered about the night of the robbery was the sound of two fire engines racing to a nearby blaze. After bidding farewell to colleagues, Marmion was driven home in a police car. His hopes of progress had been checked. He was frustrated.

When he let himself into his home, Ellen came bustling into the hall to welcome him with a kiss. She then stood back to appraise him and recognised the signs.

'Has it been that bad a day?' she asked.

'I'm afraid so, love.'

'I'll make a pot of tea.'

'A stiff whisky would be more welcome.'

'You only call for that when things are really bad.'

'Then I'll settle for the tea,' he replied, straightening his shoulders. 'Put the kettle on and I'll join you in the kitchen.'

While his wife went off, he removed his hat and coat and hung them on a peg. Marmion then turned to the full-length mirror and studied himself. He was shocked. With sagging shoulders and a mournful face, he looked fifteen years older than his real age. He straightened his back, adjusted his tie and jacket then went into the kitchen.

'I'm sorry to dump my disappointments on you, Ellen,' he said, kissing her.

'That's what I'm here for.'

'It's so unfair on you.'

'Not really,' she said. 'I know that you'll solve this case in due course but there will be setbacks along the way. To begin with, you don't have Joe at your side.'

'Cliff Burge is a good deputy.'

'But he has nothing like Joe's experience – not to mention that knack Joe has for coming up with good ideas. You always call him a born detective.'

'Well, he's going to be something else in a few weeks' time,' remembered Marmion. 'Joe Keedy is going to be married to our daughter and move into that nice little house of theirs. I'll not only be his boss – I'll be his father-in-law as well. That could create problems.'

'You'll solve them. You always do.'

'I wish that I could be so optimistic,' he said, pulling a chair from under the table and sitting on it. 'This case is depressing me, love, and I don't know why.'

'Wait until you've made your first arrest in connection with the bank robbery. You'll realise that you've been having a wonderful time.'

He gave a hollow laugh. 'If only . . .' Pulling himself together, he sat up. 'Forget my problems. What have you been doing all day?'

'Well, I spent this morning at the sewing circle,' she explained. 'It's still cold on the Western Front so they're always grateful for socks and gloves and things that warm them up. Also, of course, I had a lovely gossip with the other women.'

'What was it about today?'

'What else but the bank robbery? They seem to think I have inside knowledge about it.'

'I'm sorry if they ganged up on you.'

'I don't mind. Anyway, after lunch I treated myself to a couple of hours with my novel.

'The hero should have been caught by now.'

She frowned. 'How did you know he'd be arrested?'

'Because that's what always happens to British spies in the books you get from the library. They lead lives of wild excitement, but they're always caught by the enemy and interrogated. Back home, meanwhile, the woman who loves the secret agent is distraught. She's desperate to rescue him but can't think how to do it. Then, of course, he escapes . . .'

'Does he?'

'He's the hero, Ellen. He must escape so that he can turn the tables on those bloodthirsty Germans. In fact—'

'Don't say another word,' she scolded. 'I wish I hadn't told you what the book is about now. You're spoiling it for me.'

'I'm sorry, love. I didn't mean to. Let's talk about something else.'

'That's what I want to do.' She glanced up at the cupboard on the wall. 'Do you remember when that money was stolen from the cup I always keep it in?'

'Yes, I do. You were afraid that Paul might have taken it.'

'Who else would have known where I hide the housekeeping money?'

'That's a fair point,' he agreed. 'And there was no sign of a forced entry.'

'Paul has a key to the house. He must have let himself in.'

'Don't dwell on it, Ellen. It won't happen again because we've hidden the housekeeping money in a safer place. Paul would never find it. Anyway,' he added, 'we can't be certain that he was the thief. That was just a guess.'

'No, it wasn't. I'm certain it was him.'

'Why do you say that?'

'I'll show you.'

Ellen went to the cupboard and opened it before taking out a cup. When she put it on the table, Marmion could see that it contained money. She pulled out the note and coins.

'This is exactly the amount that was stolen,' she said, 'so please don't tell me that the thief was not Paul. Who but our son would take money then repay the full amount? Can you hear what I'm saying?'

'Yes – it wasn't stolen, it was borrowed.'

'Then paid back in full. We ought to be glad.'

'Well, I'm not,' he said, angrily. 'If Paul is on the loose and back in the area, why the hell doesn't he get in touch with us? We're his parents, for heaven's sake! If he needed money, I'd have been happy to lend it to him. Forget the sewing circle tomorrow,' he said. 'Stay here so that a locksmith can change the lock on the front door. I'm not having someone letting himself in here at will, even if he is our son. What sort of a stupid game is he playing with us?'

'I don't know, Harvey. What I can tell you is that you won't find a locksmith who will come here tomorrow because it will be Sunday – the day of rest. The lock on the front door will have to wait until Monday.'

Evening in Glasgow was cold and cheerless. After a fruitless day in search of a missing banker, Burge and Reed were starting to feel dejected. They had been in touch with several banks and a much larger number of churches and chapels, but their efforts had so far yielded nothing. After suppressing a yawn, Reed glanced up at the clock on his wall.

'It's time to call it a day, Cliff,' he suggested.

'Couldn't we just try one more telephone call?' asked Burge.

'We did that half an hour ago and it was a waste of time. It looks as if Neil Paterson is no longer in the city – or, if he is, he's living under an assumed name.'

'It might be his wife's maiden name, perhaps?'

'But we don't know what it is.'

'True.'

'Let's start afresh tomorrow, shall we?'

Burge yawned. 'I don't see the point, Hector. There's nowhere else to look.'

'You can't go back to London empty-handed.'

'No, I suppose not. We'll just have to grit our teeth and start again.'

'Tomorrow is Sunday. I should be taking my wife and children to our local kirk.'

'In that case, I'll soldier on alone.'

'I can't let you do that. Glasgow is foreign country to you.'

'You're entitled to a day off with your family.'

'I'll work something out,' said Reed.

The telephone rang and he snatched it up before putting it to his ear.

'No,' he said, 'this is not Detective Sergeant Burge but he's sitting beside me. I'll hand you over.' He lowered his voice to a whisper. 'It's Father Drummond.'

'Let me speak to him,' said Burge, taking the receiver. 'Is that you, Father?'

'Yes, it is,' replied Drummond, 'and I must first begin with an apology. We had an emergency in the church, and I had to sort it out. Unfortunately, it took several hours to get everything back on an even keel. I was only able to honour my promise this evening.'

'And?'

'I may be able to help you.'

Burge was galvanised. 'What did you find?'

'A Neil Paterson was married in this church almost twenty years ago to a young woman named Flora Anne Goddard. That was before I moved to St Alban's, so I have no memory of the event.'

'Do you have an address for either of them?'

'Yes, but it's in London. I assume that that's where they moved after the wedding. Would you like me to give you the address?'

'No,' said Burge, trying to master his disappointment. 'I've already been there. It was Paterson's neighbours who told me that he and his wife had returned to Scotland.'

'Did they say why?'

'Mrs Paterson wanted to move closer to her parents.'

'That would be Mr and Mrs Goddard. Those names ring a bell.'

'In what way?'

'I'm not quite sure, Sergeant Burge. I'll need time to think.'

123

'Could I come over to St Alban's to talk to you?'

'Please do – you'd be most welcome.'

'I'll be on my way in a few minutes.' Burge put the receiver down.

Reed was delighted. 'You look as if you've just struck gold.'

'He's found the record of Paterson's marriage.'

'Is he absolutely sure?'

'I think so. The wife's maiden name was Goddard – Flora Goddard.'

'Then let's get over there at once,' said Reed, getting up from his chair. 'We've had a spot of luck at long last.'

'It's really cheered me up.'

'Your inspector was right. Persistence pays dividends.'

'God bless him.'

When he came into the living room, Raymond looked almost bemused. Both Lily and Keedy noticed his expression of incredulity.

'Who was on the telephone?' asked his wife.

'It was Harvey – with an amazing tale to tell.'

Keedy was interested. 'Does it concern the case in hand?'

'No, it doesn't, Joe. It's to do with Paul – at least, they think it is.'

'What on earth are you talking about?' asked Lily.

'Let me sit down,' said her husband, 'and I'll tell you.'

After lowering himself onto the sofa, he needed a moment to gather his thoughts. Raymond then told them about the discovery of the money that had been stolen and, apparently, returned. Marmion had been baffled by the development.

'Ellen is convinced that Paul put back the money that he had stolen earlier,' said Raymond.

'And what does your brother think?' asked Keedy.

'He's not sure that Paul is involved in any way.'

'But he must be. Who else would be able to let himself into the house with a key? Instead of stealing that money, Paul must simply have borrowed it for a while until he was able to pay it back. That's the obvious explanation.'

'Harvey thought it was too obvious.'

'What's his theory?'

'He thinks that Paul is deliberately playing games with them, and it's really angered him. His first move is to have the lock of the front door changed. Paul's key would then be useless.'

Keedy had doubts. 'Are they certain that the thief really was their own son?'

'Who else could it be?' asked Raymond.

'Someone Paul met on his travels. He might have confided to him that he still had a key to the family home. This other person could have stolen it from him. He knew where the money was kept so he helped himself to it.'

'You're forgetting something,' said Lily. 'The money was returned in full.'

'How many thieves would do that?' asked Raymond. 'My brother rang me because he wanted my opinion. He knows how many homeless people we pick up off the streets. They're in desperate need of food and shelter. We help them as much as we can, but we also keep a close eye on them. Some are on the run from the police and others simply can't resist the urge to steal.'

'Paul doesn't belong in either of the categories you mentioned,' said Keedy.

'He may have changed.'

'How has he managed to survive all this time?' asked Lily.

'He's probably picked up work along the way.'

'What sort of money can an itinerant like him earn?'

'Not enough to get him through a hard winter,' said Keedy, weighing up the facts. 'Paul was obviously lurking in the area. Where did he hide?'

'My brother had one suggestion,' said Raymond. 'He recalled that young man in Shepton Mallet prison who had documents to prove that he was, in fact, Paul Marmion. They'd been on the run together and exchanged identities.'

'What is the real Paul calling himself now?'

'And how could he have got into the family home with a key that he handed over to that other man? This gets more confusing by the minute.'

'I can see why Ellen wants it to be her son,' said Lily. 'In her position, I'd feel the same.'

Keedy shook his head. 'This is such a distraction,' he said, clicking his teeth. 'Harvey has enough on his hands, leading a murder investigation. The last thing he wants is more trouble from Paul – if Paul is really involved, that is.'

'I'm not sure that he is,' decided Raymond.

'Lily believes that he must be – just like Ellen.'

She nodded vigorously. 'Call it maternal instinct, Joe.'

'It may blur your vision, my love,' said her husband. 'The question is this – how can we help my brother to solve this mystery? He's working around the clock at Scotland Yard. We're not. We have a bit more freedom.'

'So do I,' said Keedy.

'You're a patient, Joe. You need rest.'

'Not when an emergency like this crops up. I'm even more available than you and Lily. You've told us how upset Harvey and Ellen are, but Alice is going to be concerned as well. Helping to solve this problem,' said Keedy, 'will be a wonderful wedding present for her.'

When they reached the church of St Alban's, they discovered that Father Drummond was a diminutive, middle-aged man in clerical attire. His biretta was perched on the top of a head covered in silky white hair. The church was lit by a series of candles, carefully placed to show off its distinctive features. Reed shivered slightly when they stepped into the nave, but Burge was warmed by the feeling that he was on the edge of a significant discovery. All three of them went into the vestry. Reed was struck by the quality of the statues there, but Burge's eye was fixed on the large, leather-bound book on the table. It was open at a particular page.

'Here you are,' said the priest, indicating the ledger. 'It's visible proof that Neil Hugh Paterson and Flora Anne Goddard were married in the sight of the Lord in this very church.'

Burge saw the two names and admired the elegant calligraphy. The priest had a surprise for them. His eyes twinkled and he gave a broad smile.

'I remembered something else as well,' he told them. 'When I put my old brain into gear, I recalled that we had had another Goddard in the congregation. His name was Fraser Goddard, and he is linked to the man you are seeking.'

Burge was excited. 'In what way?'

'He was Flora's father. Unfortunately, he passed away some months ago. I did not take the funeral, so I had no real memory of it in my mind, but I do recall hearing that a larger than usual congregation of mourners had turned up.'

'Did they include his daughter and son-in-law?'

'Most assuredly.'

'It could be the reason why they moved back to Glasgow,' said Reed. 'Flora might have been keen to live close to her mother.'

Burge turned to Drummond but the question he was about to ask was already anticipated.

'Yes,' said the priest, 'I do have an address.'

'That's wonderful!'

'It makes all our efforts worthwhile,' added Reed.

'I've written it down,' said Drummond, opening a drawer in the table to take out a sheet of white paper. He handed it over to Burge. 'I hope that this will be of help to you.'

The two detectives were thrilled.

Sidney Mills was feeling much better. He'd had a good meal with his friends and had drunk half of a flagon of beer. He was no longer as edgy as he had been.

'Shall I put some more wood on the fire?' he asked.

'Yes,' said Gadney, 'we must keep it alive all night. This is the only warm place there is.'

'I'm starting to feel really drowsy.'

'Don't you dare nod off. Terry and I are the ones that really need sleep. You're on guard.'

'But I'm tired, Max.'

'So are we. Someone must stay awake. I'll take over in a few hours, then Terry can relieve me in turn. You can snore away for the best part of eight hours – when you've done a few jobs, that is.'

'What kind of jobs?'

'Clear everything away then dig a hole outside to hide the rubbish.'

Mills was horrified. 'It's bleeding cold out there!'

'You'll soon warm up when you get busy with a spade,' Hillier told him.

'Why can't we leave everything here?'

'Because it's evidence, you fool,' hissed Gadney. 'It must be hidden. The most that we can stay is a few days, then off we go without leaving any trace behind us.'

'Max is right,' said Hillier.

'Why can't one of you dig the hole?' complained Mills.

'It's because we robbed a bank. You just drove the car.'

'I also started that blaze then called the fire brigade.'

'There was no real risk in that, Sid.'

'Don't argue with him, Terry,' said Gadney, getting to his feet. 'The only thing he understands is a kick up the arse.' Mills cowered in fear. 'You've got a poor memory, Sid, haven't you? When we said you could join us, I told you I was in command. Then comes Terry and the last in line is you.' He lowered his voice to a growl. 'Now get out there with a spade and dig that hole – or I will dig a much bigger one and bury you in it.'

CHAPTER TEN

Clifford Burge let his imagination run away with him. Now that they had an address, he believed, they were certain to find Neil Paterson and his wife. The couple might even be living with Flora's mother in the wake of her husband's death. Burge felt that he would be able to confront and wrest a confession of guilt from Paterson. As he travelled in a police car with Hector Reed, he started to believe that he was about to make the most important arrest in his career. The trip to Glasgow had finally borne fruit.

When they arrived at the house, they saw that it was a detached property in a pleasant neighbourhood. The detectives knocked on the door and it was soon opened by a middle-aged woman with a gaunt face and an unwelcoming glint in her eye. When Reed introduced himself and Burge, she was taken aback.

'What are you doing here?' she demanded.

'We wish to speak to Flora Goddard's mother.'

'She is my mother as well,' said the woman. 'I am Flora's sister.'

'May we know your name, please?' asked Reed.

'I'm Miss Goddard – Miss Celia Goddard.'

'Is it possible to speak to your mother, please?'

'If you must,' said the woman, defensively, 'but let me warn you that she is not in the best of health. That's why I moved in here to look after her.' She sniffed. 'It's what a daughter ought to do.'

She stood aside to let them step into the house then closed the front door. After telling them to wait in the hall, she went into the living room for a few minutes. When she emerged, she issued a warning to them.

'Mother is very frail,' she explained. 'You have to treat her gently.'

'We'll bear that in mind,' said Reed.

'And there's another thing . . .'

'Is there?'

'She may fall asleep at some point. It happens all the time.'

'Oh dear!' murmured Burge.

Celia led them into the living room. Seated beside the fire was an old woman in a thick dressing gown. There was a surface resemblance to her elder daughter but what struck the detectives most were the hollow cheeks, the dull eyes, and the constant nodding of the head. Celia indicated the sofa, and they sat down beside each other. The daughter stood protectively beside her mother. The old woman's voice was a croak.

'Why are you here?' she asked.

'We are trying to find your son-in-law, Neil,' replied Hector.

'What's he done wrong?'

'We don't know that he's done anything wrong, Mrs Goddard. I'll let Detective Sergeant Burge explain. He's come from Scotland Yard.'

'That's right,' said Burge. 'There was a robbery at a bank where your son-in-law used to work.'

'It's not to do with Neil, is it?' demanded Celia. 'He's got his faults and many of them, but he would never stoop to crime. I'll say that for him.'

'He may be able to help us with information about his former colleagues,' Burge continued. 'It would be a great help to us if you could give us his address.' Celia snorted. 'Is there a problem?'

'We don't have an address for him,' she snapped.

'But we understood that he's moved back to Glasgow.'

'Yes,' said Reed. 'He and his wife attended your father's funeral.'

'That may well be, but we didn't speak to either of them.'

'Tell them the truth, Celia,' urged her mother.

'My parents didn't like Neil,' said Celia. 'They were against the idea of Flora marrying him.'

'I see.'

'To start with, he'd been offered a job in London so they would be leaving Scotland.'

'That's odd,' said Burge. 'I understood that Mr Paterson was interested in politics. He wanted an independent Scotland.'

'It was another reason we took against him. He kept spouting nonsense at us.'

'But why did he move so far away from a country he loved?'

Celia's face hardened. 'He wanted to take Flora well away from us.'

'And good riddance to her!' added her mother. 'She's not one of the family any more.'

'That's very sad,' said Reed.

'We did warn Flora.'

'It's why we don't care where she is,' said Celia, coldly.

Reed exchanged a glance with Burge. Clearly, they were

wasting their time. Having entered the house with high hopes, Burge was crestfallen. Their search for Neil Paterson and his wife would have to continue. He might be staying at the Spurrier Hotel for some time yet.

Joe Keedy was not a regular churchgoer. Sundays were, for the most part, anything but a day of rest in his case. He would usually be at Scotland Yard, working on the latest case or out in pursuit of a suspect. On the rare occasions when he did have free time, he would spend it with Alice. The two of them were now sitting side by side in the parish church of All Saints', waiting to hear the banns of marriage being published for the second time. Ellen was seated beside them. Keedy felt completely out of place in the congregation. While he was looking forward to the wedding itself, he found the preliminaries irritating and a trifle unnerving.

As he had admitted earlier, the actual wording of the banns worried him. When he read them aloud, the vicar, the Reverend Harold Sanders, would ask anyone who knew of a reason why the couple should not be joined together in holy matrimony to come forward. That worried Keedy. Before he and Alice had got together, there had been other women who had been close to him, some of whom might feel that they still had a claim on him. One of them, Maisie Bell, had come back into his life recently when he was rushed to hospital after being shot. Maisie was one of the nurses who looked after him and pleasant memories of their earlier friendship had been rekindled. What if the woman decided that she had a first claim on him and stood up in church to declare it? The thought made Keedy shudder with embarrassment.

As the moment approached, he became increasingly

uncomfortable. He tried telling himself that the banns had already been published once without any interruption, but that did not still his unease. When the vicar addressed the congregation, Keedy tensed. Was he about to face public humiliation?

'I publish the banns of marriage . . .'

The only thing that Keedy heard was the appeal to anyone who knew of a reason why the marriage should not take place. There was a long, excruciating moment where he half-expected a female voice to cry out. But it never came. The vicar carried on.

'This is the second time of asking . . .'

Keedy breathed a huge sigh of relief.

They were so downhearted that most of the ride back to police headquarters passed in silence. It was Burge who finally spoke.

'Funny, isn't it?' he said.

'What do you mean?'

'Well, Paterson was supposed to be in favour of an independent Scotland but, as soon as he gets married, he goes off to England.'

'Perhaps he just wanted to get away from his in-laws.'

'That elder sister was a real harridan, wasn't she?'

'Fair play to her,' said Reed. 'She's taken on the task of looking after her mother. As for Scottish Nationalism, cries in favour of it have died down a great deal. We've got a bigger problem to worry about and that's being invaded by the Germans. It's why so many Scotsmen volunteered to join our regiments and fight against the Huns. They're doing it to protect the whole of Great Britain, not just Scotland.'

When they left the church, Keedy was intensely grateful that the banns of marriage had been read for the second time without interruption from a female voice. Overwhelmed with relief, he had no time to enjoy the feeling because several members of the congregation made a point of introducing themselves to him. They had seen newspaper reports of his bravery during the siege and wanted to congratulate Keedy. Older ladies were especially touched that they had a hero in their midst.

'Now that you're finally out of hospital,' said one of them, 'we hope to see you on a Sunday far more often.'

'Yes,' he replied, 'unless I'm on duty at Scotland Yard, of course.'

'You and the future Mrs Keedy are an inspiration to the rest of us. You make us feel safe.'

'Thank you,' said Alice, stepping in to rescue him from his female audience. 'What on earth was wrong with you, Joe?' she asked when they were out of earshot of other people.

'I was only being polite to them.'

'I'm not talking about those women. I'm thinking of what happened when the vicar published the banns of our marriage. Your face was white, and your teeth were gritted. It was almost as if you didn't want to marry me.'

'Don't be silly,' he said, hugging her. 'Of course, I do – the sooner, the better.'

'Weren't you feeling well?'

'I was . . . a bit overcome, that's all.'

'You should have felt as happy as I did. Instead of that, you were trembling.'

'I'm sorry,' he said. 'I'll be fine next time.'

'Was it that much of an ordeal?'

'No, of course not.'

'Then what was going through your mind?'

'I don't know, Alice . . .'

Before he could say anything else, he was interrupted by Ellen who had been talking to some friends of hers. His future mother-in-law was glowing.

'Everyone is so delighted to meet you at last, Joe. Mrs Morissey is very jealous that we have someone like you coming into the family. She thought that you and Alice were ideally suited.'

'I didn't feel at ease in there,' admitted Alice.

Ellen was surprised. 'Why do you say that?'

'It doesn't matter, Mummy. I had a moment of discomfort, that's all. To be honest, the occasion was a bit much for me.'

'And for me,' said Keedy. 'It's the first time I've been in a church for ages. And I'm just not used to being out of hospital at last.'

'You'll soon adjust to it,' said Ellen.

Before she could continue, the vicar swooped down on them. He was a fleshy man in his fifties with a benign smile. He shook Keedy's hand for the best part of a minute.

'It's so good to see you again at last, Sergeant Keedy,' he said. 'You caused quite a stir among the ladies. It's not often that we have such a hero in the congregation.'

Keedy shrugged. 'I was only doing my job, Vicar.'

'It's such a blessing that you lived to tell the tale.'

'We're trying to put all that behind us,' said Alice.

'Quite right, too. You'll have a wonderful life together ahead of you. Look to the future.'

'They will,' said Ellen, fondly.

'Don't go back to work too soon,' advised the vicar. 'You need rest.'

'I've had plenty of that,' said Keedy. 'I thrive on action. I want to be back in harness more or less immediately.'

'If you'd returned to work, what would you be doing on a Sunday morning?'

'He'd be at Scotland Yard,' said Ellen, 'just as my husband is right now.'

'And if I hadn't come to church today,' said Keedy, 'I can tell you exactly what I would have been doing at this very moment.'

'Having a lie-in, perhaps?' guessed the vicar.

'No – I'd be playing the big drum in a Salvation Army Band.'

They sat either side of a table in the canteen at police headquarters. Their cups of tea stood untouched in front of them. They could not even bring themselves to nibble a biscuit. It was Hector Reed who eventually broke the silence.

'That kind of thing happens from time to time,' he said.

Burge looked up at him. 'What sort of thing?'

'Having high expectations, Cliff.'

'I was foolish enough to think that we'd found Neil Paterson.'

'Everything pointed that way. We had his wife's family's address. That meant that we were only one step away from discovering where he and his wife lived.'

'Instead of which,' said Burge, 'we discovered that Paterson was not even on speaking terms with his in-laws. In short, all our assumptions crumbled.'

'We'll find him eventually.'

'How?'

'I've put out an appeal to every major city in Scotland for information about Paterson. Sooner or later, we'll run him to ground.'

'I can't stay here indefinitely, Hector.'

'You must do. We know that he's back north of the border.'

'But do we?' asked Burge. 'He lied to the neighbours in

London. What if he's stayed somewhere in England all this time?'

'Paterson has no reason to do that.'

'If he was involved in that bank robbery, he has a very good reason.'

'That's a fair point,' conceded Reed. 'If he provided the robbers with all the information they needed, he'd want to stay reasonably close to them so that he could get his share of the money.'

'Are you saying that I'm wasting my time in Glasgow?'

'Not necessarily.'

'Then why do I feel that I am?'

'It's because we've had a setback, Cliff. Think it through. If Paterson did help to organise that bank robbery, he'd surely want to stay in contact with the men involved. Once he'd been paid, I fancy that he'd head back here to the country he loves.'

'What about the robbers themselves?'

'They're keeping their heads down.'

'But where?'

'Your guess is as good as mine,' said Reed. 'Take heart.'

Burge shook his head. 'I feel that we're completely in the dark.'

'Then my advice is this. You should get in touch with Inspector Marmion. Tell him that the search may take longer than you imagined.'

'He won't be pleased with what happened up here today.'

'Perhaps not, but he's an experienced detective. He knows that whenever you fail, you must try twice as hard to succeed. Paterson was born and brought up here. He doesn't care that his in-laws have turned their back on him. I bet that he longs to be on Scottish soil again.'

'With his share of the money.'

'It will be a tidy sum.'

Burge frowned. 'How will he explain his sudden wealth to his wife?'

'That might be tricky,' admitted Reed. 'Then again, if she loved him enough to cut her ties with her own family, Flora will stand by him whatever he does.' He inhaled deeply. 'I still sense that he's back this side of the border. All that we need to do is to find and arrest him.'

'You're asking for a miracle, Hector.'

'Why not? It's Sunday, isn't it?'

Marmion was in his office at Scotland Yard, poring over reports from the various detectives he had deployed. His mind, however, was elsewhere. He kept thinking about his son, Paul, wondering if the latter really had gone into the family home on two occasions. His wife was convinced that it must have been Paul, stealing money out of necessity, then repaying it when he had earned enough to do so. Marmion had doubts. Paul might be estranged from them but even he would have stopped short of stealing from his own home. The only explanation, Marmion decided, was that someone else had the key to the house. Paul had befriended another person on the run, and they had exchanged identities. It was the other young man who sneaked into their house when it was unoccupied.

But would such a person return and repay the money stolen? It seemed unlikely. Besides, the person who was caught with Paul's papers on him was in custody. Alice and her mother had met him face to face in Shepton Mallet Prison. What had happened to him after that?

Before he could find out, Marmion was interrupted by the

arrival of Claude Chatfield. Without bothering to knock, the superintendent opened the door and came in.

'Any word from Sergeant Burge?' he asked.

'No, sir,' replied Marmion. 'He rang yesterday to tell me that he was staying at a hotel they had booked for him, and that he had been given the services of a Detective Sergeant Reed. Burge did warn me not to expect immediate results.'

'Let's hope that sending him there was not a mistake.'

'I'm sure that it wasn't, sir.'

Chatfield glanced down at the pile of papers. 'What have you been doing?'

'I've been going through these lists of deserters, said Marmion, 'trying to work out which regiment the bank robbers might have been in.'

'What conclusion did you reach?'

'The Royal Fusiliers.'

'Why choose them?'

'The City of London Regiment has the most interesting battle honours. They fought at a bewildering variety of places on the Western Front. While most of their men distinguished themselves in combat,' said Marmion, 'the regiment has nevertheless had its deserters.'

'They're nothing but cowards,' sneered Chatfield, 'and should be shot on sight.'

'They need to be caught first.'

'Do we have any names?'

'We have one who may be of interest. The man's name is Gadney – Max Gadney, to be exact. The one thing that Constable Lee told me about confronting the bank robbers was that one of them was called Max. We're hoping to have his home address very soon.'

'Excellent. His associates will be from the same regiment, I daresay.'

'We've asked for full details of all their deserters.'

'Then we've made an excellent start. The commissioner will be delighted.'

'There's still a long way to go, sir,' warned Marmion.

'You'll track this man down somehow.'

'I owe it to Sam Collard. He was murdered by Gadney.'

'You have all the motivation you need,' said Chatfield. 'Any word of Sergeant Keedy?'

'He's settled in well at my brother's house.'

'I daresay that he's dying to get back to work – especially on a case like this.'

'The doctor's advice is that he needs rest in a calm environment.'

'But he thrives on action.'

'Yes, he does.'

'He'll have to control his natural urges.' The superintendent narrowed his eyelids. 'I hope that you haven't been giving him details of this investigation.'

Marmion looked offended. 'It would never occur to me, sir.'

When they had finally left the church, Keedy returned to their family home with Ellen and Alice. He was still enjoying the feeling of relief at having survived what he had feared might be an awkward moment during the reading of the banns. But he had not forgotten about the mysterious return of money that had previously been stolen from the house.

'May I borrow your telephone, please?' he asked.

'Yes, of course,' said Ellen. 'There's no need to ask.'

'Do you want to talk to Uncle Raymond?' asked Alice.

'I'll have plenty of chance to do that when I go back to their house,' he said. 'The person I want to speak to is the governor of Shepton Mallet Prison.'

'Why?'

'It's this business about stolen money being returned, Alice.'

'We're still undecided about that,' she said.

'I'm not,' insisted Ellen. 'It was Paul who paid us back.'

'Are you sure?' asked Keedy. 'Don't forget that Paul had exchanged his papers with someone else. You went to the prison and met that young man calling himself Paul Marmion.'

Ellen pulled a face. 'He was revolting.'

'Yes,' added Alice. 'He really enjoyed leading us astray.'

'I was shocked that Paul had befriended someone as cruel as that.'

'Do you know what his real name was?' asked Keedy. Both women shook their heads. 'Then let's try to find out, shall we? I'll ring the prison now.'

'We have the phone number,' said Alice.

'Do you remember the governor's name?'

'Scarman . . . Mr Gerald Scarman.'

'He was a very nice man,' recalled Ellen.

'We were grateful for the way that he treated us and so relieved to discover that it wasn't Paul who was behind bars. It was someone pretending to be my brother,' said Alice. 'He taunted us, Joe. He was vile.'

'The governor may not be there on a Sunday,' said Keedy, 'but somebody will be. Let me have the number, please, and I'll ring the prison. I'll soon find out if the fake Paul Marmion is still locked up there.'

Clifford Burge was very much aware of the fact that he had deprived Hector Reed of a Sunday with his family. He was tempted to urge him to go home but he knew that he would not make any progress without the man's expertise and knowledge of the city. Also, Reed was not brooding. Nor was he resentful towards his English counterpart. He simply adjusted to their earlier disappointment and remained hopeful.

'It's ironic, isn't it?' he said.

'What is?'

'Well, Scotland is a country brimming with people named Paterson, yet we can't find the one that we want. Even if we narrow the search by adding Neil, we still have endless possibilities.'

'But they're not all married to a Flora Goddard.'

'A woman who defied her family to walk down the aisle with him.'

'There's one advantage, I suppose,' observed Burge.

'Is there?'

'To all intents and purposes, Paterson doesn't have a mother-in-law.'

Reed laughed. 'That could be seen as an advantage,' he said. 'Mind you, not every mother-in-law keeps a watchful eye on her daughter. Mine is a lovely woman and she was very supportive when the children were born. They adore her. Do you have children, Cliff?'

'I'm not married.'

'Do you have a Mrs Burge in mind?'

'I've had several, but they never stay the course. As soon as they discover the hours we work, they change their minds. I don't blame them.'

They were in Reed's office, watching heavy rain pummel the outside of the windows.

'Let's get back to Neil Paterson,' suggested Reed. 'What do we know about him?'

'He was very good at his job when he lived in London.'

'Why did he leave it?'

'I'm hoping we'll find out, eventually.'

'Was he a vengeful man?'

'It looks as if he might have been,' said Burge. 'The other suspects are in the clear. Walter Greenlow retired for health reasons and Martin Beale left for a better job in another bank. He liked Paterson, by the way. They were friends.'

'Yet you told me that Paterson didn't give Beale his new address when he left London.'

'That could be a telling detail.'

Lost in thought, Reed was silent for a couple of minutes. When he spoke, he had a suggestion.

'Let's forget about Neil Paterson,' he said. 'He may be completely innocent, after all.'

'I doubt it,' said Burge.

'If you were the mastermind behind a bank robbery, what would you be careful to do?'

'I'd select people who were completely trustworthy.'

'A relative, perhaps?'

'Definitely – and he'd be the leader of the gang.'

'What would your main concern be?'

'Stealing the money then going to a place of safety,' said Burge. 'I'd have chosen an abandoned house somewhere out in the countryside. And I'd have had a second hideaway lined up in case the first one was discovered.'

'Then you'd have done a lot of planning in advance.'

'It would be vital, Hector.'

'What about the money?'

'In the short term, it would be kept by the gang who stole it. They'd have the sense not to spend any of it. Crisp new banknotes would give the game away.'

'Well done – you're thinking like a crook.'

'When would they divide up the spoils?'

'When it was safe,' decided Reed. 'That might be weeks later . . . months, even.'

'Neil Paterson – or whoever the former employee was – wouldn't wait that long.'

'Why not?'

'The robbery was his idea, after all. He'd want some recognition of that, so he'd set a date when they all got together. He'd want his share sooner rather than later.'

Mills was becoming increasingly restive. While the others warmed themselves near the fire, he paced up and down with the remains of a cigarette between his lips. When he'd inhaled for the last time, he hurled the stub into the flames.

'Sit down,' said Gadney.

'I'd rather stay on my feet,' replied Mills.

'Why? You're going nowhere.'

'I'm entitled to do what I want, aren't I? It's not as if we're still in the army. Everything we did there was because of an order barked at us. We're free now, Max.'

'And who helped you to get free?' asked Gadney.

'You did – along with Terry.'

'Don't ever forget it.'

'I did my share,' insisted Mills. 'Who knocked that guard out when he challenged us? I did.'

'At my instruction.'

'Yes,' said Hillier, 'but you didn't hit him hard enough, Sid. I had to finish him off.'

'But that's as far as either of you would have gone without my help,' boasted Gadney. 'With no map, you'd have been lost. That's why I went to such lengths to steal one. I guided you both safely across France under the cover of darkness.'

'That's true,' conceded Mills. 'What are we going to do when we get our share of the loot?'

'Well, I'm not going back to work in that garage,' said Hillier. 'That's for certain. My girlfriend always complained about me having oil on my hands.'

'Forget her,' advised Mills. 'You'll be able to buy women from now on.'

'Buy them, use them, then get rid of them,' said Gadney with a crude laugh. 'We'll have to be on the move all the time.'

'What about your job in the abattoir, Max?'

'That's dead and buried. We're new men with completely new lives from now on but only as long as we don't make stupid mistakes. Agreed?' The others nodded obediently. 'Never forget it. Don't breathe a word of what we did to anyone. Do as I bloody well tell you and you'll survive. Strike out on your own and you're bound to be caught.'

Before he made the telephone call, Keedy took the precaution of having a pad and a pencil beside him. Alice and Ellen, meanwhile, were in the living room, catching only the odd phrase of what Keedy was saying. After a long time, they heard the receiver being replaced. Keedy entered the room.

'Well?' asked Alice. 'Did you speak to the governor?'

'He wasn't on duty,' said Keedy. 'I talked to his deputy

146

instead, a Stephen Hobson. It took me some time to convince him that I was a detective sergeant from Scotland Yard. It was only then that I began to get answers.'

'What was the name of that repulsive young man?' asked Ellen.

'Garth Price.'

'Is that the name Paul is using now?'

'Who knows?'

'Is Garth Price still locked up safely in prison?' asked Alice.

'No, he isn't. He was a deserter. His regiment sent men to reclaim him.'

'Then he's in for a very rough time.'

'Unfortunately,' said Keedy, 'he isn't.'

'Why not?'

'Somehow, he managed to escape. Price jumped from a moving vehicle with a pair of handcuffs on. They're still searching for him.'

'In that case,' said Ellen, anxiously, 'he could have been the thief who broke in here.'

'No,' said Keedy. 'I think it was Paul. If it had been Price, he'd never have come to put the money back. He'd have stolen anything he thought he could sell. But be on your guard. Get that locksmith here tomorrow to change the front door lock.'

'Why do you say that?'

'The deputy governor told me about Price's behaviour in prison. He caused them endless trouble. And he still knows this address, remember. He might decide to pay a visit here when you least expect him. Take no chances. Garth Price is a menace.'

CHAPTER ELEVEN

Marmion had a full day at Scotland Yard, gathering reports from his detectives, reassuring the superintendent that they were making headway and promising the commissioner that he anticipated an arrest before long. He also spent time wondering how Burge was getting on in Glasgow and why he had not received a full report from him. Had he sent Sergeant Keedy to Scotland instead, the latter would have kept him fully informed at every stage. He realised that Burge might be a promising detective, but that he was not yet the finished article.

Out of the blue, he received an unexpected telephone call. He picked up the receiver.

'Marmion here . . .'

'Hello, Inspector,' said Stuart Fryer. 'I'm sorry to disturb you. I had a feeling that you'd be hard at work even on a Sunday.'

'We're like the Pinkerton Agency – We Never Sleep.'

'Even you must have a rest now and again. May I ask how the investigation is going?'

'It's going slowly but surely, sir.'

'Do you have any idea who the bank robbers were?'

'We have one possible name but we've yet to establish if the man really was involved.'

'I see,' said Fryer. 'The reason I rang is this. Since I'm in charge of security at the bank, I have a particular interest in how one of the robbers got into the premises. When business came to an end yesterday, I stayed behind and went up into the attic. I gave it a more thorough search this time and found more evidence that someone had been there.'

'What sort of evidence, sir?'

'Tucked away in a corner was a tattered French newspaper, dated well over a week ago. It had details of events on the battlefield.'

'That confirms my belief that the robbers were deserters from our army. When they fled their regiment, they might have picked it up on their way to the coast. Once here,' said Marmion, 'they had no further use for it.'

'There were some dirty marks on it – as if something had been wrapped inside it.'

'A weapon of some kind, perhaps?'

'Possibly. Are you in touch with regiments based in France?'

'Of course, Mr Fryer. We leave no stone unturned.'

'Your thoroughness is reassuring.'

There was a long pause. Marmion eventually broke the silence.

'Is there something else you wish to tell me, sir?' he asked.

'As a matter of fact, there is,' confessed the other. 'It's about Neil Paterson.'

'Go on.'

'Well,' said Fryer, 'when I told you that we had always been friendly towards each other, I was not being entirely honest. Neil was in line to be the next deputy manager, and he rather let it get to his head. When I was appointed instead of him, he was quivering with rage. He managed to hide it from everyone else, but he left me in no doubt that I'd stolen something from him. In short, we were no longer colleagues. I'd made an enemy.'

'Were there any clashes between you?'

'It took the form of angry glares at first. Whenever we were alone, Neil would stare at me as if I were his worst enemy. Then came nudges and, on one occasion, a punch. I can't tell you how relieved I was when he resigned. Going to work became a pleasure again.'

'The search for Paterson continues,' said Marmion. 'I have one of my detectives in Glasgow at this very moment. If Paterson is there, he will be found.'

'Will he have some of the money stolen from the bank with him?'

'That's a distinct possibility, sir.'

'I'll feel so guilty if it turns out that Neil was behind the raid. In essence, it was my fault. By taking on a role that Neil had coveted for so long, I shattered his dreams. I'm terrified to think that I might somehow have been responsible for the robbery.'

'Don't lose sleep over it,' advised Marmion. 'If Paterson is involved – and we yet to have proof that he was – he was not driven by jealousy. The crime was planned down to the last detail by a man who could not resist the opportunity to steal a large amount of money. That shows how cool and collected he was. He assembled a gang of men capable of obeying his orders. The one thing he did not tell them to do was to kill a policeman on duty in the vicinity.'

'Yes, that came as a dreadful shock.'

'It's one of the main reasons why I'm happy to sacrifice a Sunday to work on this case.'

'That's very commendable of you, Inspector.'

'I don't need congratulations, sir,' said Marmion. 'I just want the satisfaction of catching the man who killed a good friend of mine. That's what drives me on.'

After spending the afternoon at the family home, Alice Marmion and Joe Keedy were being driven by Raymond Marmion back to his house. The couple had agreed to have supper there with their hosts. The ride gave them a chance to review their respective days.

'What was it like to hear the banns of marriage being published, Joe? asked Raymond.

'Scary,' admitted Keedy.

'I've never seen him so nervous,' said Alice. 'Joe is brave enough to take on vicious criminals, but he was trembling when our names were read out.'

'I had a guilty conscience, that's all.'

'There was no need.'

'I know that now, Alice. At the time, I didn't.'

'Whatever happened,' said Raymond, 'you're one step closer to the wedding. Has the vicar had a serious talk with the both of you?'

'Not yet. We had to wait until I came out of hospital. Though, to be honest, I'm not entirely sure that we need it. Alice and I have been together for years.'

'Once you're married, you'll be together for decades. Apart from your commitment to the Church, you need to discuss the problems that lie ahead, including the possibility of having a family.'

'We certainly hope to have one,' said Alice.

'In time,' added Keedy. 'We'd like to enjoy being together first.'

'But we have discussed the idea of having children. I know that Mummy is waiting for the day when it happens. She'll be a wonderful grandmother.'

'For what it's worth,' said Raymond, 'my advice is to be patient. It seems unfair to bring children into a world that is trapped in the dark shadow of a war. Their childhood would be blighted from the very start.'

'We don't want that to happen, Uncle Raymond.'

'I can understand that.' He slowed the van so that he could ease it around a corner. 'Did you have a chance to discuss that business with the money that turned up?'

'Yes, we did.'

'I don't believe that Paul put it there,' argued Keedy.

'What makes you say that?' asked Raymond.

'When he was on the loose, he exchanged identities with a young man by the name of Garth Price. You'll remember that Price was arrested and imprisoned.'

'That's right. Alice and her mother went to Shepton Mallet to meet him.'

'Only because we believed that the prisoner might actually be Paul,' she recalled.

'Your mother told us what a dreadful experience it was for you.'

'It was frightening, Uncle Raymond. Price really enjoyed dashing our hopes. I can't believe that my brother would befriend such a horrible person.'

'Yet he did,' Keedy pointed out. 'It's very worrying.'

'What happened to this fellow?' asked Raymond. 'Is he still in prison?'

'No, he isn't. I took the liberty of ringing the place and spoke to the deputy governor. Garth Price was a deserter. He was handed over to his regiment but – when they drove him away – he somehow escaped. And he might still have had the key to the house in his possession.'

'That's worrying, Joe.'

'It frightens me,' confessed Alice. 'Until we have a new lock on the front door, we simply won't be able to feel safe there.'

Since the rain had eased off, Hector Reed took the opportunity to show Burge around the city. As they drove around in a police car, Reed pointed out the important buildings. What struck Burge was the amount of noise they heard. Whenever they passed factories, lights were on in the windows and the sound of machinery boomed out at them. War had turned Sunday into a normal day. Every time they glimpsed the Clyde, they saw men hard at work alongside its banks, contributing to the war effort with unflagging commitment.

'How much longer will it last?' sighed Burge.

'I've been asking myself that for years, Cliff.'

'I blame the Russians.'

'Why?' asked Reed.

'Well, they used to be on our side. That meant they could harry the Germans on the Eastern Front. Then they had that revolution last year and dropped out of the war altogether. That changed the balance of power immediately,' said Burge. 'The Germans suddenly had huge reinforcements they could bring to the Western Front. It's made a big difference.'

'Did you ever think of joining the army?'

'Of course – we all did.'

'What kept you in the police?'

'The fact that I was sorely needed, Hector. There's a war to be fought on the Home Front as well and I was ready to do my bit here. I've hardly had a day off for years.'

'It's the same with me. We've had to make sacrifices.'

'I sometimes think we've made too many of them and we're not appreciated. It's no wonder there are whispers about a police strike. We deserve better pay.'

'I agree with you there.'

'Maybe it's time we stood up for ourselves,' said Burge. 'We should make demands.'

Reed tensed. 'Would you take part in a strike?'

'I'd certainly think about it. What about you?'

'I'm against the idea,' insisted Reed. 'What would happen if policemen suddenly stopped work? There'd be utter chaos. Crime would rocket everywhere. The Huns would be delighted.'

'Why?'

'It's because we'd be in complete disarray.'

'We're entitled to fight for more pay and better working conditions,' argued Burge.

'Then do it when there's no war on.'

'We can't wait that long.'

'In that case, you'll be helping the enemy to win the war. You'd also be letting our armies down. One day,' said Reed, 'our lads will be coming home at last. They deserve to find a country that's welcoming and peaceful, not one that's tearing itself to pieces.'

The rest of the journey was in complete silence.

Left alone in the house, Ellen had settled down with her novel. As her husband had anticipated, the hero was captured by the enemy and interrogated by a German officer. Locked up in a dark attic, he made a courageous escape over the rooftops, dropping to the ground eventually and vanishing into the darkness. Gripped by the narrative, Ellen pressed on until she came to the end of the story and felt a profound sense of relief. Setting the book aside, she sat back and reflected on the way that the novel had kept her entranced for hours.

Without any warning, she was suddenly gripped by a sense of alarm. There was somebody else in the house. Had it been her husband, she would have been aware of his return. Ellen felt hopelessly alone. Her first instinct was to defend herself, so she grabbed the poker and began a tentative search of the house. There was nobody in the hall and the kitchen was also empty. She tried to shake off her fears, telling herself that nobody else could possibly be inside the house because the front door was securely locked. Confidence restored, she went back into the living room and put the poker back in its place. Ellen even felt brave enough to sit back on the sofa.

Her composure did not last long. She soon became aware that it had gone cold. There was a fire in the grate, but it no longer filled the room with warmth. Grabbing the poker once more, she opened the door slowly and stepped out into the hall. The drop in temperature was even more noticeable. A cold draught was coming from upstairs. Ellen tightened her grip on the poker and cried out with as much authority as she could manage.

'Who's there?' she demanded.

There was no answer. A sudden breeze blew into her face and made her shiver.

'Is that you, Paul?' she asked.

Once again, no reply came. What she did notice was how much colder it was getting. The wind seemed to be coming from Paul's room at the top of the stairs. Poker in hand, Ellen went slowly up the steps and shivered in the cold. The door to Paul's room was slightly ajar, allowing the breeze to come through unchecked. Ellen was confused. Should she allow herself to be frightened by her own son? He was entitled to be back in the house.

'Paul!' she shouted. 'Is that you?'

By way of reply, the wind increased in volume and the door of the bedroom slammed shut.

The three of them sat close to the fire. Hillier had dozed off to sleep, Gadney was sharpening his bayonet and Mills was staring at the leather bag beside Gadney, knowing that it contained the money they had stolen from the bank and wondering when it would be shared out.

'What if someone sees smoke coming from the chimney?' he asked.

'They won't,' said Gadney.

'Why not?'

'Because it's pouring with rain outside and almost dark. Nobody's going to stop to look at an abandoned farmhouse that's falling to bits. Stop finding things to worry about, Sid.'

'The police are after us, Max.'

'What's left of them, that is. They don't have the numbers to do the job properly and they certainly wouldn't send a search party this far outside London.'

'Then why do I feel so uneasy?'

'You were born uneasy.'

'I still think we should keep on the move.'

'And get soaked in this downpour?' asked Gadney in disbelief. 'Put your trust in the person who set up the bank robbery. He offered us a golden opportunity to make a lot of money. And he made sure that we'd have a safe hiding place.'

'I don't feel safe.'

'That's your problem.'

'You killed a copper, Max. That means they'll never stop looking for us.'

'It doesn't mean they'll catch us. We're trained soldiers. We know how to look after ourselves and keep ahead of danger.'

'I'm scared,' admitted Mills.

'The only thing that scares me is that you're so frightened. It's a threat to all of us. If you look so guilty, people will realise that you've done something bad. As for that copper,' said Gadney, baring his teeth, 'he got what he deserved. I used to make a living at it, remember. When I worked in the abattoir, I slaughtered animal after animal. To my mind, a copper is no different to an animal.' He held up the bayonet to examine it. 'Besides, I've wiped his blood off it now. I'm ready for the next person who gets in my way.'

'Why have you kept that bayonet?'

'It's a souvenir. I've killed Huns by firing a rifle, but I never actually saw them die. With a bayonet, I get to watch the victim suffer.'

'You're cruel, Max.'

'It's necessary sometimes.'

'Doesn't anything frighten you?'

'Yes – it's the sound of you losing your nerve.'

'I can't help it.'

'Try harder.'

'I will.' Mills yawned. 'What day is it?'

'Sunday – say your bloody prayers.'

* * *

157

When they reached the house, Raymond unlocked the front door and ushered them in. Lily Marmion gave them a cordial welcome, then told them to sit down. She recalled a visitor to the house.

'Oh, there was a letter for you, Joe,' she said.

'Was there?' he asked in surprise.'

'It was shoved through the letter box.'

'Oh, I see. Who could possibly know where I was living?'

Lily took a letter off the mantelpiece and handed it over. She then went into the kitchen with Raymond. Alice was curious.

'Who is it from, Joe?' she asked.

'Heaven knows. I don't recognise the handwriting.' He tore open the envelope and took out a leaflet. 'Ah, I was waiting for this.'

'What is it?'

'Nothing you need bother about,' he replied, folding the leaflet before putting it in the inside pocket of his jacket. 'It's private.'

She was irritated. 'We agreed that we had no secrets between us.'

'It's police business, Alice.'

'I'm a policewoman, remember?'

'It . . . doesn't concern you.'

'Then why are you being so secretive?'

'I just don't want to talk about it, that's all.'

'Joe, I'm going to be your wife in a few weeks.'

'I know and that day can't come early enough for me, I promise you.'

'Does that mean I get to see the letter of yours when we're married?'

He laughed. 'You're so damned nosy!'

158

'Yes or no?'

'No,' he replied. 'You won't see it after we're married because you can read it right now.' He took out the letter. 'Here you are.'

Alice took it from him and glanced at it. Her eyes filled with dread.

Marmion had never been driven home so fast. Ellen's phone call had been so wild and incoherent that he left Scotland Yard immediately and sought a driver. When he was dropped off outside his house, he jumped out of the car and ran to the front door. Jamming his key into the lock, he turned it in the hope that the door would swing open, but it was firmly bolted on the inside. He banged on it with his fist and heard footsteps approaching. When the door was opened by his wife, she flung herself into his arms.

'Thank God you're back!'

'You sounded so desperate on the telephone.'

'I'm so sorry.'

'Let's get inside out of the cold.'

Helping her into the house, he closed the door behind them. Then he took her by the shoulders and held her at arm's length.

'Now – very slowly – tell me what happened. You said that someone was here.'

'I'm certain of it, Harvey.'

'Did you see them?'

'No, I just felt that . . . an intruder was in the house . . .'

'And what made you think that?'

'I suddenly felt cold,' recalled Ellen, 'and I knew for certain that I'd closed all the doors and shut all the windows. Yet this draught of air was coming from upstairs. I simply had to go and find out what caused it.'

'You should have been more cautious,' said Marmion.

'I took a poker with me.'

'What use would that be against a burglar?'

'I thought it might be Paul,' she said. 'The cold air was coming from his room. When I got there, I heard a sudden gust of wind and the door slammed shut.'

'Did you try to open it?'

'Yes, I did – after a while, that is. I was a bag of nerves, Harvey, but I felt that I had to see if it had been our son. I forced myself to open the door and saw that the window was wide open. The room was empty, and the curtains were being blown about.'

'What did you do?'

'I rushed to the window and looked out but there was no sign of anyone. If Paul or someone else had been there, they'd got away by jumping down onto the path.'

'Did you close the window?'

'Yes, I closed it and locked it.'

'And were you certain that someone had been in the room?'

'Yes,' she replied, 'drawers had been pulled open and the wardrobe was ajar. Paul – or someone else – had stolen a lot of clothing. That proves we had a burglar.'

'Calm down, calm down, love,' he advised, putting his arms around her. 'Take a few deep breaths.' She did as he suggested but the anxiety in her face remained. 'Did you check the money?'

'What money?'

'The housekeeping that was returned. Someone put it back in the cup.'

Ellen shrugged. 'It's still there, as far as I know.'

'Let's go and see.'

'If it was Paul who put the money back,' she said, following him into the kitchen, 'then he'd have left it there. All he was after was warmer clothing.'

'I wonder . . .'

Marmion opened the cupboard and reached in for the cup. When he showed it to his wife, she gasped in horror. The cup was completely empty.

When he had finally been left alone, Clifford Burge had felt a sense of relief. He had found Hector Reed both friendly and extremely helpful. They had worked well together. Then came a sudden change. Burge had mentioned the possibility of a police strike and admitted that – if it happened – he might take part in it. It was a stance that Reed did not share. Indeed, he spoke sharply against the idea. A gap suddenly opened between the two men. It reached a point where Burge insisted that Reed should go home to his family. After agreeing to meet up the following morning, Reed offered Burge the use of his office and telephone, then left him on his own.

Sad that they had fallen out, Burge hoped that the slight hostility between them would disappear before they next met. Meanwhile, he had work to do. Seated at the desk, he took out his notebook and reminded himself what had happened during his visit to Glasgow. Though there was no good news to report, he nevertheless rang Marmion's number at Scotland Yard.

'Why didn't you tell me?' demanded Alice.

'There was nothing to tell,' claimed Keedy.

'You've been in touch with them, haven't you?'

'No, I haven't.'

'Then why did they send you that leaflet?'

'They probably sent a copy to everyone in the Metropolitan Police Force.'

'I'm only interested in you, Joe.'

'I can't see why you're so upset.'

'It's because you're not telling me the truth.'

'Of course, I am,' he said, hotly.

'Then how did they know that you were living here with Uncle Raymond and Auntie Lily?'

His face clouded. 'Well . . .'

'The only explanation is that you must have told them.'

'What if I did? I'm entitled to know what's going on.'

After a meal with Raymond and Lily, they were alone in the living room of the house. Having suppressed her anger, Alice now let it show. Her voice was raised, her eyes alight and her finger jabbed him repeatedly on his chest.

'You know what Daddy would say, don't you?' she told him.

'I'm entitled to my own opinion.'

'He'd call it a betrayal.'

'And so would I,' he replied, voice rising. 'We've been betrayed by this government for too long. They expect us to work all hours but offer no reward in the form of extra pay and better working conditions.'

'Don't side with them, Joe.'

'It's a fair argument.'

'But it's not one that you should be making right now. We're still at war, Joe. It's the worst possible time for us to strike.'

'We think that it's the ideal time – when the government is under such pressure. They'd soon realise just how much they need us.'

'Daddy is going to be very cross about this.'

'Your father knows where I stand,' he said. 'Now can we please stop arguing? It's making me feel upset. I should never have shown you that leaflet.' He took her in his arms. 'It's an idea, Alice. It may never happen. But it's a threat that might be used – don't you see that?'

'No, I don't.'

'Let's talk about something else, shall we?'

She broke away. 'I'm too upset.'

'I'm sorry.'

'I'm not sure that you are, Joe.'

He took a deep breath. 'Look, we're seeing the vicar next week. What is he going to tell us?'

'He'll say that we must be honest with each other.'

'That's exactly what we are being, Alice.'

'Then why are we arguing like this?'

Keedy had no answer.

They were mystified. Someone had come into their house and stolen money and items of clothing from their son's bedroom. They could not decide if the thief had been Paul or the person he had befriended along the way. Marmion and his wife talked anxiously about what had happened. It was only when the telephone rang that they were jolted out of their conversation.

'Hello,' said Marmion, speaking into the receiver.

'Is that you, sir?' asked Burge.

'Ah, you've broken cover at last, have you? Why haven't you been in touch sooner?'

'There was nothing to report, sir.'

'Well, I hope that you've got something now.'

'Not really,' admitted the other.

Burge delivered his report as succinctly as he could, stressing how much help he'd had from the Glasgow Constabulary. Marmion listened intently but heard nothing that would take their investigation to a more positive stage. When he rang off, his face reflected his disappointment.

'Bad news?' asked Ellen.

'Cliff Burge has got nowhere in Glasgow.'

'Oh dear!'

'I've told him to keep at it for a couple of days.'

'Did you mention what's happening here?'

'No, Ellen,' he said. 'This is our problem. We need to solve it ourselves.'

'I'm terrified that it might be that evil young man we met in Shepton Mallet Prison.'

'I'm equally frightened that it might be our own son. What possessed Paul to come here and act like a burglar? This is his home. He belongs here.'

'I don't think that he realises that, Harvey. He's a fugitive – or at least he acts like one. Why did he take that money from the cupboard for a second time?'

'He needed it, Ellen – and he needed that clothing.'

'But supposing that it wasn't Paul at all?'

Marmion grimaced. 'It doesn't bear thinking about.'

Sir Edward Henry had been troubled by the headlines in the morning papers. He went along to Chatfield's office to complain about them.

'The German Army is making greater advances,' he said.

'I'm sure that it will be at considerable cost to them, Sir Edward. Our soldiers always fight back like terriers.'

'The problem must be with our generals.'

'Yes, they haven't adapted swiftly enough to the tactical changes made by the enemy.'

'I sincerely hope that they soon will,' said the commissioner. 'Do you have more cheering news on the Home Front?'

'I'm afraid not,' confessed Chatfield. 'Had you come ten minutes earlier, you'd have heard Marmion's latest report. Sending a man to Glasgow was an excellent idea but it has yet to prove of any real benefit. This fellow Paterson is far too elusive.'

'That could be an indication of his guilt.'

'He's bound to get in touch with the bank robbers at some point.'

'I agree, Sir Edward, though he might be keeping clear of them until they can meet in a place of safety. Since the raid was so carefully planned, we can expect that everything else has been considered beforehand. Paterson – if he really is behind the robbery – will have found the perpetrators a hiding place outside London.'

'And outside our reach,' sighed the commissioner.

'Village bobbies are easier to dodge than trained detectives like ours,' said Chatfield.

'We simply can't let these villains get away with it.'

'We won't, Sir Edward. It's only a matter of time before they slip up.'

'Is Marmion optimistic?'

'He's always optimistic,' said Chatfield. 'No matter how many setbacks there are, he'll chase these men until he catches them. Constable Collard, a close friend of his, was murdered by one of the robbers. The need for revenge is burning inside Marmion like a forest fire. He's working around the clock to find the bank robbers.'

CHAPTER TWELVE

The weeks spent in hospital had accustomed Keedy to an early start every morning. There was so much noise and movement that it was impossible for him to sleep. When Monday morning had dawned, therefore, he was wide awake. He went straight to the bathroom to wash and shave. By the time he went downstairs, however, he was still too late to catch Raymond. Evidently, the demands of running a Salvation Army hostel were heavy.

Keedy found Lily in the kitchen.

'Has your husband gone already?' he asked.

'I'm afraid so. Raymond has had his breakfast and started work.'

'And I thought that being in the Metropolitan Police Force was a hard life.'

'It is,' said Lily, smiling. 'At least we don't have to confront fear and threat every day. That's what Harvey found when he joined the police. I remember him telling us about needing eyes in the back of his head. We don't have that problem, thank God.'

'Is there anything I can do?'

'Yes, you can sit down and wait until I serve breakfast.'

'I'd like to help in some way.'

'Then stay in the kitchen and talk to me. Time passes more quickly when I natter.' She looked down at the items of food and sighed. 'There's not much choice, I'm afraid. Since they brought rationing in, we seem to have been worse off somehow. Sugar, butter, margarine and lard are in short supply. As for tea, cheese and jam, they're rationed by local food committees.'

'How on earth do you manage?'

'Luckily, we have a farmer who believes in the work we do. He sells us as many eggs as we need at half the normal price. Would you like yours boiled or fried?'

'Boiled, please. Hard-boiled.'

Lily filled a saucepan with water and put it on the gas stove. Two eggs were soon bobbing around inside it. She spoke over her shoulder.

'Raymond tells me that you and Alice were very quiet last night,' she recalled. 'When he drove the pair of you to her flat, you hardly said a word.'

'We had a disagreement, that's all.'

'Nothing serious, I hope.'

'No, no,' said Keedy with a laugh, 'of course not. It was . . . just one of those silly rows that couples like us have. We still love each other just as much.'

'Alice was tortured by anxiety while you were in hospital.'

'I know. She's talked about it.'

'Then, of course, there's the problem with Paul. She just can't understand why he left in the first place. It's so unlike her brother.'

'Blame the war for his behaviour,' said Keedy. 'He was a happy-go-lucky lad before he joined the army. There's not much happiness in his life now. He's been cut adrift.'

'It was his decision. That's what upsets Ellen.'

'I know. She's worried sick – and so is Harvey. He's just better at hiding it.'

'We keep praying for Paul's safe return.'

'Is that such a good idea?'

'What do you mean?'

'He's changed out of all recognition,' said Keedy. 'When Alice met that man who had Paul's papers, she was horrified. She couldn't believe that Paul would befriend someone as revolting as that. And yet he obviously did.'

'It must be so confusing for his parents,' said Lily. 'They brought Paul up to be an honest, straightforward, hard-working young man. When he enlisted with his friends, they were very proud of him.'

'That was then, Lily. They can't possibly take pride in him now.'

When the locksmith arrived, Ellen had felt a huge sense of relief. Stanley Gault was a short, whiskery, stooping man in his fifties with a businesslike manner. Invited into the house, he put his toolbox down and sized up the front door.

'Yes,' he promised, 'I can fit a new lock here and it will be perfectly secure. I'd also suggest another bolt at the top of the door. It's an extra precaution.'

'Very good, Mr Gault. And when you've finished that, we'd like you to put a lock on one of the windows upstairs.'

'Doesn't it have a standard lock?'

'Yes, but we wanted to feel even safer.'

'Fair enough.'

'Would you like a cup of tea before you start?' she asked.

'No, thank you, Mrs Marmion.'

'I'm about to make one for myself.'

'Let me do something to deserve it. I'll tackle the door first then I'd like to have a look at this window of yours.'

After breakfast at his hotel, Clifford Burge walked the short distance to Police Headquarters. Conscious of what had happened last time they were together, he knocked on Hector Reed's door with slight trepidation. Invited in, he opened the door and entered the office. Reed was on the telephone, jotting something on a pad. He gave a warm smile of welcome. Burge relaxed. There was no hint of the awkwardness between them generated by a discussion of a possible police strike. It was a new day with new priorities.

Ending his phone call, Reed replaced the receiver then stood up.

'Don't take your raincoat off, Cliff,' he said. 'We're going out.'

'Where?'

'In search of Neil Paterson.'

Burge was delighted. 'You've tracked him down?'

'I may have. There are two possibilities. First, we're going to Erskine – that's to the north-west. If the Neil Paterson we find there is not our man, then we'll see if the one we want is living in Hamilton. That's to the south-east.'

'This is great news!'

'Don't get too excited.'

'Why?'

'You obviously haven't realised what day it is, have you?'

'It's Monday.'

'Monday, 1st of April,' said Reed. 'It's April Fool's Day.'

* * *

Sidney Mills was in the woodshed, gathering up the remaining logs to put into a wheelbarrow. He was feeling increasingly resentful at having to do the most onerous jobs. While his two friends were indoors, sipping cups of tea, he was outside in the cold. What irked him most was that they had not told him exactly how much of the stolen money would go to him. As their leader, Max Gadney would have the largest amount. Without him, there would have been no bank robbery. They'd simply have been three deserters, struggling along somehow and being hunted at every stage. Luckily, Gadney had a friend who had offered them the opportunity to make a new life for themselves. They had seized the opportunity bravely.

But it meant that a fourth person would expect his reward as well. Terence Hillier had entered the bank and helped Gadney to steal the money. They had therefore taken the major risk and were challenged by two policemen as they left the premises. Mills was ready to acknowledge that. But he also felt that he deserved a substantial amount of money because he had stolen the car that carried all three of them to the farm. It was time to stand up to the others and to demand a fair share. As he loaded the last of the logs into the wheelbarrow, he resolved to ask for details of how much money he would get.

When he got back to the kitchen, however, there was no sign of his friends. After unloading the logs, he tossed a couple on the fire then went in search of Gadney and Hillier. The place felt strangely empty. Had they sneaked away without him? That was impossible, he told himself, because the car was still locked. So where were they? More to the point, where was the money? He was gripped by a sudden fear. Had they fled with the proceeds of the robbery? Was he being discarded by his erstwhile friends? Gadney always carried the leather bag that held the money. He slept with it beside him. Find the money, Mills told himself, and he would find Gadney.

Mills began a frantic search for the two men. Rushing from room to room, he opened doors and looked everywhere. When he raced upstairs, he was met with the same story. They had abandoned him. Having used him, they had discarded him completely. A thought struck him. The one place he had not searched was the cellar. Racing down to it, he tried the door and found that it was not locked. Ignoring the feeling of damp, he went down the steps in the gloom. When he reached the bottom, he looked around in despair.

Without warning, two figures jumped out in front of him and cackled.

'April Fool!' shouted Gadney and Hillier in unison.

Alice Marmion and Iris Goodliffe walked side by side on their beat. The rain had stopped and the clouds had cleared. There was the promise of a fine day.

'Has something happened?' asked Iris.

'What do you mean?'

'Well, you've hardly said a word to me this morning. As a rule, you've always got plenty to talk about. Didn't you and Joe see each other?'

'Of course, we did.'

'Then what happened?'

'We . . . had a lovely time together, Iris.'

'You don't sound as if you did,' said her friend. 'How is Joe?'

'He gets better by the day.'

'Haven't the two of you slipped back to the house to be on your own?'

'We've had other things to do, Iris.'

'Such as?'

'We've been making plans, that's all.'

'That's an exciting thing to do, yet you seem so . . . well, subdued.'

'Look,' said Alice, 'please stop probing. If you must know, Joe and I had a tiff but it's water under the bridge now.'

'What was it about?'

'I'm doing my best to forget.'

'Then I won't press you. It's none of my business, really.' She brightened. 'Is everything ready for the wedding?'

'No,' admitted Alice.

'What's the problem?'

'It's one that's been haunting us for some time. Mummy thinks that Paul is back.'

'Oh dear!'

'She can't understand why he let himself into the house a while ago,' explained Alice. 'It was upsetting to think that he got in there while she was at her sewing circle.'

'He'd know the times when your mother wasn't at home.'

'Paul would know something else as well, Iris.'

'What do you mean?'

'We've had lots of replies to the invitations we sent out for the wedding. Some of them came in the shape of pretty cards. Mummy and I put them on the mantelpiece.'

'That's a lovely idea.'

'Is it?' asked Alice. 'If Paul let himself into the house, he's sure to have seen the cards. In other words, he knows exactly when and where Joe and I are going to be married. What if he decides to interrupt it somehow?'

* * *

Marmion was used to receiving telephone calls from the bank manager, asking what progress had been made. Instead of waiting for Douglas Boucher to ring that morning, he decided to pay a visit to the bank to speak to him in person. A police car drove him to Paddington. Boucher was delighted to see him and suggested that they were joined by the deputy manager. Stuart Fryer was summoned immediately. His eagerness to help was palpable.

'I don't have anything specific to report,' Marmion warned them. 'This is just a courtesy visit to bring you both up to date. Details of the bank robbery have been in all the newspapers and police forces throughout the country have been given all the available information. The robbers have gone to ground somewhere.'

'Do you have any idea where?' asked Boucher.

'No, but I'm certain that a hiding place had been chosen for them ahead of the robbery.'

'What about the car they used?'

'There have been no sightings of the vehicle. They fled in the middle of the night and probably reached their destination before daylight. They're simply keeping their heads down.'

'And counting our money,' said Fryer, bitterly.

'Don't be disheartened, sir. We're building up a clear picture of these men. Thanks to you, we know how they got into the bank in the first place. It's because one of them was a daredevil who climbed up to the roof. Only someone fit and fearless could have done that.'

'I agree, Inspector.'

'How did they know that it was the best way to gain entry?' asked Boucher.

'Someone had tipped them off – Neil Paterson, in all probability.'

'Are you sure that he was involved?'

'I'd say it was a safe bet, sir.'

'And you've got a man in Glasgow,' said Fryer, 'searching for him.'

'If he's there,' promised Marmion, 'we'll find him.'

'But he was such a loyal man,' argued Boucher. 'I put complete trust in Paterson.'

'Neil did have another side to him,' said Fryer, 'and it revealed him in his true light. That's why I have no doubt that he is behind the robbery.'

'You knew him better than I did, Stuart.'

'And he was so annoyed that you'd been appointed above him,' said Marmion, 'that he confronted you. Indeed, he punched you at one point.'

Fryer nodded. 'That's true, I'm afraid.'

'Would he have been able to mastermind the robbery?'

'I firmly believe so.'

'How did he come to choose the men?'

'He might have had contacts with friends in the army. Who knows? One of them might have been a relative. Paterson offered him a tempting opportunity. If the man was considering desertion, he was resorting to a desperate measure. It would have seemed far less desperate if there was a huge financial reward at the end of it.'

'Do you have any idea who the leader of the gang is?'

'We're still sifting through the names of deserters.'

'How did Neil expect to get away with it?' asked Fryer.

'If he had the ability to plan the robbery to the last detail,' said Marmion, 'he will have worked out a way to cover their tracks. They may even be all together, toasting their success and laughing at our vain effort to catch them.'

Boucher was puzzled. 'I thought that Paterson was in Glasgow.'

'Wherever he is, sir, I guarantee that we will find him.'

In view of their earlier disappointment, Burge did not let his hopes rise too high this time. All that they had been told was that a man named Neil Paterson was living in Erskine, having retired from working in a bank. Burge was perplexed. Could a man of Paterson's age afford to retire? Seated beside him, Hector Reed seemed to read his thoughts.

'Yes, he could afford to give up work,' he said, 'if . . .'

'If what?'

'If he had a share of the money stolen from that bank.'

'Don't let's make any assumptions. We haven't even met the man.'

'It's our turn to have some luck for a change.'

'I'm bracing myself for disappointment.'

'Have faith, Cliff. This could be him at long last.'

'Do you want to place a bet on it?'

'No – I'm too canny.'

Situated in the Clydebank area, Erskine was near the outer ring of the Glasgow conurbation. It was hovering somewhere between a large village and a small town. One of its main features was the Princess Louise Scottish Hospital for Limbless Soldiers and Sailors. Built two years earlier, it provided much more than convalescence for the military. Burge was told that patients could learn new trades there so that they could have an income when they were finally discharged. When the detectives found the property they sought, he was surprised. The charming old house outside which the police car stopped was set in a plot of land that afforded it a front and back garden. Evidently, the owner was a keen gardener because he could be seen pottering about among some bushes near the bay window. He was a slim man in nondescript clothing. His face was half-hidden by the brim of his hat. Noticing the police car, he ambled towards it, taking off his gardening gloves as he did so.

Burge and Reed stepped onto the pavement and appraised him.

'Neil Paterson?' asked Reed.

'Aye, that's me.'

'I'm Detective Sergeant Reed from the Glasgow Constabulary and this is Detective Sergeant Burge from Scotland Yard.'

Paterson grinned. 'Scotland Yard is no in Scotland.'

'Have you ever worked in England?' asked Burge.

'Aye, I have.'

'In London, perhaps?'

'Aye, for a short while.'

'Was it in a bank in Paddington?'

'No,' said Paterson, 'It was in a bank in Camberwell.'

'Oh,' sighed Burge.

'Isn't it too early for you to retire, sir?' asked Reed.

'Doctor's orders.'

'What's the problem?'

'I've got a dicky heart,' said Paterson, tapping his chest. 'I was told to retire and to get plenty of fresh air. If it's not raining, I'm out in the garden most days.'

'Could you afford to retire?' said Burge.

'No hope of that, I'm afraid. Bank clerks are not well paid. My father made it possible. When he died, he left me this wonderful old house and a fair bit of money saved from the days when he was a bank manager in Aberdeen. Looking after people's money runs in the family, you see. My brother's working in a bank in Dundee.'

'I'm sorry to have disturbed you, sir,' said Reed, hiding his disappointment. 'Excuse us.'

'You're welcome to a cup of tea.'

'That's very kind of you but we have . . . somewhere else to go.'

The detectives got into the rear seat of the car and turned to each other.

'Ah, well,' said Reed, philosophically, 'at least I wasn't stupid enough to put a bet on him.'

Marmion was missing Keedy. When he left the bank, therefore, he asked his driver to take him to his brother's house, hoping that the detective sergeant could make a useful contribution to the case. Alone in the house, Keedy was delighted to see him. Taking him into the living room, he indicated the pieces of paper on the table.

'I've been taking a leaf out of your book, Harv,' said Keedy. 'These are the people involved in the investigation. The suspects are in capital letters.'

'There should only be three of them – you seem to have four.'

'I've reinstated Stuart Fryer.'

Marmion gaped. 'You still think he's a suspect?'

'Yes, I do.'

'But he's been extremely helpful to me.'

'That could just be a smokescreen. Let me explain.'

'I'm sorry, Joe,' said Marmion, sitting beside him, 'but it's a ridiculous idea.'

'I thought that when I mentioned it to Raymond. In fact, it seemed so unlikely that I scrunched up the first piece of paper with Fryer's name on it and threw it away.'

'Quite right.'

'Then I remembered what he'd told you and my suspicions returned. It was the deputy manager who worked out exactly how someone got into the bank.'

'He's a shrewd man, Joe. He used his head.'

'He even took you up into the attic. You saw the door to the roof.'

'I went through it. I was shown the drainpipe that one of the burglars must have climbed up. That was quite a feat in the dark.'

'How did the man get into the attic?'

'He must have picked the lock somehow. That was Fryer's explanation.'

'There is another one – Fryer had left the door to it unlocked.'

'That's ridiculous, Joe!'

'Let me finish,' said Keedy. 'I've had a lot of time to think about it. You told me that to get into the attic, you had to climb up a ladder. How was the trapdoor locked?'

'There was a thick bolt underneath it.'

'Then how did the burglar open the trapdoor from the other side?'

'Well . . . I suppose that he could have inserted a thin blade through the gap around it and gently nudged the bolt back. Once he'd done that, he could lift the trapdoor up and jump down into the room before rushing off to disable the burglar alarm.'

'I'm not sure about that.'

'That's how it must have been done, Joe,' argued Marmion. 'Timing was essential. The intruder had to open the trapdoor at exactly the moment when the fire engines were racing past nearby. The ear-splitting noise would have drowned out the sound of the burglar alarm. Mr Fryer told me that it could have been switched off very quickly.'

'He would know. He would also have the combination of the safe that was opened and emptied. That was what the robbers had come for – with Fryer's help.'

'Slow down, Joe. You're making wild assumptions.'

'That might be the only way to solve this case.'

'The deputy manager is above suspicion in my view.'

'I think that he may have planned the whole thing, Harv.'

'What was his motivation?'

'He'd have a decent chunk of the stolen money for a start,' said Keedy. 'Then there's the satisfaction of creating what looks like a perfect crime.'

'I'd never call it that. You're forgetting that Sam Collard was murdered,' said Marmion, angrily. 'Was that part of Fryer's master plan?'

'No, it was just bad luck on Sam's part.'

'I'm sorry, Joe, but I've met Fryer and I think he's a decent, honest man.'

'It could be that he's just pretending to help.'

'You're not going to bring this investigation to an end by playing with a few pieces of paper.'

'It worked for you once,' Keedy reminded him.

'I just got lucky.'

When he went for a walk around the farmhouse, Sidney Mills saw how badly damaged the property had been. Hearing a noise from the barn, he went to investigate and found Terence Hillier cleaning the car with an old rag.

'Why are you bothering, Terry?' he asked. 'It's not yours.'

'I'm fulfilling a dream, Sid. I'd always promised myself that if I did ever own a car, I'd clean it whenever I could.'

'I'd get a chauffeur to do that for me.' They laughed. 'It's funny,' he went on, 'I've worked on boats all my life, yet I never wanted to own one.'

'Since you were a sailor, why didn't you join the navy?'

'All my friends joined the army, so I followed suit. The sad thing is that most of them are probably dead now.'

'Max and I survived somehow. And while we knew how to steal a boat, we didn't have a clue about sailing it across the Channel. Thank heavens we had you, Sid! You were our saviour.'

'Someone should remind Max of that.'

'Just keep out of his way.'

'How in hell am I supposed to do that?'

'You'll manage somehow.' He stood back to admire the sheen on the car. 'That'll do, I fancy.' He turned to Mills. 'When you get your money, what are you going to do?'

'Get as far away from Max as possible.'

'We owe him everything, Sid. He was the one who climbed into the bank. Just think of the risks involved in that. Do what he tells us and there'll be no problem.'

'His orders are that we have no contact with our families.'

'I agree with that,' said Hillier. 'If we get shelter from them, we'll put them in danger of arrest. We can't be too careful.'

'But I miss them, Terry.'

'We all do but it's one of the penalties we must suffer. We're deserters, remember. Even when we get our share of the money, it's not going to be plain sailing.'

'Why not?'

'Well, to start with, we've got no ration books. That gives the game away.'

'We can afford to bribe shopkeepers.'

'We'd be reported immediately.'

'But we're going to be rich, Terry,' said Mills. 'We can enjoy life.'

'Yes, we can – until they catch up with us, that is.'

Hamilton was far bigger than Erskine. Situated in Lanarkshire, it was a bustling town with over thirty-five thousand people living there. Cotton and coal industries had blossomed, and the railway was on hand to distribute the goods throughout Scotland and beyond. Looking around, Hector Reed dared to feel optimistic.

'This is more like it,' he said. 'In a place this size, we'll find as many people named Neil Paterson as we want.'

'Will the man we're after be among them?'

'Your guess is as good as mine, Cliff.'

'I'm desperate for some good news to report.'

'Tell that inspector of yours that you're coming home in triumph.'

'Am I?'

Reed grinned. 'Let's go and find out, shall we?'

Minutes later, the police car drew up outside a bank. The detectives got out and went into the building. When they asked to see the manager, they were conducted to an office at the rear of the property. Hugh Mallory was a tall, lean man with faint blue veins decorating his bald head. When he heard why the detectives were there, he was thrown on the defensive.

'It can't be our Neil Paterson,' he assured them.

'May we judge for ourselves?' asked Reed.

'Yes, of course . . .'

Mallory left the office at once and closed the door behind him. They had the opportunity of looking at their surroundings. Shelves lined two walls and filing cabinets stood against a third one. The focal point was the fireplace in which flames were dancing merrily. Burge studied the painting above the fireplace. It featured a stag, standing proudly on the peak of a mountain.

They were still admiring it when the door opened, and the manager brought in one of his employees. Burge's heart lifted immediately. Neil Paterson fitted the description he had been given to perfection. He was the right age and the correct height. He had the pleasant manner and natural grace described by his former employer. It had to be him.

After introducing Paterson to the two detectives, Mallory stood his ground. If someone in the building was going to be subjected to an interrogation, the manager was determined to be there.

'Why don't we all sit down,' he suggested.

When they were seated, Paterson looked mildly surprised.

'May I ask why you wish to speak to me?' he asked.

'It's to do with a bank robbery that took place in London recently,' said Burge.

'Ah, yes, I saw the reports in the newspapers.'

'How did you respond to what you read?'

'I was naturally upset,' said Paterson. 'Robberies of any kind are bad enough, but they have a special piquancy when a bank is involved.'

'I don't follow,' said Reed.

'Banks are symbols of safety. When people deposit their money there, they are entitled to feel that it is well protected. We go to great lengths to make sure that it is.'

'I couldn't agree more,' said Mallory. 'Security is vital.'

'It was the same for the bank in London,' said Burge. 'But you know that, Mr Paterson, because you used to work there at one time.'

'I don't deny it.'

'In fact, you were in line to become deputy manager.'

'That was ages ago, Sergeant,' said Paterson with a flick of his wrist. 'I moved back to Scotland to be among my own people.'

'And during his time with us,' observed Mallory, 'he has given such devoted service that he really has become a deputy manager. Frankly, I couldn't survive without him.'

'You may have to,' suggested Reed.

'Why?'

'Please let Sergeant Burge question the man, sir.'

Mallory nodded. 'Yes, of course.'

'Did you enjoy working in London, Mr Paterson?' asked Burge.

'I did, as a matter of fact,' replied the other.

'Then why did you leave?'

'The call of Scotland was loud and unceasing.'

'I can't believe that you wished to get back to your mother-in-law?' He saw Paterson wince. 'Yes, I have met the lady, sir. She did not speak well of you.'

'The feeling is mutual,' said Paterson, coldly.

'Given her hostility, you had every reason to stay away from Scotland.'

'My wife and I had other reasons for returning here.'

'Do you have any relatives serving in the British Army?'

'I'm sad to say that I don't.'

Burge was disappointed. 'That's a pity.'

'Your questions are increasingly bizarre, Sergeant Burge.'

'Then let me be blunt, sir. We have reason to believe that you may have been involved in the bank robbery, if only from a distance. Statements taken from your former colleagues suggest that you left in a huff with an urge for revenge.'

183

'Martin Beale would never have said that about me and his is the only opinion I respect.'

'Why did you leave England without telling anyone where you were going?'

'It was none of their business.'

'Did you miss your home country?'

'Yes, I did,' said Paterson, 'and so did my wife, Flora. When I saw an advertisement placed by Mr Mallory, I applied for the post and was delighted to be given it.'

'One of the best decisions I ever made,' mumbled the bank manager.

'When did you last cross the border into England, Mr Paterson?' asked Burge.

'I vowed never to do so again,' replied the other. 'I feel at home here.'

'We have the power to compel you to return to London, sir.'

Paterson was mystified. 'Why ever would you exercise it?'

'It's so that you could face a more rigorous interrogation at Scotland Yard.'

'You would be wasting the taxpayers' money,' said Paterson, acidly. 'Take me back if you must, but you will be highly embarrassed by the outcome.'

'You seem very sure of yourself, Mr Paterson.'

'I have nothing to hide, I promise you.'

'I second that,' affirmed Mallory. 'Can this meeting now be terminated, please?'

'I'll decide when we do that,' said Burge, sharply.

There was a long, tense pause. Mallory was grinding his teeth, and the detectives were having second thoughts. The only person who was completely at ease was Neil Paterson. Burge and Reed became increasingly uncomfortable. When they looked at each other, it was clear that they had reached the same depressing conclusion. After the thrill of tracking down the man they were after, they were forced to accept an obvious fact. Paterson was no criminal. He was simply a man who had returned to Scotland in search of a better job and the opportunity of persuading his fellow countrymen of the virtues of Scottish independence.

It was Burge who eventually felt the need to speak.

'I owe you an apology, Mr Paterson,' he said, forcing the words out. 'We were acting on insufficient evidence. It's patently clear that you were in no way involved in a bank robbery in London. We can see that now.' He turned to Mallory. 'Our apologies to you as well, sir. Sergeant Reed and I will intrude no further.' The detectives rose from their seats. 'We've made hasty assumptions about you, Mr Paterson, and we regret that deeply. Goodbye.'

Heading for the door, he led Reed out and they left the building as quickly as they could. Only when they were back in the police car did they feel able to exchange a few words.

'I'm sorry to involve you in this mess, Hector,' said Burge.

'We did finally track him down. At least we deserve congratulations for doing that.'

'I'll catch the next train to London.'

'Don't take all the blame, Cliff. This embarrassment was not entirely your fault.'

'It's good of you to say so.'

'You'll feel much better when you catch the real culprit behind the bank robbery,' said Reed. 'And I don't think it will be long before you do that.'

Burge groaned inwardly. 'I do,' he murmured.

CHAPTER THIRTEEN

Instead of merely going for a walk, Keedy decided to jog around the nearby park. He kept up a steady rhythm and was delighted that he felt no discomfort afterwards. When he returned to the house, he decided that a daily run would be part of his recovery from now on. Meanwhile, there was a major crime to solve, albeit from a distance. By the time that Raymond returned to the house, Keedy was seated at the table once more with the pieces of paper set out before him.

Looking over his shoulder, Raymond was surprised.

'I see that you've got the deputy manager back again.'

'Yes,' said Keedy, 'he's my prime suspect.'

'I thought you'd decided that he was clearly innocent.'

'I was . . . having doubts about his guilt,' admitted Keedy. 'Not any longer.'

'Does my brother know about this game you're playing?'

'It's not a game. It's a serious attempt to contribute to the investigation.'

'Have you told Harvey that you're pointing the finger at Mr Fryer?'

'Yes, I have. He called in to see how I was getting on.'

'What was his reaction?'

'He disagreed strongly.'

'That makes two of us,' said Raymond.

'Then why does Fryer's name keep buzzing around in my brain?' asked Keedy. 'Yes, I know that your brother has met the man and is certain he's in no way involved in the robbery. But Harvey has made mistakes before.'

'Not many of them, Joe.'

'I agree, but I feel he's making another one now. Fryer was in the best possible position to organise the robbery and to cover his tracks afterwards.'

'What is his link with the robbers?'

'It's a very close one, obviously.'

'Have you and my brother been involved in bank robberies before?' asked Raymond.

'We have, as it happens. We've dealt with five or six.'

'And was an employee of the bank involved in all of them?'

'No, he wasn't,' said Keedy.

Raymond hunched his shoulders. 'There you are, then.'

'But a former employee was closely implicated in every case. They supplied information about the security arrangements and details of how to open the safe. The only difference here is that Fryer is still working at the bank that was the target.'

'Then he must be an accomplished actor.'

'I don't follow.'

'If he can convince my brother that he's innocent, he's a very clever man. If someone is lying to him, Harvey's suspicions are usually aroused. Are you saying that Fryer has deceived him?'

'It's more than a possibility, Raymond.'

'Give me one valid reason why you're making that claim?'

'It's because Stuart Fryer is trying too hard to help,' said Keedy.

'That's what anyone in his position would do, surely?'

'He not only told your brother exactly how the robbers got into the bank,' argued Keedy, 'he's given Harvey information that incriminates Neil Paterson.'

'He's just doing his best to help the investigation.'

'Is he? Or is Fryer simply muddying the waters?'

'I have no means of knowing that, Joe. You and Harvey are the detectives. What I do feel is this. Stuart Fryer would never have been given the job of deputy manager unless he'd been judged to be completely trustworthy.'

'I stand by my theory.'

'Well, I think you should tear up that piece of paper with his name on.'

'I did that once before,' Keedy reminded him, 'and look what happened. Fryer has popped up once more as the man in the best position to plan the robbery.'

Having worked steadily throughout the day at the bank, Stuart Fryer checked the time on his watch then got up from his desk. After collecting his overcoat, he went to the manager's office and knocked before opening the door. Boucher was seated behind his desk.

'I'd forgotten that you were leaving early today,' said the manager.

'It was the only time that the doctor could fit me in.'

'Well, I hope that he can give you something to help you get a decent sleep for once.'

'It's the robbery, sir,' explained Fryer. 'I simply can't get it out of my mind.'

'I'm the same. It preys on me.' He stood up. 'I must say that it was good of Inspector Marmion to come here in person, even though he had no good news to report.'

'I admire his commitment. It will bring a reward in due course – I'm sure of it.'

'I sincerely hope so. Anyway,' said Boucher, 'off you go. Find the right sleeping tablets. I need a deputy manager who is not yawning at me all day.'

'I do apologise, sir.

Fryer left the room and then slipped out of the bank, pulling on his hat as he did so. After walking briskly for a few minutes, he turned into a major road. Seeing a taxi approach, he hailed it. When it stopped at the kerb, he stepped into the vehicle.

'Where to, guv'nor?' asked the driver.

'Paddington Station.'

Clifford Burge was also heading for a railway station in London though he was still almost two hundred miles away from it. His mission had been a failure. Having achieved his aim of confronting Neil Paterson, he had been shocked to realise that the man had no connection whatsoever with the bank robbery. Indeed, Paterson had been justifiably shocked to discover that he had even been considered as a suspect. All that Burge could do was to apologise and withdraw. He was sorry to part from Hector Reed, but his orders were to return to London as soon as Paterson had been located.

Having braced himself for a long train journey south, he tried to focus on a burning question. If Neil Paterson had not been in league with the robbers, then who had helped them?

* * *

Left alone in the house once more, Keedy studied the information delivered to the house with his name on the envelope. What he had not admitted to anyone was the fact that he had been in touch with the National Union of Police and Prison Officers while he was in hospital. As soon as he had been discharged, he had contacted NUPPO to make them aware of his new address. Keedy believed in the aims of the banned organisation. He had also been pleased when some sympathetic Labour politicians had tried to persuade Sir Edward Henry to recognise the union, arguing that its constitution prevented its members from striking. Unfortunately, the commissioner had rejected the appeal, refusing to accept NUPPO as a legitimate organisation.

Keedy, by contrast, had agreed with its objectives and knew many others who did so. The problem was that his support of NUPPO was frowned upon by his future father-in-law. Marmion could see the merit in the union's demands, but he believed that a police force should never be allowed to go on strike. During a bitter war, he stressed, it would be disastrous for the country and ruinous for the reputation of the police. Keedy had pointed out that pay rates had not improved for years and that there were thousands of policemen forced to take out loans to support themselves and their families. Protecting the British public came at a high price. Much as he respected the man with whom he worked at Scotland Yard, he favoured strike action while hoping that it might prove unnecessary. If it ever went ahead, he realised, he would face intense domestic friction.

Marmion had delayed passing on the bad news to the superintendent, but it was something he was forced to do in the end. After knocking on his door, he entered the office and found Claude Chatfield seated behind his desk with a sheaf of documents in front of him.

'Is this a good time, sir?' asked Marmion.

'Not really . . .'

'I'll come back later.'

'No, no,' said Chatfield. 'If you've something to say, I need to hear it.'

'Clifford Burge has been in touch.'

The superintendent sat up. 'Good news, I hope.'

'Not exactly, sir.'

'Was he unable to find this fellow, Neil Paterson?'

'Oh, he did find him eventually. In fact, he found more than one person with that name. When he confronted Paterson, however, he was shocked to find that the man was in no way connected to the bank robbery and had simply returned to Scotland with his wife because they both missed their homeland.'

'Did Burge believe that explanation?'

'It happened to be the truth, sir. He was convinced of that.'

Chatfield gritted his teeth. 'Then it was a waste of time sending him there.'

'I disagree,' said Marmion. 'Burge pursued the man relentlessly until he finally confronted him. That shows his determination.'

'What use is determination if it failed to deliver the result we needed?'

'Neil Paterson was completely innocent.'

'Is the bank manager aware of our dismal failure?'

'With respect, sir, I still believe that sending a man to Glasgow was a sensible course of action.'

'Even though it was a complete waste of time and money?'

'Yes,' said Marmion, stoutly, 'even then. As for Mr Boucher,

I've told him of our disappointment.'

'Then you must have spoken to him before you passed on the news to me,' said Chatfield, slapping his desk to express his disapproval. 'I should have come first.'

'I disagree, sir. The bank manager took precedence because it was his bank that was robbed. Also, of course, Neil Paterson had been a trusted employee of his. Mr Boucher was anxious to learn if the man had been party to the crime.'

'I always come first, Inspector. Obey the structure of command.'

'In that case, I should have spoken to the commissioner before you.'

'Don't be so insolent,' cried Chatfield. 'You answer to me. Do you understand?'

'Of course, sir.'

'This is not the first time I've had to remind you.'

'It will be the last, sir.'

'I sincerely hope so. Now,' said the superintendent, glowering. 'How is Keedy faring?'

'He's delighted to be back on his feet again.'

'Can he give us a date for his return to work?'

'That depends on his doctor's opinion,' said Marmion. 'If the decision was left to him, Sergeant Keedy would be back at Scotland Yard right now.'

'Impress upon him that we need his expertise.'

'I'm afraid that my daughter has a prior claim on him, sir. As you can imagine, Alice went through a very difficult time when he was in hospital. The man who stalked Joe Keedy also tried to follow her from the hospital one night. Luckily, she managed to shake him off.'

'It must have been a frightening experience for her.'

'It certainly was but Alice soon recovered.'

'Be that as it may, Sergeant Keedy's first duty is to the Metropolitan Police Force.'

'He is aware of that.'

'His work here must take precedence.'

Marmion smiled. 'I fancy that he has a more pressing commitment, sir,' he said, thinking of his daughter.

As soon as she finished work that evening, Alice travelled by bus to her uncle's home. She was pleased to find Keedy alone and noticed how healthy he appeared.

'You look wonderful, Joe!' she said.

'I could say the same about you.'

'Have you been taking a magic potion of some sort?'

'You're my magic potion,' he said, putting his arms around her and kissing her. 'I took an important step forward today, Alice. For the first time since I came out of hospital, I tried jogging in the park and there were no after-effects.'

'That's amazing!' she said.

'I didn't overdo it. I just resolved to run a little further each day.'

'As it happens, I did my share of running today. When Iris and I were on our beat, we spotted a man trying to break into a shed. As soon as he saw us, he took to his heels. We went after him.'

'I bet you won the race. You're a sprinter whereas Iris can only wobble along like a jelly.'

'Don't be unkind!' she protested.

'Did you catch the man?'

'Yes, I did,' she said, 'and he struggled like mad. It was only when Iris helped me that we got him under control. He cursed us for ages.'

'All thieves do that, Alice. The one you arrested had an additional reason to be upset. He'd been caught by two women.'

'Two policewomen,' she insisted.

'I'm sorry – two policewomen.'

'So,' she said, 'what have you been doing all day?'

'Thinking about you, of course.'

She laughed. 'Stop teasing.'

'It's true. I also thought about this latest case, of course, and came to the same conclusion. The man who planned the robbery must have been the deputy manager.'

'But he's been a great help to Daddy.'

'That shows how cunning he is. Fryer knows that the best way to avoid suspicion is to appear to assist the investigation. It means that he's able to mislead the police.'

'What does my father say?'

'He dismissed the idea out of hand.'

'Well, he's in the best position to know the full details of the robbery, Joe.'

'Let's not argue about it. Every second I'm alone with you is precious to me.' He embraced her again. 'We should make the most of it.'

'What if someone comes in?' she asked as he tried to kiss her.

'I don't think that your Uncle Raymond will be shocked. I daresay that he went through this stage when he was courting Lily.'

'What stage are you talking about?'

'I'll show you.'

Arms around her, Keedy pulled her close and kissed her full on the lips.

* * *

Clifford Burge was the recipient of a small miracle. The train that brought him back to London was almost an hour faster than the one that had taken him to Glasgow. He was deeply grateful. After the failure of his trip, it was a relief to have something to lift his spirits. Even though he found the capital beset by heavy rain, he was not dismayed.

Burge made his way to Scotland Yard and was delighted to find that Marmion was still there. The inspector was alone in his office, sifting through details of the bank robbery. When Burge came in, Marmion was on his feet at once.

'Welcome back, Cliff!' he said.

'I'm sorry that it was a wasted journey, sir.'

'That's not your fault. Take off those wet things and sit down. I want to hear every detail about your trip to Glasgow.'

After hanging his coat and hat on a peg, Burge settled gratefully into a chair.

'It's good to be back,' he said.

'At least we've eliminated one suspect,' observed Marmion. 'And you've had a close look at the workings of the Glasgow Constabulary.'

'They were very helpful – especially Detective Sergeant Reed. Apart from anything else, I could understand every word that he said. Some of the others talked in a foreign language.'

'What was Neil Paterson like?'

'Exactly how he was described,' said Burge. 'We'd found the right man at last. Unfortunately, he had no link whatsoever with the bank robbery in Paddington.'

'It's a pity.'

'I did ask him about his former colleagues and his comments were interesting. He didn't have much to say about Walter Greenlow, but he was very fond of Martin Beale. If they went for a drink together, they used to talk politics. Paterson is a fierce Scottish Nationalist. Beale used to tease him about the fact. Also, they had a shared interest in football. Paterson argued that Scottish players were much better than their English counterparts.'

'Did he mention Mr Boucher?' asked Marmion.

'He described him as a slave driver who always kept their noses to the wheel. But he thought him a decent man at heart – until he chose someone else as deputy manager, that is.'

'Does that decision still fester?'

'Very much so.'

'What about Fryer?'

'Ah,' said Burge, 'he had a lot to say about him. He admitted that Stuart Fryer was efficient, but it was the only thing in the man's favour. According to Paterson, he was sly, dishonest and two-faced. Also, when he became deputy manager, he lorded it over the other members of staff. Just before he left the bank altogether, Paterson punched him. That's how much he loathed Fryer.'

'Did he think that Fryer could be in anyway connected with the robbery?'

'Oddly enough, he did. He reckoned that the deputy manager would stoop to anything, and that we ought to take a very close look at him.'

Marmion thought about the name written on a piece of paper by Keedy.

As usual, Stuart Fryer arrived early for work next morning. There was a distinct spring in his step. After letting himself into the building, he went straight to his office and spared a few moments to look at the newspaper he had bought. The front-page headlines concerned severe losses on the Western Front by the British Army. Full details were given over the next three pages. The bank robbery, he was pleased to see, had been reduced to a relatively brief mention. They were no longer caught in the full glare of publicity.

The door opened and the manager walked into the room.

'Good morning,' he said.

'Good morning, sir,' replied Fryer.

'I wanted a word before the bank opens.'

'What about?'

'Well, first of all, I'd be interested to know how you got on at the doctor's yesterday.'

'It was a successful visit,' said Fryer. 'He sympathised with my problem and was surprised that I hadn't been to see him earlier. When people have a profound shock, he pointed out, they often have difficulty sleeping.'

'Did he prescribe any tablets?'

'He did indeed, and they certainly did the trick. I had the best night's sleep since the robbery. In fact, my wife had to wake me up this morning.'

'That's excellent news,' said Boucher, smiling. 'Let's move on to another problem . . .'

After his jog that morning, Keedy returned to the house and let himself in with a key. The first thing he noticed were the pieces of paper he had been using to familiarise himself with the bank robbery. What he had never done, he realised – and it was a definite handicap – was to see the bank itself. If he did so, he might have a clearer idea of what had happened there during the robbery. When he had washed and changed, therefore, he set off on a journey of discovery.

A bus took him a few stops, then deposited him outside a suburban railway station. There was a direct line to Paddington. Having caught the first available train, he felt elated. He was behaving like a detective again. Instead of speculating in the privacy of the house where he was staying, Keedy was joining the investigation, albeit in secret. When he reached Paddington Station, he asked a policeman for directions to the site of the robbery. The closer he got, the more excitement he felt. He turned a corner and had his first look at the building.

It was impressive. Big, solid, and slightly forbidding, it reminded him of a medieval castle. Keedy decided that getting into it at night involved all kinds of challenges. Having the assistance of someone who had worked there seemed the only way it could be done. He saw the thick pipe that one robber had climbed up to reach the roof. Though the man was a criminal, Keedy felt a degree of admiration for him. It had been a dangerous way to gain entry – tricky in daylight, perilous in the dark. He would never have taken such a risk himself.

He studied the building for a long time before a memory surfaced. Robbing a bank was not the only crime that had been committed. Two policemen on night duty had also been involved. When they challenged the robbers, one of them had been knocked unconscious and the other had been killed by the thrust of a bayonet. Keedy had known Sam Collard and had met his wife. It was Nora Collard who directed his mind back to the leaflet from NUPPO. The union was not simply asking for an increase in wages for serving policemen. It was also seeking to improve the amount paid out in widow's pensions. Nora was a case in point. Having been told that her husband had been brutally murdered, she would find that the widow's pension she received was woefully inadequate.

Keedy had one more reason to support the call for strike action.

Ellen Marmion was hopelessly confused. She could still not decide if her son, Paul, had broken into the house or if the burglar had instead been Garth Price, the young man who had exchanged his identity card with Paul. Since the most recent theft had occurred in her son's room, she was bound to think that Paul was involved because the clothing stolen belonged to him. Ellen then reminded herself that Price had been roughly the same height and weight as her son. The clothing would easily fit him as well. She recalled their visit to Shepton Mallet Prison. Expecting to see Paul, they were instead confronted by a grinning, heartless individual who gloried in their shocked response. She could easily imagine Price letting himself into the house and stealing money. Only Paul would dream of repaying what was stolen. Yet it had now been taken once more. That made Garth Price the more likely burglar.

There was one cheering thought. The lock on the front door had been changed and another had been fitted to the window in Paul's bedroom. Alone in the house as she now was, Ellen felt much safer. Nobody could let themselves in. When she walked into the living room, her eye settled on the cards spread along the mantelpiece. They were all from relatives or friends, accepting the invitation to the wedding. Whoever had gained entry to the house most recently was bound to have seen the display. If it had been Paul, he might have been tempted to come along to the church on the day itself and watch from a distance. If, on the other hand, the most recent burglar had been Price, anything might happen. He was such a malign young man that he might take pleasure in disrupting the proceedings. Having met Price at Shepton Mallet prison, she knew that he was capable of anything.

Ellen looked forward to the wedding with foreboding.

As he sat in his office, Marmion was lost in contemplation. Burge's trip to Glasgow might have been a failure but it had unearthed new facts about the relationship between some of employees of the bank that had been robbed. Having listed three suspects, they had soon whittled the number down to one. Marmion had become so convinced of Neil Paterson's guilt that he sent Burge off to track the man down in Scotland. When their only suspect was found, he turned out to be completely innocent of the charges against him. But he had given Burge a new name to consider. The sergeant was unconvinced.

'I don't think that it was Fryer,' he announced. 'He's a man who loves his job and who is proud of the bank where he works.' When he got no answer from Marmion, he raised his voice. 'Did you hear what I said, sir?'

'Yes, yes,' said the inspector, coming out of his reverie.

'Mr Fryer is innocent.'

'Innocent until proven guilty, Cliff.'

'Paterson just wants revenge. He's trying to get Fryer in trouble because the pair of them fell out.'

'They did a lot more than that,' said Marmion. 'They obviously had some sort of feud.'

'Fryer is far too law-abiding.'

'That's the impression he gives, I grant you. He looks as if he'd never dare to do anything that was remotely illegal. It could just be a mask.'

'I fancy that it is, sir.'

'Why do you believe that?'

'It's because Paterson spoke so vehemently about the man. They did work together, after all. You get to know a colleague very well if you spend almost every day alongside him.'

'The trouble between them seems to have started when Fryer was promoted above him. What Paterson told you might just be a case of sour grapes.'

'I disagree. He was in earnest.'

Marmion paused for a moment to consider the evidence. When he finally spoke, he told Burge what his future son-in-law had claimed. Burge was surprised.

'How much have you told him about the case?' he asked.

'Enough to arouse his interest. Needless to say,' added Marmion, 'nobody must know that I've divulged confidential details of an ongoing investigation – especially Chat.'

Burge nodded. 'My lips are sealed.'

'I think that we should look at Fryer more closely.'

'I was coming around to the same point of view. Paterson really believed that Fryer is involved in some way. You'd never guess it to look at him, but we've known criminals before who looked as if they were one step away from sainthood.'

Marmion grinned. 'I once arrested a Cistercian monk.'

'What was his crime?'

'He was siphoning off some of the beer they brewed and selling it at a profit.'

'So much for a vow of obedience!'

'What's the best way to proceed, I wonder?'

'We need someone who can watch Fryer like a hawk.'

'Are you volunteering for the task?'

'Why not?' said Burge. 'If both Paterson and Sergeant Keedy

have named the deputy manager as the culprit, I'll be interested to find out if he's as honest and conscientious as he appears.'

Stuart Fryer had spent over an hour with the bank manager, discussing clients who were causing them problems. Boucher was inclined to be ruthless. His way of dealing with troublesome accounts was to terminate them. Fryer had more sympathy for people unable to pay off loans, pointing out that there were usually extenuating circumstances. When they had finished, the manager sat back in his seat and appraised his deputy.

'I'm so pleased you had a restful night.' Boucher said.

'Me too.' replied Fryer. 'Those tablets are wonderful.'

'What are they called?'

'Who cares? I just pop them into my mouth, and, minutes later I'm snoring.'

'I'd want to know what the ingredients are.'

'They work. That's all that matters to me.'

'Then the bank is the beneficiary.'

'Yes, sir, I'm pulsing with energy now.'

'You certainly are, Stuart.'

'No more sleepless nights for me. I'm firing on all cylinders once more.'

While they awaited instructions, they played cards to pass the time. Gadney had suggested that, to spice up the games, they played for money. His friends agreed. Gadney kept a record of each game he won and how much he was owed by his two companions. Of the trio, Mills was the most frequent loser.

'You keep dealing me a useless hand, Max,' he complained.

'Stop moaning,' said Gadney, shuffling the pack. 'I can't help it if I have a run of good luck.'

202

'I still think we should play with real money,' argued Hillier.

'Not a chance!'

'But we've earned it, Max.'

'It stays where it is.'

'I'd like the feel of it in my hands.'

'Then you'll have to wait, Terry. It's not up to us to share it out. That's a job for my friend.'

'When is he going to show up?'

'When he's good and ready,' said Gadney, silencing him with a glare. 'Right, it's your turn to deal, Sid,' he went on, handing the pack to Mills. 'Let's see if you have more luck this time.'

Burge embraced his new role with enthusiasm. Standing within sight of a bank in the Paddington area was a far easier assignment than travelling all the way to Scotland for what turned out to be a waste of his time and energy. He was not entirely persuaded that the deputy manager had helped the bank robbers, but he agreed that the man needed watching. As he lurked in a doorway nearby, he watched a trickle of employees leaving the bank and hurrying off to their individual homes. Last to appear was Stuart Fryer. Since the deputy manager was responsible for security, Burge reasoned, he would have activated the burglar alarm before he left. The man's final task was to insert keys in two separate locks in the front door. Once that was done, Fryer took a moment to look around then he set off at a brisk pace.

Burge followed at a discreet distance. Having taken the trouble to find out Fryer's home address, he had consulted a map of the area and realised that the deputy manager lived within walking distance of the bank. Fryer would not need to travel by bus or taxi. It meant that Burge could not be shaken off. With his overcoat on and his hat pulled down, Fryer marched on for hundreds of yards before turning a corner. Burge reached the corner and peered around it. He was just in time to see his quarry going into a tobacconist's shop further down the street. Minutes later, the man came out again and put his briefcase down on the pavement. He then took a cigarette from the packet he had just bought and slipped it between his lips. When the cigarette was alight, he inhaled it with satisfaction then blew out smoke from his lungs.

In a flash, Burge's opinion of him changed. It was as if he'd suddenly found a chink in the man's armour. When he had first met Fryer inside the bank, the deputy manager had seemed a model of rectitude. He had looked and sounded like a dedicated employee. Burge had now seen him in a different light. Fryer smoked a cigarette as if desperate for tobacco.

The man was a human being, after all. Fryer had a weakness. He was therefore subject to temptation.

CHAPTER FOURTEEN

It was not often that Marmion had good news over the telephone. Sheer surprise brought him to his feet. After replacing the receiver, he went straight to the superintendent's office. Claude Chatfield was alone. He was surprised when there was a loud knock on the door before it opened to allow Marmion to burst in. The superintendent sat up.

'Why are you in such a rush?' he asked.

'I have a breakthrough to report, sir.'

'What is it?'

'I've just come off the telephone,' said Marmion. 'I was speaking to someone from that regiment I mentioned. As you'll remember, I asked if anyone by the name of Max had deserted.'

'And you got a positive response?'

'There has been another deserter with that Christian name, it turns out.'

'Who is he?'

'Max Phillips – and he seems a more promising suspect than Gadney.'

'Why is that?'

'Phillips was born and brought up in Paddington.'

Chatfield rubbed his hands. 'That sounds interesting.'

'In other words, he'd probably know the bank that was targeted.'

'Did you have an address for Max Gadney?'

'Yes, sir, they gave me that as well – he lives in Dorset.'

'That's a fair distance away from Paddington.'

'Phillips takes priority. I'll visit the London address immediately.'

'Take Burge with you. If this fellow is there, he may be a handful.'

'I think it highly unlikely he'll be there, sir,' said Marmion. 'Phillips is another deserter. If he's caught, he'll be condemned to death by a court martial. Do you think he'd be stupid enough to imperil his family by hiding at home?'

'I see what you mean.'

'His parents may not even know that he's on the run.'

'Or that he may have been involved in a bank robbery.'

'Quite so. As for Burge,' continued Marmion, 'he's tied up elsewhere. I'll take a couple of detectives with me. One of them can cover the rear of the house.'

'Good luck!'

'I may need it, sir.'

Marmion darted out of the office and closed the door behind him.

Burge loitered near the tobacconist's shop until Stuart Fryer continued his walk home. When he reached his house, he put down his briefcase and spent several minutes enjoying his cigarette. Eventually he tossed it into the gutter and stamped a foot on it. Picking up the case, he took out a bunch of keys and let himself into his home. Burge got close enough to look at the house. It had the typical features of a small Victorian dwelling and was in good condition. The low hedge at the front helped it to stand out from its immediate neighbours.

After wondering why Fryer had finished his cigarette before entering the house, Burge walked back to the shop and went in. A short, curly-haired man in his fifties was behind the counter.

'What can I get you, sir?' he asked, politely.

'Oh, I don't want to buy anything. I just wondered if you could help me.'

'Did you want directions?'

'No, I'm in search of confirmation. A short while ago, you served a gentleman. He stepped outside and lit a cigarette.'

'That would be Mr Fryer, sir.'

'Oh,' said Burge with mock disappointment. 'I hoped it was someone else.'

'Mr Fryer works in the bank that was robbed.'

'Really? He's the absolute double of a friend of mine who is a solicitor. I should have realised that it couldn't have been David Radford.'

'Why is that?'

'David quit smoking years ago.'

The shopkeeper chuckled. 'Then it certainly couldn't have been him. Mr Fryer loves his cigarettes. The problem is that he can't smoke inside the house.'

'Oh? Why is that?'

'His wife suffers badly from asthma, poor woman.'

Alice Marmion was glad to reach the end of her shift with Iris Goodliffe. It had been free from any real incidents, but Alice still felt jangled. The problem was that Iris was in one of her moods, shifting between elation and despair at regular intervals.

Inevitably, they had discussed the forthcoming marriage. One minute, Iris was looking forward to getting married herself; the next, she was convinced that no man would give her a second look. Alice was tired of having to bolster her friend's confidence.

As they were on the point of parting, Iris felt the need to apologise.

'I'm so sorry, Alice,' she said. 'You must have wanted to hit me.'

'Don't be silly. We're friends.'

'I haven't behaved like one. I spent the whole shift talking about the wedding then moaning that I'd never have one of my own.'

'Yes, you will, Iris.'

'No man would give me a second look.'

'That's ridiculous. Of course, they would – and one day, you'll meet someone who adores you. Look at the way those American soldiers always whistle at you when we walk past.'

'They're whistling at you, Alice – not at me.'

'Maybe it's both of us, but they're always looking at you.'

Iris frowned. 'I could never marry an American.'

'Why not?'

'It would mean leaving my family to go thousands of miles away.'

'That would be an adventure.'

'I'd be too scared to leave this country.'

'Then you'll have to settle for a British husband.'

'But where will I find him?' asked Iris with a gesture of despair.

'I'll bring a magazine for you tomorrow. Mummy passed it on to me,' said Alice. 'There's an article in it about how many women find the man of their dreams at someone else's wedding.

It's something to do with the feelings you get at such a happy event.'

'Have you invited anyone who might be interested in me?'

'Well, there'll be a few younger men who work in reserved occupations. They're friends of Joe's – and I know they're single. Read the article. It may cheer you up.'

'Then I'd love to see it. Thank you, Alice.'

'And stop worrying. You'll find someone soon.'

'You're right. I must be more confident. Men are not interested in wallflowers.'

'You're an attractive woman with so much to offer.'

'Yes, I am,' said Iris, brightening. 'I'm in my prime and I should be proud of it.' She hugged Alice. 'Thank you so much. You always know how to cheer me up. There's bound to be a man out there who will take me seriously. All I need to do is to find him.'

Marmion took precautions. When he was driven to the house, he took two detectives with him. Dropped off at the end of the street, he saw that there was a lane at the rear of the houses. He therefore sent one of his men to stand guard outside the back entrance of the property he was about to visit. Once the detective was in place, he and his companion walked along the terrace. When they reached the house they wanted, they saw that it was badly neglected. Grass had sprouted between the flagstones, the paint on the walls had faded badly and there was a long crack in one of the windowpanes upstairs. Curtains were drawn in the front bedroom.

Marmion used the knocker forcefully. He got an immediate response. The door was soon flung open by a beefy man in his sixties with an aggressive manner.

'Bugger off!' he said. 'We don't want to buy anything.'

'We're not selling anything, sir,' replied Marmion, displaying his warrant card. 'I'm Detective Inspector Marmion from Scotland Yard and this is Detective Constable Riggs.'

'Why the hell are you bothering me?'

'I think you already know the answer to that, Mr Phillips. That is your name, isn't it?'

'So what?'

'And your son is Private Max Phillips of the Royal Fusiliers?'

'Don't mention that useless bastard.'

'Are you aware that he has deserted his regiment?'

'Of course I am. The army sent me a warning letter.'

'Then they'll have told you what the penalty is for sheltering a deserter.'

'Max wouldn't dare come here,' growled the man, 'because he'd know that I'd turn him in at once. Well – after I'd given him a good hiding, that is.'

'Have you any idea where he might be?'

'Not a clue. I don't know and I don't care. The only decent thing Max ever did was to join the army, but it scared the pants off him. I knew he'd run away sooner or later. He's a coward, Inspector, a low, disgusting, yellow-bellied coward. I'm ashamed of him.'

'I see,' said Marmion. 'We're sorry to disturb you, Mr Phillips.'

'So am I,' grunted the man before closing the front door abruptly.

Having gone there with a degree of optimism, Marmion was leaving with disappointment.

* * *

Sidney Mills was still chafing at the delay. It was maddening. He had neither seen nor handled the money stolen from the bank. The leather bag in which it was kept remained at Gadney's side. Mills was not even allowed to touch the bag, let alone the money. He felt that it was unfair on him. The bag contained his hopes for the future. Why wasn't he at least able to look at his share of the money? It was cruel to deny him that right.

His chance finally came. Hillier was outside, gathering scraps of wood. Gadney rose to his feet to announce that he was going to the privy. For the first time, he did not take the leather bag with him. Mills could not believe his luck. He waited long enough to be certain that he was alone then he crept towards the bag. Before he could grab it, however, he heard the door open. Hillier came in, carrying a pile of logs and small branches. He took the load across to the grate and stacked it in a pile. He then turned to Mills.

'What's up?' he asked.

'Nothing,' said Mills, feigning innocence.

'You weren't going to touch Max's bag, were you?'

'No, no, Terry . . .'

'You'd be committing suicide if you did.'

'I was just . . . wondering what the money looked like.'

'You'll get your share before long, Sid.'

'Why not now?'

'Max makes the rules,' warned the other. 'Obey them.'

Now that he was taking proper exercise, Joe Keedy was feeling much better. The sense of freedom he enjoyed while he was out for a walk or a run was almost intoxicating. His mind was fully occupied as well. At the hospital he had been used to saying the same things to the same people every day. His mind had been numbed by repetition. It was now able to cope with serious concerns. Keedy was not only involved with a bank robbery – albeit at a distance – he was able to support the idea of a police strike and to consider the worrying visits to the Marmion household made by Paul Marmion or a friend of his. What occupied his mind most, of course, was the prospect of his forthcoming marriage. Now that he had survived a morning in church when the banns of marriage had been read, he felt a sense of release and had a rush of confidence. Keedy was even looking forward to taking Alice to the vicarage for a conversation with the priest about to marry them.

Before that happened, there was a major crime to solve, and he was excited to be a kind of unofficial consultant. Having seen the bank involved, he had realised that the robbers must have been fit, determined men who had planned the robbery carefully in advance with the aid of someone who worked in the bank. Now that he was back at the house, Keedy was able to give the matter his full concentration.

Seated at the table, he scattered the array of names in front of him and stared at each one. Unaware that Neil Paterson had been eliminated, he still had the man's name in capital letters, but it was Stuart Fryer who held pride of place. The deputy manager could have assisted the robbers and then misled the investigation while appearing to cooperate fully with it. Fryer remained the prime suspect in Keedy's mind, but another person now caught his eye. Because the name was not written in capitals, he had effectively forgotten about Martin Beale. He now decided that he had been too quick to dismiss the man. Paterson and Fryer were more obvious suspects because they knew details of the security arrangements to the bank – and those details had made the robbery a realistic possibility.

Keedy remembered being told that Beale and Paterson were good friends. They often went to a pub together and enjoyed a chat. It was conceivable that – apart from arguing about Paterson's hope for Scottish Independence – they had talked about the safety measures taken at the bank. Evidently, Beale was a clever man. He had moved to a job in a rival bank that gave him more authority and a higher income. It was possible – Keedy decided – that he could have waited until he and Paterson had enjoyed a few drinks together, and then slowly drawn information out of him about the code for the burglar alarm.

Reaching for the piece of paper with Beale's name on it, Keedy turned it over and wrote the name in capitals. He felt a sense of discovery.

When he got back to his office, Marmion found Clifford Burge waiting for him. The sergeant gave him a detailed account of trailing the deputy bank manager to his home. Marmion was surprised to hear that the man was a confirmed smoker.

'He looks far too fussy about his clothing to get ash on it,' he said. 'That suit he wears makes him look so smart. I wouldn't be surprised if his wife presses those trousers for him every morning.'

'He's obviously very considerate towards her,' said Burge. 'He keeps the cigarettes hidden away when he's at home.'

'How does he manage when he's at work? Confirmed smokers need a fag at regular intervals. There's not much hope of him doing that at the bank.'

'No, I suppose not.'

'Wait a moment, though,' said Marmion. 'I was forgetting somewhere.'

'Oh?'

'The attic. Do you remember what happened when he took us up there?'

'Yes, I do. He went up that ladder as if it was something he did every day. Then he pulled back the bolt, flipped open that trapdoor and climbed up into the attic.'

'And what did he show us when we went up after him?'

'He unlocked that door and took us out on to the roof.'

'Where better to have a fag than out in the fresh air? If he is addicted to smoking, that's where he can go. The wind would blow any ash off that smart suit of his.' He pointed a finger. 'I want you to follow him again tomorrow – starting from his house this time.'

'Righto.'

'Only you'd better go in disguise, Cliff. He's seen you in what you normally wear. Put on some old clothes and a cap you can pull down over your face. And it might help if you have a walking stick to lean on. It will make you lose several inches.'

Burge nodded. 'Leave it to me.'

'Don't get too excited,' warned Marmion. 'That was the mistake we made with Neil Paterson. We allowed ourselves to feel certain that he was involved in the robbery.'

'I felt such a fool when I challenged him.'

'Then let's not make any assumptions this time. Fryer is a person of interest to us. At this stage, that's all he is. Only when we have enough hard evidence can we consider an arrest. It's up to you to gather that evidence.'

'I'll do my best,' promised Burge.

When she left the shop, Ellen Marmion had two bags of groceries. Rationing meant that staple items were only sold in small quantities. Like everyone else, she and her husband had to adapt to wartime shortages. Inevitably, she wondered how her son was coping. Since he had no ration book, how did he get enough food? And how did he survive without any money? It was a constant worry for her. When the house came into view, she was troubled. A new lock on the front door and another on the window in Paul's bedroom had given her a feeling of security, but what sort of mother kept her own son out of the house? It felt wrong.

Ellen wondered if she should have tried to reach out to Paul. If he had, in fact, broken into the house to steal money, then there was a chance he might come back. Should she have left a message for her son, assuring him that he was welcome to return home? Unlike his odious friend, Garth Price, he was not a criminal. Price was a deserter whereas Paul had been discharged from the army after serving in France. He had left home of his own accord. Shocked by his disappearance, Ellen had come to realise how much easier life at home was without him. But that did not stop her from thinking about him constantly and hoping that he was well.

She had almost reached the house when a voice rang out behind her. Ellen turned to see Maggie Horton, a neighbour, bustling towards her. When she reached Ellen, she was panting slightly.

'I'm so glad I caught you,' said the neighbour.

'Why is that?'

'Someone called at your house earlier. He took out a key and tried to let himself in, but the door wouldn't open. He was so angry that he kicked the door before marching off.'

'Was it Paul?'

'It might have been him, but I couldn't be certain. He was a young man with a full beard. All I got was a glimpse of his face as he turned around. He stalked off.'

'Thank you for telling me, Mrs Horton.'

'It frightened me. Since the war started, we've had far too many strange men wandering about. Speak to your husband. Something must be done about them.'

At the end of the working day, Stuart Fryer was in the manager's office, discussing the investigation into the bank robbery. They both expressed confidence in Marmion but accepted that it might take time before the robbers were caught and imprisoned.

Boucher simmered with anger.

'I think that bank robbery should be a capital offence,' he said bitterly.

'In this case,' Fryer pointed out, 'that's exactly what it will be. On their way out of here, the robbers killed a policeman. They'll hang for his murder.'

'I wish I could be there when it happens.'

'That's out of the question, I'm afraid, sir.'

'Pity!'

As they were putting on their coats and hats to leave, Boucher remembered something.

'How is Mrs Fryer these days?' he asked with concern.

'Valerie is still suffering, alas,' said Fryer, 'but she never complains.'

'Is there no cure for asthma?'

'Unfortunately there isn't but there are ways to control it.'

'Your wife sounds like a real Trojan.'

'It's a problem to which she's had to adjust.'

'Please give her my regards.'

'I will, sir,' said Fryer. 'Valerie is a wonderful support. She understands what we must be going through in the wake of the robbery.'

'We're going through hell,' hissed Boucher, 'and it's starting to fray my nerves.'

When he gave his report on the progress of the investigation, Claude Chatfield could see that the commissioner was only half-listening. Sir Edward's mind was elsewhere. As soon as Chatfield ended, the commissioner reached for a copy of the evening paper.

'Have you seen this?' he asked.

'Unfortunately I have, Sir Edward.'

'The German artillery bombardment started hours before dawn yesterday. It hit targets over an area of one hundred and fifty square miles. Just think of the skill needed to coordinate such an attack.'

'My sympathies go to the British Fifth Army. They were the main target.'

'One estimate reckons that the Germans fired over a million shells in five hours.'

'I find that frightening.'

'It must be the biggest barrage of the entire war.'

'I'd hate to think what our losses will be,' said Chatfield. 'According to that article, the British Third Army suffered heavy casualties as well.'

'When will it ever end?' moaned the commissioner.

'There is one benefit, Sir Edward.'

'I fail to see it.'

'Because so much space is taken up by the war,' Chatfield pointed out, 'there's no mention whatsoever of the bank robbery. It's such a relief to be spared the unfair criticism of our failure to make early arrests.'

'That's true, I suppose, but it brings me scant comfort.'

'There is something else to report, Sir Edward.'

'What is it?'

'Bad news, I'm afraid,' said Chatfield, showing him a leaflet. 'This was found in the canteen. Someone must have left it there deliberately.'

'How did this ever get into the building?' demanded the commissioner, tearing it up and tossing it into the wastepaper basket. 'NUPPO is a renegade organisation, threatening to organise a police strike. I refuse to acknowledge its right to speak on behalf of the police service.'

'What action shall we take, Sir Edward?'

'I want notices put up in every part of this building.'

'What message will they send?'

'It's not a message,' said the other, sharply. 'It's a threat. I think that it's high time I launched my own Spring Offensive. Any serving policeman found in possession of one of these leaflets from NUPPO will be liable to summary dismissal.'

Alice Marmion was spending the night at the family home so that she and her mother could finalise the seating plan for the wedding reception. When she arrived there, she found Ellen in a state of agitation. She guessed the reason at once.

'It's Paul, isn't it?' she said.

'Yes, it is.'

'Has he been back?'

'I don't know. He may have been.'

'What gives you that idea?'

'One of the neighbours spoke to me this afternoon,' said Ellen. 'It was Mrs Horton who lives further down the road. She saw something that really upset me.'

'Go on.'

'While I was out shopping, a man came to the house and tried to open it with a key. Since we'd had the lock changed, of course the key didn't fit.'

'What did the man do?'

'According to Mrs Horton, he kicked the front door angrily then walked away. I've got a horrible feeling that it must have been Paul.'

'Surely not,' said Alice. 'Mrs Horton would have recognised him.'

'She couldn't be sure. Besides, she was twenty or thirty yards away. She told me it was a young man with a full beard. She saw it when he turned away from the house.'

'How was he dressed?'

'He looked a bit like a tramp.'

'If it was Paul, he is obviously living rough.'

'That's what disturbs me the most,' said Ellen. 'He came back home and found himself locked out. Despite what he's done, I feel sorry for him.'

'Well, I don't,' said Alice, firmly. 'If it was my brother, he only came to steal from you. Changing the lock was the right thing to do. He now knows that he can't just let himself in here and take what he wants. Besides,' she went on, 'he was here only a couple of days ago, wasn't he?'

'Yes, he took some of his clothing.'

'And some money.'

Ellen bit her lip. 'I find it hard to believe that Paul would do that, Alice.'

'Then perhaps it wasn't him who Mrs Horton saw.'

'That is even more worrying. The idea that the wicked

young man with Paul's papers had let himself in here makes me shudder.'

'Well, he won't let himself in here again, Mummy. You changed the lock on the front door.'

'We had to, Alice. I didn't feel safe when I was here alone.'

'Nobody can let himself into the house now.'

Ellen's face puckered. 'If it's Paul, he has a right to come in.'

'He doesn't have the right to behave like a burglar,' insisted Alice. 'He was friends with Garth Price, remember. He probably had a copy of the front door key made so that he could give one to Price. That's how much Paul cares for us. He tells his friend when to come here and how to let himself in. That's a terrible thing to do to his parents.'

Joe Keedy was reminding himself what NUPPO was advocating. As he read through its list of demands, he could see that it would gain a degree of support from members of the Metropolitan Police Force. He was, however, conscious of the fact that many policemen who agreed with the demands in principle would not be prepared to cease working to achieve their goal. Others opposed the very idea of a strike, claiming that the police should be banned from taking such action. London suffered constant outbreaks of lawlessness. Without a body of trained officers to control them, criminals would exploit the situation to the full.

When he heard a vehicle pulling up outside the house, he assumed that it must be Raymond's van. In fact, it was a police car, stopping to drop off Marmion. As soon as he caught a glimpse of him through the window, Keedy quickly put the material from NUPPO out of sight. He then went to open the door and give Marmion a welcome.

'Have you made any arrests yet?' he asked.

'No, Joe, but we have targets in mind.'

'I've got another one to suggest.'

'Who is that?'

'Come in out of the rain and I'll tell you.'

Keedy stood aside so that Marmion could enter the hall, hang his coat and hat on a peg, then go into the living room. The newcomer saw the pieces of paper on the table.

'Still playing your little game?' he asked.

'It's starting to yield results, Harv.'

'Really?'

'I've got a new name to focus on – Martin Beale.'

'But he has nothing to do with the bank in question.'

'He did have,' said Keedy, 'and I believe that he still might be linked to it.'

'No,' said Marmion, 'Beale is not connected with the robbery in any way. I've met him. He was very willing to help me.'

'Suppose that he was pulling the wool over your eyes?'

'Lots of people have tried to do that, Joe. Most of them are still in gaol.'

'Let me tell you what I believe might have happened.'

Marmion sat down on the sofa. 'Right – I'm all ears.'

Keedy explained how he had reached the point where Beale had come into the reckoning. He stressed the importance of the man's friendship with Neil Paterson, and the fact that they often went for a drink together. Beale, he argued, would have been able to extract details of the bank's security system from his friend.

'But he soon left the bank,' Marmion reminded him.

'He'd got what he wanted, Harv. All he needed were men capable of carrying out the robbery.'

'I'm sorry, Joe, but this is nonsense.'

'Hear me out, please. Let me have my shot at identifying the man behind the robbery. It could well be Martin Beale.'

'Impossible.'

'How can you be so sure?'

'I took a long look at him and realised he had nothing to do with the robbery.'

'I'd advise you to take a second look.'

'Waste of time. I'd rather concentrate on the person who did plan the bank robbery.'

'And who is that?'

'We're not entirely sure,' admitted Marmion.

'But you have someone in mind, I daresay.'

'Yes, we do.'

'Who is he?'

Marmion tried to overcome his discomfort by blurting out the name.

'Stuart Fryer.'

'I picked him out first,' complained Keedy. 'You poured scorn on the idea.'

'I've had second thoughts.'

'I'm glad you finally came to your senses.'

'There's no need to gloat,' warned Marmion. 'A moment ago, you were shouting Martin Beale's name into my ear. Now you've gone back to Fryer.'

'He was always my prime suspect.'

'We're taking a very close look at him.'

Marmion explained how he had become convinced that the deputy manager might be a party to the robbery. He told Keedy that he had the man followed home from work and how Fryer would be tailed the moment he left his house next morning.

'I'm glad you finally appreciated my advice,' said Keedy, smiling.

Marmion became serious. 'Let me give you some advice of my own in return.'

'Go on.'

'Are you still attracted to that lunatic idea about a police strike?' Keedy shook his head. 'I think you still are, Joe. You might still be in touch with NUPPO.'

'That was all in the past,' lied Keedy.

'It's just as well. The commissioner was shown a leaflet of theirs that was found in the canteen. Sir Edward went berserk, apparently. According to Chat, he wants warnings pinned up all over Scotland Yard.'

'What sort of warnings?'

'Anyone found with material from NUPPO on his person may be kicked out of the police force immediately.' Keedy blenched. 'Yes, Joe. It's that serious.'

'It's going much too far.'

'It shows you how serious the commissioner is. I advise you to remember that you're about to get married very soon. You'll need a regular income. If you get booted out of your job as a detective, you may find it hard to find employment elsewhere. In fact,' added Marmion, 'the only person who will offer you a job will be your brother. How do you fancy working for Dennis?'

Keedy quailed.

Clifford Burge was up early the next morning. After breakfast in his flat, he hid his suit under a large, wrinkled raincoat. A wide-brimmed old hat completed his disguise. He had already asked his landlady if he could borrow the walking stick in the hallway stand. When he stepped out into the street, he found that leaning on the stick with his full weight made his whole body shrink. Even if Stuart Fryer saw him from a short distance, he would not recognise the detective.

When he got to the street where the deputy manager lived, he waited near a corner some thirty yards or so away. After several minutes, the front door of the house opened, and Fryer emerged. Burge had a glimpse of his wife, a short, slim, pale woman in a thick dressing gown. After planting a kiss on her cheek, Fryer set off. When he reached the tobacconist's shop, he paused to take out a cigarette packet. Extracting a cigarette, he put it between his lips and lit the end, tossing the match into the gutter. Case in hand, Fryer set off once more, oblivious to the fact that he was being watched by the man behind him.

Sidney Mills was accustomed to being awakened in the small hours. During his time in the army, it had been the sound of explosions that usually disturbed his slumbers. At the hideaway, it was the firm feel of Terry Hillier's hand on his shoulder.

'Wake up, Sid,' he said. 'You're on guard duty.'

Mills used a hand to suppress a yawn. 'Is it that early already?'

'Yes, it is. Up you get or Max will prod you out of bed with that bayonet of his.'

The threat brought Mills fully awake. Pulling back the tarpaulin under which he had slept fully clothed, he stretched himself then glanced towards the window. 'What's happening out there?'

'Nothing,' said Hillier.

'Then why do we have to be on guard throughout the night?'

'Just do as you're told.'

'What time is it?'

'It's well past eight o'clock in the morning. Now get out there.'

Mills lowered his voice. 'Where's Max?'

'Fast asleep. He was on duty during the night. I relieved him.'

'Did he have the leather bag with him?'

Hillier sniggered. 'Need you ask?'

'I'd just like to know how much is in there, Terry.'

'Well, don't you dare ask him. Now get out there and do your stint. Oh, and put a hat on.'

'Why?'

'It's just started to rain.'

Mills groaned. 'That's all I need!'

He reached for his hat and raincoat then trudged off down the stairs. Hillier, meanwhile, lay down on the bed and pulled his raincoat over himself. Within seconds, he was asleep.

Joe Keedy was still reeling from the news. It had made him think again about his support of the idea of a police strike. Taking the leaflet from NUPPO with him, he went off to his bedroom, leaving Marmion talking to his brother, Raymond. Once alone, Keedy remembered what he had been told. Mere possession of the document was a crime in the commissioner's eyes. Sir Edward Henry was not a man to issue wild orders. If he was threatening to dismiss anyone caught with NUPPO propaganda, he would find a way to do it. Keedy still believed that he and like-minded friends had the right to demand higher wages and a significant increase in widows' pensions. But he decided to keep his opinions to himself.

Losing his position as a detective would be a disaster for him. Apart from depriving him of the pride that he took in helping to enforce the law, it would have an immediate effect on his income. Since he and Alice had spent their respective savings on the house, he needed money to furnish it properly. Police pay might be inadequate in his eyes, but it was needed to support him and his wife. What other job could he do that brought the same satisfaction? Other employers might well look askance at the fact that he was dismissed from Scotland Yard. Where would he turn?

Being forced to go back to the family undertaker business would be a humiliation. Keedy took a last look at the NUPPO leaflet and tore it into pieces. Though he still agreed with its objectives, he would be careful not to discuss them with colleagues from now on. He had to put Alice first. She was looking forward to marrying a detective sergeant in the Metropolitan Police Force. His future wife took pride in his career. Even though he was shot during a siege, neither she nor Keedy had believed for one moment that he should quit his job. It was expected that the moment he was fit enough, he would return to active duty. Alice accepted that gladly.

He could imagine her disappointment if he were summarily dismissed. She would feel his loss of status as much as he would. Alice would also look at him differently, although she would still love and support him. He was pleased when she confessed that she had kept a scrapbook of press cuttings about the various successes that Keedy and her father had enjoyed. There would be no more photographs of the two of them appearing in the daily papers. Keedy would fade into anonymity. It was a painful thought.

There was an additional problem. If ejected from the police service, he would suffer another blow. Keedy was still in his thirties. He would be eligible for conscription and deemed fit enough to serve his country in the army. No sooner had he married the woman he loved than he would be off to a training camp. Instead of enjoying marital bliss, Keedy would be a soldier with a very uncertain future. He began to wish that he had never listened to the call for a police strike.

CHAPTER FIFTEEN

Claude Chatfield had been involved in a series of meetings that morning, so Marmion had to wait until the man was free. When he entered the superintendent's office, he could see that Chatfield was in a fretful mood. Something had clearly upset him.

'Well?' snapped Chatfield.

'I've come to report a development in the case, sir.'

'At long last!'

'I need hardly tell you that investigations as complex as this one take time.'

'Let's dispense with the excuses. Bring me up to date.'

'We have a new suspect, sir.'

'Who is he?'

'Stuart Fryer.'

Chatfield blinked in disbelief. 'The deputy manager?'

'That's the man.'

'But you've spoken so well of him until this moment. You told me how eager he has been to help you.'

'Fryer was rather too eager.'

'I thought that he actually worked out how the robbers got into the bank.'

'And I was very grateful to him at first,' said Marmion. 'But I think that he supplied that information in order to win our confidence.'

'I find that highly unlikely.'

'Hear me out, please.'

'I've got a horrible feeling that I've heard enough already.'

Chatfield sat back in his chair with his arms folded and glared at his visitor. Marmion explained how they had come to suspect the duty manager of being involved in the robbery. Apart from the manager, Fryer was the only person who knew how to open the various safes in the bank. He had somehow passed on that information to the robbers. They would have received additional help from Fryer. Marmion argued that he had left the door to the roof unlocked so that one of them could enter the attic easily, then wait until the agreed time for the fire brigade to be summoned.

'What puzzled me,' said Marmion, 'was how the robber got from the attic into the upper level of the bank. The trapdoor that would give him access was bolted from below.'

'Go on,' said Chatfield, exuding hostility.

'The answer was simple. Fryer must have released the bolt so that the trap could be lifted upwards. In short, the intruder waiting in the attic could easily drop down into the bank and disable the burglar alarm. His next job was to let an accomplice into the bank. They then opened a safe with the combination given by Fryer.'

'This is utter nonsense!'

'I disagree, sir. The deputy manager is clearly implicated. It's the reason I had him followed.'

Chatfield was shocked. 'Why ever did you sanction that?'

'The evidence against Fryer justified it, sir.'

'And what did you learn?'

'I learnt that he is a chain smoker.'

'Dear God!' cried Chatfield. 'What possible use is that piece of information?'

'If you'll let me, sir, I'll tell you.'

Marmion went on to explain why he thought Stuart Fryer's reliance on cigarettes was important. The superintendent's face was a study in incredulity. He waved both arms.

'Stop, stop!' he cried. 'I can't take any more.'

'I know that it sounds unlikely, sir . . .'

'It's more than unlikely – it's completely ridiculous.'

'The only place where he could have smoked at work was up on the roof. That must have been how he devised the plan to rob the bank. Because it was not connected to the burglar alarm, the attic was its weak spot. Fryer must have realised that.'

'Enough!' yelled Chatfield, standing up. 'I won't listen to any more.'

'Inside help was vital. Fryer supplied it.'

'In between the occasions when he was smoking a sly cigarette, I suppose. I'm sorry, Inspector. You're a brilliant detective with an unrivalled run of success but you have let yourself down this time. Just because Fryer was seen to buy a packet of fags, you've identified him as the man who planned and made possible the bank robbery.'

'He must be viewed as a suspect, sir.'

'No! He must be treated as the dedicated, hard-working man that he clearly is. I'll forget that you even mentioned his name. Stuart Fryer is completely innocent.'

After letting himself into the room, Fryer locked the door behind him. He then clipped the ladder in place and climbed the rungs. When he reached the trapdoor, he drew the bolt back and pushed the trapdoor upwards. He climbed into the attic and switched on the light. Walking to the door, he unlocked it and stepped out onto the roof. The fresh air was invigorating. Within seconds he had lit a cigarette and taken his first pull on it. He exhaled smoke with a feeling of deep satisfaction.

The bank robbers were on the move. While Gadney and Hillier were clearing up everything inside the house, Mills was digging a hole outside so that all their rubbish could be buried. No sign was to be left of the fact that they had been hiding there. Hillier drove the car out of the garage and Gadney climbed in beside him. The latter was in a truculent mood.

'I wish that we could leave Sid behind us,' he said.

'That'd be unfair, Max.'

'He's our weak link.'

'You didn't think that when he got us safely across the Channel. Without him, we might have been drowned.'

'Yes, he's a good sailor,' admitted Gadney, 'I'll give him that. But he worries me.'

'Sid gets a bit jittery sometimes, that's all.'

'He doesn't have any plans of what to do when he gets his share of the money. You and I have worked out exactly how we can enjoy life when keeping our heads down. My fear is that Sid will open his big mouth and we'll all be in trouble.'

'What do we do?'

'Watch him closely.'

'And if he steps out of line?'

'There's only one solution,' said Gadney. 'It's him or us. If he does something stupid, Sid will get all three of us in trouble. Do you want to be forcibly returned to our regiment to face trial?'

Hillier shivered. 'No thanks!'

'Then we have to put ourselves first.'

'Don't be too hasty, Max.'

'I've made far too many allowances for him.'

'Let me speak to Sid,' insisted Hillier. 'I know how to knock sense into him.'

'If you fail,' warned Gadney, 'he has to go.'

'Fair enough.'

'All it needs is a thrust from my bayonet. That's how I killed that copper.'

'Sid is one of us,' Hillier reminded him.

'Yes, he is – at the moment.'

Joe Keedy was glad that he had decided to jog around the park that morning. It helped him to clear his head and allow him to think clearly. What had rattled him was a threat made by the commissioner. Sir Edward might well regret his sudden anger. He might also find that a decision made on the spur of the moment might not be so easy to enforce. Apart from anything else, the threat would create a lot of ill feeling among those involved in law enforcement. Constabularies throughout the country would be angered at what they would see as a snap decision. Instead of being suppressed, the desire to strike might spread.

Panting from his exertion, Keedy sat down on a bench to review his own position. While there was, in theory, a danger of being dismissed from the Metropolitan Police Force, he believed that his record might save him. Marmion would certainly speak up for him and so would Chatfield, if with less enthusiasm. Other senior officers held Keedy in high regard. It might well be felt that he would be far more effective as a detective sergeant than he would as a nameless soldier in the ranks. And he was not the only one. Other detectives had told him of their approval of NUPPO's objectives. When he realised just how many good men he would lose, Sir Edward might well come to see how damaging to the force his peremptory demand would be. One fact was certain. Seasoned officers were like gold dust. They had rarity value.

While he had given himself a measure of comfort, Keedy was still concerned about the future. In Alice's view, she was marrying a fearless detective in the Metropolitan Police Force. How would she feel if he were sacked from his job and instantly conscripted? Alice would simply be one more army wife, praying for the survival of her husband and hoping that he returned from combat without any hideous injuries. Getting up from the bench, he broke into a gentle trot. Mind in turmoil, he was torn between fear and reassurance.

'What exactly did he say, sir?' asked Burge.

'I'd rather not repeat his exact words, Cliff.'

'Didn't he realise that Fryer simply has to be a suspect?'

'He dismissed the notion with contempt,' said Marmion.

'Then he's as blind as a bat.'

'Chat called me far worse names than that.'

They were alone in Marmion's office, reviewing the discussion between the inspector and the superintendent. Both were angry at the latter's response to the claim that Stuart Fryer might be instrumental in the robbery at his bank.

'What do we do, sir?' asked Burge.

'We get on a train to Dorset.'

'Is that what Chat recommended?'

'No, it isn't,' said Marmion. 'It's my decision. Max Gadney

is the deserter who interests me most. If we can find him – or at least have some idea of his whereabouts – we'll be close to the man who probably stabbed Sam Collard to death. That matters more to me than any money stolen from the bank.'

'What about the superintendent?'

'What about him?'

'Shouldn't you tell him where we're going?'

'No,' said Marmion. 'We must take independent action of our own sometimes. We just need to be sure that we bring back concrete evidence.'

'Where does Max Gadney live?'

'In Dorchester, the county town of Dorset.'

'I hope that we have more luck than I had in Glasgow.'

'We will, Cliff, I promise you. I have a good feeling about this man Gadney. And when that happens, I know that I've picked up a trail.'

Hillier drove the car with great care, maintaining a relatively low speed and staying on quiet country roads. The few people they passed hardly gave them a second glance. Seated beside the driver, Gadney was relaxed. Mills, by contrast, was moving around the back seat as if he were sitting on a beehive. He kept looking anxiously through the back window.

'Sit still, for God's sake!' ordered Gadney.

'Why did we have to leave the farmhouse?' asked Mills.

'I told you before. We need to keep on the move.'

'It felt safe there, Max.'

'Sooner or later, someone would have seen the smoke coming out of the chimney and realised that the place was occupied.'

'Where are we going now?'

'Somewhere that's even more isolated.'

'Will we share out the loot at last?'

'Stop moaning about the money.'

'I deserve my cut.'

'You'll have to be patient, Sid,' advised Hillier. 'Like me.'

'Meanwhile,' added Gadney, 'you can shut up and do what you're told. Agreed?'

Mills was cowed. 'If you say so . . .'

On duty together, the policewomen had had a busy day. Things had now settled down. As they walked side by side on their beat, Iris became aware of the fact that her partner had not said a single word for several minutes.

'Is anything wrong?' she asked. Getting no reply, Iris raised her voice. 'Did you hear me, Alice?'

'There's no need to yell at me, Iris.'

'It's the only way to get your attention. You're in a world of your own.'

'I'm sorry . . .'

'Something's bothering you, isn't it?'

'Yes, it is,' confessed Alice. 'I keep thinking about Paul.'

'I'm not surprised. His behaviour must be maddening.'

'It's so out of character.'

'Are you absolutely sure that he was the person who stole that money?'

'No, I'm not. That's what is so maddening. Was it my brother who caused all the trouble, or was it that wicked friend of his we met at the prison?'

'Would Paul really give him the key to the house?'

'That's a question I keep asking myself.'

'There is one explanation, Alice.'

'What is it?'

'Paul and his friend are working together.'

'That's a terrifying thought. I hope it's not true. They'd split up, remember. Paul and that man had exchanged identities and went their separate ways. Price ended up in Shepton Mallet Prison, claiming to be Paul Marmion. In fact,' said Alice, 'he was a deserter. When they worked out who he was, they contacted his regiment. Soldiers came to take him off to face a court martial, but Price somehow escaped. That shows you what a desperate young man he is.'

'How on earth did Paul get involved with him in the first place?'

'We may never know, Iris.'

'They're not exactly birds of a feather.'

'That's what we thought,' said Alice, 'but Price is a strong character. We saw enough of him to realise that. He might have dragged my brother down to his level.'

'Is that what your mother believes?'

'Mummy is completely confused. So am I.'

'I think that changing the door lock was a good idea.'

'But will it be enough to keep Paul at bay? I don't think it would deter Garth Price. If he can escape from two soldiers when he's in handcuffs,' said Alice, worriedly, 'then he'd find his way into the house somehow.'

When they reached Dorchester late that afternoon, Marmion and Burge discovered that it had been market day. As they walked to the police station, they saw straw and animal dung being brushed away from the cobbles and loaded into a cart. Marmion breathed in deeply then smiled.

'Smell that country air, Cliff.'

'All I can smell is the stink of cow shit.'

'Even that is better than what we sometimes inhale in London.'

Burge laughed. 'That's true.'

When they reached the police station, they were given instant cooperation. The desk sergeant was a tall, bony man in his late fifties with small tufts of hair clinging desperately to his bald head like passengers hanging on to a sinking ship. As soon as Marmion mentioned the name of Max Gadney, the man gave a snort of contempt.

'Oh, we remember Max all too well,' he said, sourly.

'Why is that?' asked Marmion.

'The little bugger caused us so much trouble, Inspector.'

'What kind of trouble?'

'Thieving, mostly. We even caught him stealing from the church one day. I felt sorry for his family. They were decent people, yet they had this delinquent on their hands. Max found Dorchester too quiet for him. That's why they packed him off to his uncle in London.'

'Which part of London?'

'Bayswater.'

'Not all that far from Paddington,' noted Burge.

'We were just glad to get rid of him,' said the duty sergeant.

'Were you aware that Gadney is a deserter?'

'Yes, his regiment notified us. Not that Max would ever come back here. He hated living on a smallholding. All he ever talked about was getting a job in a big city.'

'And what job did he get?' asked Marmion.

'He worked with his uncle in an abattoir. Killing animals suited him.'

'We'll need the uncle's address, please.'

The duty sergeant opened a ledger and ran a finger down a

list of names. When he gave them an address, it went straight into Burge's notebook. The visitors were also told where the Gadney family lived.'

'How far away is it?' asked Marmion.

'Almost a mile. A police car will take you there and bring you back.'

'Thanks for your help.'

'We'll do anything to help you catch Max Gadney.'

'Was he that bad?'

'Let's just say that he led us a merry dance.'

'Shall I mention your name when we catch him?'

'Please do – and be sure to give him my regards.'

When they first saw their next hiding place, they were disappointed. It comprised a few small huts close to a stand of trees. Gadney checked a letter to make sure that they had come to the right place.

'Is this it, Max?' asked Hillier.

'Yes, it is,' replied the other. 'It's not as big and comfortable as the farmhouse, maybe, but it's got advantages.'

'I can't see any,' moaned Mills, peering through the car window.

'To start with, we can hide the car behind those trees. Also, it's off the beaten track so we won't be troubled by visitors. And even if we are,' added Gadney, 'there's a second way out. Look at that track over there. If we need it, there's our escape route.'

'We were better off where we were,' said Hillier.

'It was time to move on.'

'I just don't like the look of this place.'

'Neither do I,' said Gadney. 'It reminds me too much of the smallholding in Dorset where I was brought up. At least, there are no animals to feed here. Drive us behind those trees, Terry.'

Hillier obeyed and parked the vehicle on the other side of the trees. The three of them got out and appraised their new home. Mills noticed something.

'There's a padlock on the door of the biggest hut,' he complained bitterly.

Gadney grinned. 'If we can get into a bank, I don't think we'll have any trouble breaking into this place. It's not as if I need to climb a drainpipe in the dark.'

He got out of the car and walked towards the main hut, picking up a heavy stone on the way. His companions followed him. It took Gadney less than ten seconds to smash the padlock apart. After tossing the stone away, he opened the door wide. They recoiled from the stink.

'You'll soon get used to it,' Gadney assured them, leading the way in.

The interior was much larger than they had imagined. It contained a table, three chairs and three old mattresses stacked against a wall. There was a sink and – as Gadney discovered – the tap provided cold water. There was even a small grate with a few logs beside it. Hillier spotted that something was missing.

'There's no electricity,' he complained, flicking on the switch.

'We'll manage without,' said Gadney. 'Bring in the food from the car, Sid.' Mills went quickly out of the hut. 'I'll find some twigs and try to start a fire.' He opened the window. 'The fresh air will soon get rid of this stink.'

'How can anyone live in a place like this?' asked Hillier with disgust.

'It would only be for a bit. I reckon this used to be a fruit farm. These huts were used by pickers hired for the summer. They're not too fussy about accommodation – neither are we.'

'Speak for yourself. I like some comfort. We have all this money,' said Hillier, bitterly, 'yet we must put up with this rubbish dump.'

'We've slept in worse places when we were in the army.'

'That's no consolation.'

'It is to me.'

'How long will we be here?

'It's only for a short while, Terry. Be patient. In due course, my friend will have sorted out somewhere much better for us.'

'Will it have a bath?'

'It will probably have a bath with a naked woman in it,' said Gadney. 'Will that suit you?'

They laughed coarsely.

Later in the afternoon, Chatfield decided that he had been too hasty in dismissing Marmion's theory about the deputy manager. After sifting through the reports of the bank robbery, he saw how often Stuart Fryer had supplied what appeared to be helpful information. The man was clearly anxious to be involved in every stage of the investigation. Chatfield wanted more information about him. When he went to Marmion's office, however, the inspector was not there. On his desk was a message in block capitals.

GONE TO DORCHESTER.

Chatfield gaped. 'What, in God's name, is he doing there?'

When they met Donald Gadney for the first time, the detectives felt sorry for him. Well into his sixties, he was a withered man with a nervous cough. Shoulders that had once been broad were now hunched. When Marmion explained why they had come, the old man became defensive.

'He's not here, Inspector,' he said. 'Max grew to hate our way of life. We grow crops and keep hens, pigs, and some cows. Our son chose to work at an abattoir, killing farm animals. That's how much he grew apart from us.'

'Do you have any idea where he might be?'

'No, we don't, and we don't wish to know. Max is the bane of our lives. My wife was getting on when we finally had a child. It seemed like a blessing at first. Then he began to grow up into this angry, violent young thug. If you live as we do, there are chores to be done every day. Max hated that. I had to take a strap to him sometimes. Then he got into trouble with the police and made our lives a misery. I began to wish that they'd lock him up for good.'

'When did he leave home?'

'He'd be barely sixteen, I suppose. We couldn't handle him. Most parents are proud of their children – not in our case. We had this lazy, foul-mouthed youth who lived off us whenever he was released from detention. In the end, I packed him off to my brother in London and told him never to come back.'

'Did you ever visit your brother's house?'

'Once or twice,' replied the other. 'Max was usually at work, so we never actually saw him, but Charlie – that's my brother – told us that he was no trouble to look after. In fact, Charlie was more of a father to Max than I was able to be.'

'Was your son ever violent when he lived here?'

'He never stopped, Inspector. I lost count of the number of parents who complained about the way he'd attacked their sons for no reason at all. Max was a bully.'

'What did you feel when he joined up?'

'I felt a sense of relief – and so did my wife.'

'Was there no tinge of pride?'

'There was at first,' admitted the man. 'We thought that the army would teach him some discipline – and it seemed to do so at first. Then my brother told me what Max said in letters to him. He boasted about playing tricks on the other soldiers and sneaking off in search of French women. I didn't dare tell my wife about that.'

'When did you hear that he'd deserted?'

'It was a week or more after it had happened. Some soldiers came to tell us and to make sure he wasn't hiding here.' He laughed bitterly. 'Fat chance of that! I wouldn't have let him in here. As far as we are concerned, we no longer have a son.'

'I'm sorry to hear you say that.'

'He's given us nothing but grief.'

'If he didn't come here,' said Burge, taking out his notebook, 'do you think that he'd have gone to his uncle?'

'It's more than likely.'

'Could you tell me where he lives, please?'

'Of course.'

As the address was reeled off, Burge made a note of it. He looked up from his pad.

'When your brother heard that his nephew was a deserter, how would he have reacted?'

'Charlie would have been shocked as much as me.'

'In that case, where would Max go?'

The man gave a shrug. 'He'd find somewhere.'

At the end of his day's work, Stuart Fryer waited until everyone had departed then he activated the burglar alarm, left the premises, and locked the main door. After glancing around, he walked off in the direction of home but did not get far. When he spotted a taxi, he waved a hand to stop it and got into the back seat. The driver studied him in his mirror.

'I've driven you before, sir,' he said.

'Then you know where to take me.'

'Paddington Station.'

On their return journey to London, the detectives did not enjoy the luxury of an empty compartment. Instead of discussing their visit, therefore, they were confined to a series of neutral subjects. It was only when they were leaving the railway station in London that they could talk freely.

Burge anticipated the first question.

'I felt sorry for the man and for his wife,' he said.

'So did I, Cliff. Nature can be cruel. Having been forced to wait several years before their one child came along, he turned out to be a little monster.'

'And he's grown into a big monster now, sir.'

'Yes,' said Marmion, 'and what did he do for a living? He slaughtered animals. When he has a bayonet in his hands, he's happy to kill a policeman as well.'

'Max Gadney is dangerous.'

'Yet his father seemed such a gentle character. He grew up in that smallholding and was happy with the life it gave him and his wife. Then their only child came into the world, and, in time, everything turned sour.'

'When do we call on the uncle?'

'First thing tomorrow,' decided Marmion. 'When we get back to Scotland Yard, I'll have to report to Chat. I hope he's in a more amenable mood than he was earlier today.'

'Don't bank on it,' said Burge.

'I won't.'

They walked on in silence until Burge remembered something.

'By the way,' he said, 'have you seen the warning that's been put up on every notice board.'

'How could I miss it?'

'It will put the fear of death into most people.'

'In my view, that's good.'

'In threatening to call a strike, NUPPO has really stung the commissioner into action.'

'I'm on his side, Cliff. The police should never be allowed to strike.'

'Then how do we get a pay rise?'

'We must earn it,' said Marmion.

Keedy was alone in the house. Since the names of the relevant people were now firmly embedded in his mind, he decided that he no longer had to keep the pieces of paper. Gathering them up, he tossed them into the wastepaper basket. Raymond Marmion entered just in time to see the small avalanche. He was amused.

'Have you given up, Joe?' he asked.

'Not at all. I've identified the villain so I can concentrate on persuading everyone else that the case has been solved.'

'You may be able to name the bank employee who planned the robbery, but you have no idea who his associates were.'

'Your brother will provide their names.'

'You seem very sure of that.'

Keedy rose to his feet. 'I've worked with him for a long time, Raymond.'

'I know,' said the other. 'Oh, I meant to ask you something. When Lily emptied the wastepaper basket in your room, she noticed that you'd thrown away a leaflet from an organisation called NUPPO.'

'The National Union of Police and Prison Officers.'

'Are you a member?'

'No, I'm not – but I have sympathy with some of their aims.'

'Then why did you throw that leaflet away?'

'It's because I'd like to stay in the Metropolitan Police Force. Somehow the commissioner has seen that leaflet. He was enraged. He's issued a threat regarding NUPPO. Anyone seen at Scotland Yard with its leaflet in their hands will be sacked on the spot.'

'Can he really do that?'

'Oh yes. He thinks the threat will stamp out any sympathy for NUPPO.'

'Where do you stand on the issue?'

'I'd be ready to strike' said Keedy, 'but I must put Alice first. Once we're married, I'll have a wife to support and a house to maintain. In other words, I'll have to watch the pennies. A wage rise for us is long overdue, but I'm not going to take on Sir Edward Henry to achieve it.'

'How will Alice react?'

'She'll support me. Alice is a fellow police officer, after all.'

'That's true.'

'She wants a husband who shares a bed with her every night – not one who's been conscripted and sent off to fight a war.'

When he got back home, Stuart Fryer tossed away the remains of the cigarette he had been smoking and stamped on it. He then let himself into the house. His wife came into the hallway to help him off with his coat. She noticed the ash on his sleeve.

'You've been smoking again, Stuart,' she scolded.

'I only had the one,' he lied.

'You promised to stop altogether.'

She opened the front door so that she could brush away the ash into the street. After closing the door, she hung his coat on a peg and turned to look at him with a frown.

'You're late,' she said.

'I did warn you that I had a meeting after the bank closed.'

'Was it with that inspector you mentioned?'

'Yes, he wanted to go over various details. It took ages. Sorry to keep you waiting,' he said, taking her by the shoulders to kiss her gently on the cheek. 'What sort of a day have you had?'

'A lonely one.'

'Did you do any shopping?'

'I wasn't well enough, Stuart.'

'What was the trouble?' he asked with concern.

'I had another coughing fit. I just couldn't stop. My chest was on fire.'

'You must go to the doctor again.'

'What's the point? All that he'll do is to prescribe the same medicine and tell me to stay in more. He makes me feel that I'm an invalid.'

'You're still recovering from . . . what happened.'

'That was months ago.'

'It was a terrible blow, Valerie – for both of us. Losing a baby is something that is bound to prey on your mind. After all this time, you're still suffering.'

'I get so lonely, Stuart.'

'Then you ought to invite some of our neighbours in for a cup of tea. They've been so sympathetic. You need the company of other women.'

'It's too painful. They always talk about their own children.'

Before he could reply, she started to cough again. Putting a comforting arm around her, he took her into the living room and lowered her into a chair beside the fire.

'I'm sorry to be such a nuisance to you, Stuart,' she whimpered.

'Don't be ridiculous. You're my wife and I love you.'

'But I can't be a proper wife to you.'

'You're the one that I want, Valerie,' he told her, 'I'll fetch your medicine.'

After giving her a smile of encouragement, he left the room and heaved a sigh of resignation.

CHAPTER SIXTEEN

When they got back to Scotland Yard, he was waiting for them. Claude Chatfield was standing outside Marmion's office, throbbing with anger. He scowled at them in turns.

'We thought you'd have gone home by now, sir,' said Burge.

'I'd have waited until midnight, if necessary,' Chatfield told him.

'The inspector left a message to tell you where we'd gone.'

'Three words on a piece of paper do not constitute an explanation. At the very least, I expected to be told your motives for making a sudden decision like that.'

'You were tied up, sir,' said Marmion. 'And we were in a hurry. As for our decision, it turned out to be fruitful. We visited the home of one of our suspects.' He opened the door of his office. 'If you'd care to step in here, I'll give you a full report.'

'I'd hoped that somebody would be kind enough to do so,' said the superintendent, icily.

He went into the room and the others followed. All three of them sat down.

'Why did you go to Dorchester?' demanded Chatfield.

'That's where Max Gadney lived, sir – or so we thought. Since he's on the run, we didn't expect to see him there, of course, but we found out exactly what sort of person he is. In brief, his father tired of his bad behaviour and threw him out.'

'Max went to live with his Uncle Charlie in London,' said Burge, 'and got a job with him.'

'Doing what?'

'Working in an abattoir.'

'You can see the irony in that, sir,' said Marmion. 'A man who grows up feeding the family's livestock every day spends his time butchering animals – a job more suited to his temperament.'

He passed on the description of Max Gadney given to them by the desk sergeant in the Dorchester Police Station. It was one that Gadney's father was ready to endorse. He and his wife were grateful when their son had finally left home. They had no desire to see him again.

'Everything I heard about him,' said Marmion, 'convinced me that Max Gadney was the man who thrust a bayonet through Sam Collard's heart. He needs to be caught quickly and made to pay for what he did.'

Chatfield sniffed. 'And how do you propose to make the arrest?'

'The first step is to visit his Uncle Charlie.'

'Well, you won't find his nephew there. Gadney is probably in hiding, counting his way through the cash stolen from the bank.'

'We're not the only people searching for him. The army is on his tail as well.'

'What about the other deserters?'

'We've finally got names, sir. One is Terence Hillier, a former garage mechanic from Paddington. The other is Sidney Mills, a fisherman from somewhere along the Thames. We'll visit their homes tomorrow.'

'Let's hope that the press doesn't get hold of those names,' said Chatfield. 'Nothing is worse than having cocky reporters trying to solve a major crime before us. Well,' he added, sitting back in his chair, 'your trip to Dorchester seems to have paid dividends. Work through me next time, however. I like to know exactly what my officers are doing.'

'Fair enough, sir.'

'What's the latest on Sergeant Keedy?'

'He can't wait to get back here.'

'Is he aware of the commissioner's stand against NUPPO?'

'Oh, I don't think it affects him in any way,' said Marmion, face impassive.

'You've told him about the edict, surely?'

'I . . . may have mentioned it in passing.'

'Make him aware of the serious consequences,' warned Chatfield. 'His reputation will not save him. If he's ever found to have that NUPPO leaflet in his possession, he'll be kicked out of the force straight away.'

Marmion was firm. 'I'll make that crystal clear to him, sir.'

They ate their meal by the light of some candles they found in the drawer beside the sink. It was agreed that each of them would sleep in a separate hut so two of the mattresses were taken to the adjoining huts. As they sat around the table, Gadney decided who would be on duty throughout the night.

'Do we really need to be on guard?' complained Mills.

'Yes, we do.'

'But this place is so remote.'

'We can't take any chances,' said Gadney. 'Now finish your

meal so that we can play cards for a couple of hours before two of us turn in.'

'Can I ask a favour, Max?'

'What is it?'

'Well,' said Mills, 'it seems silly playing for money when there's none of it on the table. Why can't we use some of the cash we stole?'

'Yes,' agreed Hillier, 'I asked the same thing last time we played cards.'

'The money stays where it is,' said Gadney, banging the table with a fist. 'You both know that. The time to handle it is when all four of us share it out.'

'But I've never even met this friend of yours,' complained Mills.

'You'll meet him soon enough, Sid.'

'Why don't you tell me his name?'

'It's because you don't need to know it. He's a good friend of ours. And he's helped to make all four of us rich.' He took a sheet of paper from his pocket and glanced at it. 'In your case, Sid, you're not quite as rich as you were. Last time we played cards, you lost twenty quid.'

Even though he was not an official member of the investigation, Keedy spent most of his time thinking about the bank robbery. As he had an early morning jog around the park, he went over the details once more. He was quick to acknowledge that they were dealing with determined and resourceful men. Keedy disapproved strongly of soldiers deserting the British army at a time when they were sorely needed, but he recognised that it took a high degree of cunning and raw nerve to plan their escape. If caught, the robbers knew that they faced a

251

death sentence. Yet they had taken the risk because they could no longer face the strictures and dangers of army life. What awaited them in England – they told themselves – was a chance to commit a crime that would give them the money necessary for survival.

Keedy was anxious to join the search for the men, but he was still following advice from a hospital doctor. It meant that he was only dealing with the crime at a theoretical level. What he yearned for was action. By the time he had reached the end of his run, he felt so fit and healthy that he decided it was time for him to take on a more proactive role.

After an early breakfast, Marmion was picked up by a police car and taken off to Scotland Yard. His wife, meanwhile, washed the dishes then spent an hour or so cleaning the house. When it was time to go out, however, she felt strangely reluctant to do so. Even though a new lock had been fitted on the front door, Ellen did not wish to leave the house. She had to force herself, stepping out into a cold wind and looking nervously up and down the street. After locking the front door, she headed for another session with the sewing circle. But when she was halfway there, she was troubled by a curious sensation.

Somebody was following her. Yet whenever she looked behind her, nobody was there.

They could smell the abattoir from some distance away. It made them wrinkle their noses in disgust. As they got closer, they could hear the noise of protesting animals being driven to their execution. When they were let into the building, Marmion and Burge got a glimpse of the yard where dogs were yapping at the heels of cattle to move them into pens. The detectives were shown into a small, cluttered office with a low ceiling. Charlie Gadney rose from his desk to glower at them. He was a short, muscular man in his fifties who exuded a sense of physical power. They noticed that one of his ears was missing.

'Police?' he guessed, eyeing them warily.

'Yes, Mr Gadney.'

Marmion performed the introductions then stifled a cough.

'Do you always have this stink in here?' he asked.

Gadney smiled. 'You learn to live with it.'

'I wouldn't,' muttered Burge.

'Then you'd be no good working here. Why are you bothering me?'

'Did you know that your nephew had deserted from the army?' asked Marmion.

'First I've heard of it,' said the other with obvious surprise. 'I thought Max would take to life with a rifle in his hands. He loved the idea of killing Huns.'

'We spoke to your brother about him.'

'Then he'll have told you what a handful Max was – always getting into trouble with the law. I'm a foreman here and Don begged me to take him on. That's what I did. Max lived with us and learnt how to kill animals quickly. Then the army came looking for him.'

'They're still looking for him,' said Marmion. 'So are we.'

'Why?'

'Your nephew was involved in the murder of a police constable.'

Gadney was shocked. 'Are you serious?'

'Very serious.'

'We believe that he took part in a bank robbery,' said Burge. 'You can see why we're so keen to find him.'

'Well, he didn't come to me,' said Gadney, firmly. 'We taught him to behave himself. And that's what he did. Something very strange has happened to him.'

'Is the name Terence Hillier familiar to you?' asked Marmion.

'Yes, he and Terry were good friends.'

'What about Sidney Mills?'

'I've never heard of him.'

'Then your nephew might have befriended him in the army. We believe that the three of them deserted from their regiment and somehow made their way back to England.'

'What's all this about a bank robbery?' asked Gadney.

'You obviously don't read the papers.'

'Why should I? All they tell us is bad news.'

'If he should get in touch . . .'

'Max will know better than to come to me.'

'I daresay that he has great respect for you.'

'Well, I don't have any respect for him,' said the foreman, angrily. 'If Max is on the run from the army and the police, he can keep on running. We're not going to take him in.'

'That's very wise of you,' said Marmion.

'But if he does turn up,' added Burge, 'get in touch with us at once.'

'We'll leave you a number you can ring at Scotland Yard. Will you do that, please?'

The foreman nodded in agreement, but they knew he would never betray his nephew.

Stuart Fryer knocked on the door of the manager's office before opening it and going in.

'Have you got a moment, sir?' he asked.

'Yes, yes, of course,' said Boucher, seated at his desk. 'Shut the door and sit down.'

'Thank you.' Fryer did as he was told. He cleared his throat. 'I am not the bearer of good news, I fear.'

'What's the trouble?'

'Two more letters from unimpressed clients,' said the other, holding up the envelopes. 'That takes us into double figures. People are losing faith in our ability to look after their money.'

'Then we have to let them go, I'm afraid.'

'We're not only losing typical clients with average savings. One of these letters is from Humphrey Melrose. His company has substantial amounts of money in our coffers.'

'In that case, I'll write to him and ask him to reconsider.'

'I was hoping that you'd respond in that way, sir,' said Fryer. 'In anticipation, I've drafted a letter on your behalf,' he went on, taking a folded sheet of paper from his inside pocket and handing it over. 'Feel free to amend it as much as you wish. I think it strikes the right note.'

'It certainly does,' agreed the manager, taking the letter and skimming through it. 'Well done, Stuart! You really have a gift. This letter is apologetic without being obsequious, and it reminds Melrose just how long we have done business with him.'

'I'm glad that you approve, sir.'

'This crisis has really brought out the best in you.' He sat back and appraised his companion. 'And to think that I considered making Neil Paterson my deputy. He could never have written a letter of this quality.'

'Neil was a good workhorse,' said Fryer. 'But that's all I can say on his behalf.'

'I'll have this letter typed up and sent off today.'

'Do you think that you should offer to speak to Mr Melrose in person?'

'I'm not sure about that.'

'You have such a persuasive manner, sir. It might just . . . tip the balance.'

'It might at that, Stuart.' Boucher smiled. 'Good advice – as always.'

'I strive to do my best,' said Fryer.

When they knocked on the door of a shabby little house not far from Warwick Avenue, they had to wait several minutes. Burge was impatient.

'There's nobody in, sir,' he said to Marmion.

'Yes, there is, Cliff. I swear that I heard movement.'

'Well, I certainly didn't.'

Marmion put a finger to his lips and pricked his ears. Moments later, the door was opened a few inches by an old woman who stared at them nervously.

'What do you want?' she asked.

'We're detectives from Scotland Yard,' explained Marmion, 'and we're looking for a man named Terence Hillier.'

'He's Terry to us and always will be.'

'Are you aware that he deserted from the army?'

'Yes, and it was very naughty of him. If his father was still alive, he'd give Terry a good hiding.'

'He'll suffer a worse fate than that, I'm afraid.'

'I think there must be a mistake. Terry was as good as gold. He never did anything wrong. That's why I agreed to look after him when his parents died.'

'And how long ago was it, Mrs . . . ?'

'Hillier – Beryl Hillier. Terry is my grandson. He moved in here five or more years ago.'

'And you say that he behaved himself?'

'Yes, he did – most of the time. It was only when he was with that friend of his that he got into trouble.'

'What was the friend's name?'

'Max – Max Gadney. I didn't like him one bit.'

'Why not?' asked Burge.

'Well, to start with,' she said, grimacing, 'there was always a dreadful stink in the air when he came for Terry.'

'Gadney worked in an abattoir.'

She wrinkled her nose. 'You don't need to tell me that, young man.'

'Did you ever meet someone called Sidney Mills?' asked Marmion.

'No,' she replied, 'who is he?'

'Someone he must have met in the army.'

'Terry never mentioned that name in his letters – but he mentioned Max every time.'

'Where did your grandson work?'

'Poulton's Garage. It's only two blocks away. Terry was good at his job. He worked hard.'

'It might be useful to speak to his employer,' said Marmion. 'Could you tell us how to get to the garage, please?'

'Yes, I can.' Tears suddenly welled up in her eyes. 'Terry is in trouble, isn't he?'

Marmion nodded. 'I'm afraid that he is.'

Alice Marmion and Iris Goodliffe had had an eventful morning on their beat. They were therefore grateful to have a much quieter time in the afternoon. As they turned a corner, they had an unexpected bonus. Joe Keedy stepped out of a doorway to confront them. Alice was delighted.

'What are you doing here?' she asked.

'I had an urge to see you,' he explained. 'Since I knew your beat, I lay in wait here so that I could pounce on you.' He turned to Iris. 'Could you excuse us for a moment, please?'

'Yes, of course,' said Iris, moving yards away.

Alice beamed. 'You're the last person I expected to see, Joe.'

'Is that a complaint?'

'Far from it!' She squeezed his hands. 'It's a real treat.'

'I just wanted to pass on some good news.'

'What is it?'

'I'm back,' he announced, spreading his arms wide. 'When I had a run this morning, I felt wonderful. No aches and pains – just a huge sense of relief.'

'That's marvellous news, Joe.'

'I've made an appointment to see the doctor tomorrow. I hope that he'll sign me off.'

'Don't bank on it.'

'I thought you'd be pleased.'

'I'm delighted, but I'm also worried that you might be rushing things. I remember how badly injured you were. You were warned that recovery would take time.'

'And I listened to that warning, Alice. I did all the exercises they gave me but had plenty of rest as well. My mind needed to heal just as much as my body. Both are functioning again.'

'I'm so pleased for you,' she said, clutching his arm.

'I'd hoped you'd see it from your point of view as well.'

'What do you mean?'

'Do I really need to tell you?' he whispered, moving closer. 'When we get married, you won't have to walk down the aisle with an invalid. You'll be on the arm of a fully fit husband, bursting with energy. How does that sound?'

By way of reply, she flung herself into his arms. Iris moved swiftly across to them with a broad grin on her face.

'Now, now, Alice,' she warned. 'We can't have that sort of thing when you're on duty.'

When she returned to the house, Ellen Marmion chose to do so by taking a different route. If she was going to be followed, she wanted to see who was behind her. She therefore went past an area with shops on both sides of the road, crossing from time to time and using their windows like rear-view mirrors to see if anyone was on her tail. Nobody was there but she still had the feeling that she was under surveillance. Was it her son or was it Paul's close friend? She never found out.

When she reached home, she let herself in and went straight to the window in the living room. Though she looked in both directions, she saw nobody watching the house.

Yet she was convinced that someone was there.

When they drove to Poulton's Garage, they learnt that its owner had no sympathy whatsoever for his former employee. Eddie Poulton, a tall, haggard, bespectacled man in dungarees and a flat cap, was blunt.

'Deserters should be put up against a wall and shot,' he said. 'Nothing's worse than betraying your country. That's what Terry did. I'd love to be in the firing squad.'

'What was he like when he worked here?' asked Marmion.

'Best mechanic I ever had. Learnt quickly and worked all hours. Then off he went to war.'

'How did you feel when he was called up?'

'I was very angry, to be honest. We needed him here.'

'His country had first claim on him, Mr Poulton.'

'Did you ever meet a friend of his named Max?' asked Burge.

'Yes,' sneered the manager, 'he was always hanging around here. Stank to high heaven, he did. Terry liked him but I thought Max was sly and deceitful. Also, he'd been in prison. I'm sorry they ever let him out. He was a nasty piece of work.'

'Who told you Hillier had deserted?' said Marmion.

'It was his granny. Poor old duck can hardly walk but she come round here to pass on the news. I feel sorry for her. She struggled hard to bring him up and what happens? Terry brings shame on the whole family.'

'Did Hillier ever mention a Sidney Mills?'

'No – Gadney was the only real friend he had.'

'Mills deserted at the same time as the others. We're after all three of them.'

'Well, if you catch them, pass on a message from me to Terry Hillier.

'What is it?'

A veritable stream of foul language shot out of Poulton's mouth.

When he'd parked the car behind the trees, Hillier lifted out the bags of food that he'd bought and carried them across to the main hut. Gadney and Mills were keen to see what he had managed to find. They were disappointed.

'There's not much,' complained Gadney.

'I needed a ration book for anything worth eating,' said Hillier.

'Couldn't you even find a loaf of bread?'

'I found it,' said Hillier, 'but it was reserved for a regular customer. I tried to get sympathy by pretending to have lost an arm, but it didn't work this time.'

'How far away was the shop?'

'Five or six miles, Max.'

'We'll pay them a visit at night,' decided Gadney. 'If they won't sell us food, we'll steal as much as we want.'

'How long are we going to be here?'

'I'm expecting word tomorrow.'

'Does that mean we get to meet your friend?' asked Mills, hopefully.

'It's possible.'

'I find it scary.'

'What do you mean, Sid?' asked Hillier.

'Well, we're just puppets, really. Somebody I've never met pulls the strings. We do the dirty work, yet he expects to take the biggest cut.'

'He deserves every penny,' said Gadney.

'But we're the ones who risked our necks,' complained Mills.

'Where else would you get that amount of money in the space of an hour? The answer is nowhere. By being brave enough and following his orders to the letter, we've earned enough money to keep out of sight and live in comfort until the war is over.'

'The army won't forget us,' warned Hillier.

'And neither will the police,' added Mills.

Gadney waved a contemptuous hand. 'Don't worry about them. They'll never catch us.'

'What about him?'

'Who are you talking about, Sid?'

'This so-called "friend" of yours. What if they catch him?'

'Impossible!' said Gadney with a snigger. 'He's far too clever. Everything was worked out to the last detail. He told me that it would take three of us – one to climb in, one to join me once I was inside, and one to have a fast car ready – that was you, Sid.'

'I was waiting outside bang on time,' recalled Mills. 'I saw those two coppers turn up.'

'Yes,' said Gadney, 'it was a pity about that. I enjoyed killing one of them and Terry took care of the other, but it would have been better if neither had turned up.'

'It was something your friend never thought about.'

'It was bad luck, Sid, that's all. We still got away, didn't we – and we had the loot with us.'

'We also have the entire Metropolitan Police Force on our trail.'

'Not any more,' said Gadney. 'We're outside their jurisdiction.'

'They'll have warned other constabularies to be on the lookout.'

'Then where are they? We haven't caught sight of a copper for days. More importantly, they haven't caught sight of us.' Gadney glared at each of them in turn. 'Let's keep it that way.'

Keedy had gone there deliberately. When he strolled past Scotland Yard, he was tempted to go into the building, declare himself fully fit and return to work the next day. Common sense held him back. Until he had been examined by a doctor, it would be foolish to make such an important commitment. As he walked past the main entrance, a police car was approaching the building. Recognising him, the driver gave a toot on his horn and waved a friendly hand. Keedy waved back in return. He had the comforting glow of someone who has been away for a long time and who has finally returned home.

Having come into central London with the express purpose of seeing Alice, he had then walked to police headquarters on the Embankment. The very sight of it was inspiring. It generated hundreds of precious memories for Keedy, along with some he wished that he could forget. Not least among them was the moment when he dashed into a house whose front door had been smashed open and found himself confronted by a man with a gun. Before he could fire his own weapon, he was shot in the stomach. The scar would always be there to remind him of his good fortune in surviving the incident. A sudden thought stopped Keedy in his tracks.

Would he ever be capable of showing such reckless bravery again?

When they got to the wharf in Barking, the detectives saw an old man with a white beard seated on a chair as he absent-mindedly sewed the broken net in his hands. There was a pipe in his mouth but no evidence of any tobacco in it. He looked up at Marmion and Burge.

'I've been expecting you,' he said.

'Why do you say that?' asked Marmion.

'I'm Frank Mills – Sid's grandfather.'

'We're pleased to meet you, sir. When we called at the house, your wife told us where to find you. Sid's father is still out with the fishing boat, is he?'

'No, he was back hours ago. Fishing is a job for those who can get up very early. I used to be able to do that in the old days – not any more.'

After sizing him up, Marmion introduced himself and Burge. Still sewing away, the old man gave a welcoming nod then released a hand so that it could move the pipe to the other side of his mouth. He closed an eye before staring at Marmion.

'Sid's not a bad lad, really,' he told them. 'He's just a bit stupid.'

'I'd have thought he had to be very clever to make a living out of catching fish. It's not easy.'

'He did as he was told, that's all.'

'Yes,' said Marmion, 'it's the reason we're here. Your grandson did as he was told by someone in the army, and they deserted with a third man. When they got back here, he did as he was told again and took part in a bank robbery.'

'That was very wrong of him.'

'A policeman was murdered during the robbery. His name was Constable Sam Collard. He was a good friend of mine.'

'Well, my grandson didn't kill him. I know that for certain. Sid would never hurt a human being or an animal.'

'What about hauling fish out of the sea? Isn't that a form of murder?'

'That's different.'

'Where is he, Mr Mills?' asked Marmion.

'I don't know – and that's the truth.'

'What would you do if he turned up at the house?'

'I'd take him by the scruff of his neck and shake the truth out of him,' said the old man with sudden anger. 'The army needs every man it can get. Running away is worse than cowardice. I'd want to know why he did it.'

'He obeyed someone else's orders, Mr Mills.'

'It's the only way it could have happened. Sid is . . . easily led astray.'

'Taking part in a bank robbery is rather more than being led astray,' said Burge. 'Then there's the small matter of a dead policeman and one who was badly beaten.'

The old man raised his palms. 'I'm not defending what my grandson did.'

'Does that mean you'd turn him in if he showed up?'

'No – it means that I'd tell him to turn himself in and I'd make sure that he did. Sid knows the difference between good and bad. What he did was bad – very bad. He deserves to be punished.'

'I'm glad that you take that attitude,' said Marmion. 'What about your son?'

'Danny's too drunk to give you an answer, Inspector. You'll find him drowning his sorrows with a bottle of rum. He'd try to rescue Sid somehow.' He looked up. 'Do you have a son?'

'I did have,' said Marmion, sadly.

'Then you've shared that bond between father and son. It's very special. If Danny was in this situation, I'd have done anything to save him. But I'm older and wiser now, Inspector. Come what will, I know that the law must take its course.'

'It certainly will, sir.'

'This can only end one way. Sid will realise that.'

'It's important that we find him,' said Marmion. 'If you have the slightest idea where your grandson is, please tell us.'

The old man took out a tobacco tin, opened it and filled his pipe with tobacco. He then lit the tobacco by striking a match on the sole of his boot. When he had inhaled it enough to produce a bright glow, he removed the pipe and looked at Marmion.

'Don't come here again,' he said. 'If Sid comes to me for help, I'll drag him all the way to Scotland Yard by the scruff of his neck and hand him over.'

When the summons came from the manager, Stuart Fryer responded instantly. He went straight to his office where he found Boucher with a smile on his face. The manager waved him to a seat.

'I acted on your advice,' he said, 'and wrote to Humphrey Melrose. I had the letter delivered by hand. Mr Melrose sent the reply immediately.'

'What did it say?'

'He's happy to come here tomorrow to discuss his accounts here.'

'Then you may well persuade him to change his mind,' said Fryer, delighted.

'I sincerely hope so. My chances of doing so would be increased if you were present.'

'I'll be happy to join you, sir.'

'You have a way of talking to our more celebrated clients.'

'I'm glad that you think so.'

'Moving on to a related matter,' said Boucher, 'have all the improvements been made to our security arrangements?'

'I supervised them personally.'

'Then I'll leave you to tell Melrose what you did.'

'The main changes concern the attic,' explained Fryer. 'I had the door to the roof replaced with one that is infinitely more robust. Three keys are needed to unlock it. The other thing that was changed was the trapdoor that gave access to the attic.'

'Did it need to be replaced?'

'I thought so. It opened upwards before. It now drops downwards and has three bolts instead of only one. During the robbery, the single bolt was somehow loosened enough for the trapdoor to be lifted. That can never happen again.'

'What about extending the burglar alarm to the attic?'

'That's also in hand, sir.'

'You've covered every eventuality.'

'It's my responsibility.'

'Mr Melrose will be duly impressed.'

'I hope so. We need clients of his calibre.'

Boucher smiled. 'We also need a deputy manager of your quality, Stuart.'

'It's kind of you to say so.'

'I'm so glad that I had the sense to appoint you.'

'I do my best to deserve your praise, sir,' said Fryer with a gentle nod of his head. 'That's why I've made the security arrangements my priority. Our reputation depends on persuading customers that their money is completely safe here. I'm confident that it's now virtually impossible for a burglar to climb a drainpipe and get into the premises.'

'That's very reassuring,' said Boucher with a smile. 'Are you equally confident that the police will catch the robbers?'

'I'm beginning to have my doubts, I'm afraid.'

CHAPTER SEVENTEEN

When he reported to the superintendent, Marmion did his best to sound as if there had been progress in the investigation. Claude Chatfield was sceptical.

'I don't feel that we've made any forward movement,' he said.

'I disagree, sir. Because we know a great deal more about the three men involved, we can guess how they operate as a team.'

'Can we?'

'I think so. Gadney is obviously the leader. He makes all the decisions. Terence Hillier gets his orders from his best friend. When they agreed to take a huge risk and escape from the army, they needed someone who could handle a boat.'

'Sidney Mills.'

'His grandfather told me that he was an experienced seaman who'd been sailing since he was a boy. My bet is that, when they'd stolen a boat, it was Mills who got them safely back to this country.'

'What about the robbery?'

'Gadney took the lead,' said Marmion. 'He climbed the drainpipe, got into the attic because someone had left the door unlocked and waited until the exact moment when two fire engines were clanging merrily away. You must admire the way they dealt with the burglar alarm.'

'I never admire criminals,' said Chatfield, coldly.

'Once it had been switched off, Gadney went downstairs and let his accomplice in.'

'Sidney Mills.'

'No, sir – Terence Hillier.'

'But Hillier is a car mechanic. Surely, he'd have stolen the vehicle in which they escaped.'

'Mills could drive as well,' Marmion pointed out. 'His grandfather told me. They have a van to carry stuff they need. As soon as he was old enough, Mills was taught how to drive it. Also,' he went on, 'Gadney and Hillier would have loved the thrill of robbing a bank. And it would mean that each of them would get a bigger share of the money than the man who simply drove a stolen car.'

'I suppose that's true.'

'What we don't know is where the robbers are hiding, but it's safe to assume that the person who helped them would have arranged somewhere in advance.'

'Do you still think that this man is Stuart Fryer?'

'It's a definite possibility, sir. At the same time, however, it might be someone completely different, an employee at the bank years earlier.'

'One who sneaked up into the attic to smoke cigarettes, I daresay,' said Chatfield, acidly.

'There's no need to be sarcastic.'

'Then don't give me a reason to question your judgement.'

'We are doing our best, Superintendent.'

'Evidently, it is not good enough,' said Chatfield. 'Demand

on our officers is unduly heavy but, should you need additional help . . .'

'That's a welcome offer but it's one that I refuse.'

'On what grounds?'

'We believe that we have already amassed a great deal of evidence.'

'I beg to differ,' said Chatfield.

'That's your prerogative.'

'Give me something to keep the press away. They're yapping at me all day.'

'You're well able to cope with newspaper reporters, sir. I've seen you in action. You know just how much information to release.'

Chatfield straightened his back. 'That comes with experience.'

'Solving a major crime like this requires patience and persistence. The trick is to pick out the evidence that really matters. That, too, comes with experience.'

Rising from his chair, Marmion excused himself and went out.

No matter how much she chided herself, Ellen Marmion could not stop looking out of the living room window or the one in the main bedroom. It was as if she were on sentry duty. Convinced that someone was watching the house, she was desperate to find out who it was. Evening shadows were starting to lengthen but she kept on checking the road outside. Nobody was ever there.

When she was about to draw the curtains in the living room, however, she suddenly saw a figure approaching from the distance. Ellen drew back instinctively. Was it Paul or was it Garth Price? When the figure passed a lamp that was shedding enough light for her to pick out the person clearly, she was able to relax. It was not a man at all but her neighbour, Maggie

Horton. Sighing with relief, she closed the curtains and went out into the road, ignoring the stiff breeze. As the other woman approached, Ellen rushed towards her.

'What's the matter?' asked the neighbour, slowing to a halt.

'Good evening, Mrs Horton.'

'Should you be out here without a coat, Mrs Marmion? It's freezing.'

'I just wanted to ask you a question. Do you mind?'

'Not at all,' said the other. 'Ask whatever you want.'

'I just wondered if you'd remembered who it was who tried to get into our house. Was it Paul or was it someone else?'

'I was too far away to be certain.'

'But you did see him try to open the front door with a key?'

'Oh, yes – he stamped his foot angrily then kicked the door. Paul wouldn't do that, surely?'

'No, no, of course not . . .'

Mrs Horton peered at her. 'Are you all right, Mrs Marmion?'

'Yes, yes, of course I am.'

'You seem so . . . jittery.'

'I feel fine, honestly. I just keep thinking about that visitor you saw at the house.'

'But he wasn't a visitor, was he? I think he was a thief. Have you had anything taken from the house recently?'

'No, no,' said Ellen, nervously, 'nothing has been stolen. But there has been someone watching the house. I'm anxious to find out who it was.'

'I don't blame you. We know there are thieves hanging about. Mrs Palmer from Coveney Street had some food stolen and there was a woman in Moorland Road who saw a man running out of her house with some of her husband's clothes. It's one of the horrors caused by this war,' said Mrs Horton, warming to her theme. 'Nobody is safe and nothing we own is secure unless there's someone at home day and night. That's why I'm grateful that my father-in-law is in our house all the time. He's our guard dog.'

'You're right,' said Ellen. 'Everything was safer before the war.'

'Yes, we had more police then.'

'I wish that we still did but thousands of them went off to join the army.'

'Well, you've nothing to worry about, Mrs Marmion.'

'I don't understand.'

'Your husband is a detective inspector at Scotland Yard. Everyone knows that.'

'Yes, I suppose they do.'

'It frightens people away from your house.'

Ellen sighed. 'If only it did, Mrs Horton . . .'

It had reached the point where Sidney Mills realised that he was never going to win a card game and that he already owed a sizeable amount of money to Gadney and Hillier. They seemed to have all the luck. Mills began to suspect that they were working together. When he lost yet another game, he threw down his cards in disgust.

'I'm finished!' he declared.

'Don't be silly,' said Gadney, checking a sheet of paper. 'Your total losses are forty-two pounds. That's chicken feed for someone who'll get thousands from the bank robbery.'

'Yes,' agreed Hillier. 'Play on, Sid. Your luck may change.'

'Not while I'm playing against you two.'

Gadney bridled. 'What do you mean by that?'

'Someone is cheating and it's not me.'

'Are you accusing us?' demanded Hillier, getting to his feet.

'We stuck to the rules. It's not our fault that you can't play cards proper.'

'Nobody's dealt me a good hand since we started,' said Mills, sourly.

'If you want a good hand,' retorted Gadney, bunching a fist, 'try this one. You apologise to Terry and me or I'll knock nine barrels of shit out of you.'

'I want my share of the loot now,' insisted Mills.

'Apologise, Sid,' urged Hillier, 'or you won't get a penny.'

'I earned it. Without me, you'd never have got across the Channel. Who steadied the boat when things got rough? Was it either of you? No, you were too busy spewing into the sea. I got the pair of you safely back to this country and what thanks do I get?'

'We cut you into the bank robbery,' said Gadney. 'That was the best thanks anyone could have. Without money, you wouldn't last more than a few days on the run. All you've done is to drive a car and moan at us. It's nearing the point where we don't need you any longer, Sid.'

Mills was horrified. 'But I'm one of the gang!'

'That was before you dared to call us cheats,' said Gadney.

'I felt I was being tricked.'

'We carried you, Sid. The night we sneaked out of camp, you were a bag of nerves. Even though it was quite chilly, you were sweating like a pancake. Me and Terry had to drag you along at one point. It was only when we reached the coast that you were any use to us.'

'Someone had to take charge of that boat,' said Mills. 'I was the only sailor.'

'Then you should have joined the navy!' yelled Gadney.

Moving quickly, he jumped off his chair and felt under the

mattress on the floor. When he brought his hand out again, he was brandishing the bayonet. Mills drew back in alarm.

'There's nowhere to run,' said Gadney, jabbing him with the bayonet and producing a yelp of agony. 'Yes, you came in useful at sea. We needed you then. But that doesn't entitle you to call us cheats. Now take back what you said, or I'll do to you what I did to that copper. What's it going to be, Sid?' he asked, holding the point of the weapon against the other man's throat. 'Do we get an apology from you, or would you rather die young?'

Shivering with fear, Mills backed away until he was up against a wall.

'I'm sorry, Max,' he gabbled, 'I really am. I know you and Terry were playing fair and square.'

'Don't you ever forget it,' said Gadney.

He was about to jab Mills when he heard a motorbike approaching the huts. Fearing discovery, Mills and Hillier froze. Gadney, however, ran to the door with the bayonet in his hand. When the motorbike came to a halt, he was ready to use the weapon. The other men needed a means of defence as well, so Hillier opened the drawer beside the sink and grabbed two knives, passing one of them to Mills. All three of them were braced for action. The motorbike's engine died, and they heard footsteps coming towards the hut. They tightened their grip on their respective weapons but, to their relief, there was no reason to use them. The footsteps stopped briefly outside the door then they retreated. Seconds later, the motorbike's engine came back to life and the vehicle drove away.

'Who the hell was that?' wondered Mills, shaking.

'Who cares?' added Hillier. 'He's gone.'

'Not before he delivered a message,' noted Gadney, picking up the letter that had been pushed under the door. 'It's addressed to me. I was hoping to hear from him at last.'

'What's in the letter?' asked Mills.

'Our instructions.'

Keedy was in high spirits. Over a meal that evening with Raymond and Lily, he told them about his appointment with the doctor on the following day. Raymond was delighted to hear how well their guest felt, but his wife advised caution.

'They told you to wait at least ten days, Joe,' she pointed out.

'My patience is exhausted,' said Keedy.

'Why not rest for another week to be on the safe side?'

'I've been resting for well over a month, Lily. I feel liberated.'

'Well,' said Raymond, 'it's your decision.'

'Alice's face lit up when I told her what I planned to do. I'm not a patient any more. I'm ready and willing to get back into action.'

'Then we wish you well – don't we, Lily?'

'Yes, of course,' she said, hiding her reservations behind a smile. 'But how on earth did you manage to speak to Alice today?'

'I ambushed her when she was on her beat.'

'Didn't she mind?'

'Alice was thrilled,' said Keedy. 'People walking past us thought it was funny to see me kissing a policewoman, but I didn't care. It's ages since I felt so full of life.'

'We don't want you getting Alice into trouble with that inspector of hers,' said Raymond, smiling. 'The woman is a tyrant. What do they call her?'

'Gale Force.'

'I don't think she'd approve of one of her policewomen being kissed on duty.'

'Jealousy!'

They laughed. Lily gathered up the empty plates and took them into the kitchen. Raymond seized the opportunity to change the subject.

'Have you had any more thoughts about joining that strike?'

'We don't know for certain that there'll be one.'

'You had that leaflet from NUPPO delivered to you here,' said Raymond. 'That means you have more than a passing interest in the union.'

'I've got other things on my mind at the moment – the wedding, for instance.'

'Are you sure that you wouldn't like a Salvation Army Band there to liven things up?'

'No thanks, Raymond.'

'We'd love them to be there.'

'You and Lily will be in the congregation,' Keedy reminded him, 'but we'd rather you didn't bring the band along as well. That's no criticism of them. Since I've been staying here, I've heard the band rehearsing more than once and they sound wonderful. But Alice and I wanted a quiet wedding.'

'Lily and I had no choice. The band was obligatory.'

'We'll hire it for our Silver Wedding Anniversary. Will that suit you?'

Raymond chuckled. 'I've started counting the days already . . .'

Stuart Fryer was among the first people to arrive at the bank next morning. Because he was going to meet one of their more affluent customers, he had put on his best suit and wore his favourite tie. Having left his overcoat and hat on pegs in his office, he used the mirror to smarten himself then went on duty. As bank employees streamed in, the deputy manager was in the entrance hall to welcome them in turn. Those who were punctual were rewarded with a smile. Fryer reserved a warning frown for the two latecomers.

Humphrey Melrose had asked for an early meeting and arrived with a minute to spare. The deputy manager was there to welcome him and to lead him to Boucher's office. After an exchange of pleasantries, all three of them sat down. Melrose was a silver-haired man in his sixties with a silver moustache complementing his flowing locks. There was an almost aristocratic air about him.

'Let's get straight down to business,' he said, crisply. 'Have the bank robbers been caught?'

'Not as yet,' admitted Boucher, 'but the police are closing in on them.'

'What do you know of this fellow in charge of the investigation?'

'Inspector Marmion has no rival in Scotland Yard. He has responded with speed and determination.'

'Does that mean he has identified suspects?'

'Yes, it does,' said Fryer, taking over. 'He is very meticulous.'

'Don't forget your own contribution,' the manager told him before turning to Melrose. 'My deputy was able to make a decisive contribution to the investigation. Thanks to him, we know exactly how the robbers got inside the building.'

Melrose was critical. 'I'd be more impressed if your burglar alarm had been proof against these villains. Don't you test it from time to time?'

'We do so on a regular basis,' said Fryer.

'Then why did nobody hear the burglar alarm and call the police?'

'It was because the sound of the alarm was masked by the noise of fire engines, rushing to a fire nearby. One of the robbers had started the fire deliberately then raised the alarm at the fire station. Whoever had climbed into the bank waited until the precise time when the fire engines were at their loudest, then he came down from the attic and set off our burglar alarm.'

'Within a very short time,' recalled Boucher, 'the intruder had switched it off.'

'How on earth did he do that?' asked Melrose in amazement.

'He found out how to do so.'

'Then he must have had an accomplice who worked here.'

'I'd absolve every member of our present staff of blame,' said Fryer. 'They are fiercely loyal to this bank. Attention has therefore shifted to . . . former employees.'

When he saw how his deputy was slowly calming their visitor down, Boucher had the sense to remain silent. Fryer was in his element, soothing a disturbed customer and assuring him that security arrangements at the bank had undergone a complete overhaul. At one point, a smile of appreciation appeared on their visitor's face. Eventually, he admitted that he had been too hasty in making his threat. In view of what he now knew, said Melrose, he would reconsider his decision to move his account to another bank. When he escorted their visitor to the front door, Fryer was given a grateful handshake.

'You've restored my faith in the bank,' said Melrose. 'I look forward to years of continued association with you, Mr Fryer. Thank you.'

'I'll show you out, sir.'

'I'd be most grateful.'

'Thank you for coming, sir,' said Boucher.

But the visitor did not even hear him. It was Fryer's persuasive argument that had won him over. As the two of them left the office, Melrose did not even bother to say goodbye to the manager. Instead, he was chatting happily to Stuart Fryer.

From the moment he heard that there had been a bank robbery, Marmion had wondered where those responsible for the crime would hide. Whoever had planned the robbery would surely have chosen somewhere to which the three men could retire in relative safety. Alone in his office with Clifford Burge, the inspector pored over a map of London and its surrounding area. He had already used a pencil to draw circles around possible locations.

'Where the hell are they?' he asked, irritably.

'I still think they may be in the city itself,' said Burge.

'Too dangerous.'

'Why do you say that?'

'We know the exact time when the bank was raided,' said Marmion. 'It was at three o'clock in the morning. If they'd gone to a house, they would have had the problem of what to do with the car. They could hardly leave it parked outside their lair. Most newspapers have carried a description of the vehicle. It was bound to be spotted and reported.'

'Yes, I suppose so.'

'They'd have headed for open countryside, Cliff. That's why I circled various places. It wasn't only houses and factories that were targeted by the German bombers. They hit farms and farm buildings as well, destroying sources of food. Some have had to be abandoned and that's where we should be looking.'

'How far outside London should we go?'

'I've been in touch with constabularies in all directions, asking them to be on the alert for signs of activity in the countryside in buildings that are supposed to be unoccupied.'

'Why haven't any of them reported seeing something?'

'It's only a matter of time before someone does.'

'How far afield might those men have gone?'

'They could be hundreds of miles away,' said Marmion. 'And they won't stay in one place for too long. It would be dangerous. They'll keep on the move.'

'In that case, they'd have needed help,' argued Burge. 'All three of them are Londoners. Gadney worked in that abattoir, Hillier was in that garage not far away and Mills lived in Barking near the bank of the Thames. They wouldn't have a clue how to find a hiding place in the countryside.'

'The man who planned the robbery would.'

'Stuart Fryer?'

'He's our best guess at the moment.'

'He looks like the sort of man who'd plan everything down to the last detail.'

'Yes,' agreed Marmion, 'then he'd reward himself with a cigarette afterwards.'

Burge laughed. 'More than one fag, surely. He'd smoke a whole pack.'

'The big question is this – when does he get in touch with the men?'

'Well, it will probably be at the weekend. It's the only time he's not tied up at the bank.'

'You must admire his patience.'

'Why?'

'Look at it from his point of view,' suggested Marmion. 'He's gone to immense trouble to organise the robbery, yet he's never had the chance to see the stolen money. That must be very frustrating. Fryer – if it really is him – must be dying to feel those banknotes when he gives everyone their individual

280

share. That's the thrill he wants to enjoy.'

'I'd feel the same in his position,' confessed Burge.

'Then you'd realise that pleasure comes with responsibilities.'

'I don't follow.'

'Fryer is a banker. He's an expert with money. He'll know exactly how to hide his share. But the three men he hired have struggled through life on low wages and low expectations. They are his weak spot. Gadney, Hillier and Mills will want to enjoy a few luxuries,' said Marmion. 'If they're not careful, they'll give the game away.'

'Isn't there some way to stop them doing that?'

'Yes, there is, Cliff. They'll have to obey orders from the man who employed them. He'll crack the whip over them. They will have to live very different lives from now on. And while they're doing it,' said Marmion, 'they must learn to keep their mouths shut.'

As they sat around a table eating their meagre breakfast, the three men were deep in conversation. Most of the questions were coming from Mills, often speaking with his mouth full.

'Why didn't he give us his orders in person?' he asked.

'Because he didn't want to,' replied Gadney.

'Why not?'

'He's a busy man, Sid. He can't get time off from work. That's why we must wait before we meet him in person.'

'Is he coming here?'

'No, we'll be somewhere else.'

'Where?'

'The directions are in that message he sent us.'

'When do we divide up the money?'

'It will happen very soon,' said Gadney. 'The first thing you must do when you get your hands on the dough is to fork out the money you owe us for losing all those card games.'

'That's not fair!' wailed Mills.

'Yes, it is,' said Hillier. 'Pay up, Sid. You can afford it.'

'Otherwise,' warned Gadney, 'we'll cut you out completely.' Mills stifled the reply he was about to make. 'I told you at the start that you had to make plans for how you live from now on. Terry and I know exactly what we're going to do. What about you, Sid?'

'I'm heading north,' said Mills. 'I want a life on water, so I'll buy a barge and go up and down the canals. Once I'm settled, I'll send money to my uncle and his family.'

'That's the last thing you must do!'

'There's no need to shout, Max.'

'Yes, there is, you idiot! Your uncle must think you've vanished into thin air. If you send him money, he'll spend it on things he could never afford. The neighbours will start asking questions about where he got the money from.'

'You have no family now,' said Hillier. 'We made that clear.'

'Yes,' said Mills, 'you did.'

'Take your money and keep your head down. It's the only way to survive.'

'Don't you ever forget it,' said Gadney.

Frightened by their intensity, Mills quailed.

When the doctor examined Joe Keedy, he was impressed by the way that the wound had healed. At the same time, however, he advised caution.

'Another week of rest would do you no harm,' he said.

'Yes, it would,' replied Keedy. 'I'd be bored stiff. I need action.'

'If you returned to work, would you be given light duties?'

'I hope not,' said Keedy, putting on the rest of his clothes. 'I've spent weeks sitting around and doing nothing. I feel ready to go back to Scotland Yard to do my job once more. I need something to make my blood race.'

'Then you're a brave man. You obviously thrive on danger.'

'Am I physically fit? That's all I need to know.'

'Yes, you are, Sergeant Keedy – physically and mentally fit.'

'I'm so relieved to hear you say that.'

Ronald Harker had been a doctor for over thirty years and since the war had started he had become accustomed to seeing patients wounded in action. Many of them had nightmares about the experience and hoped for a quieter life. Keedy, by contrast, was desperate to return to a job that was routinely fraught with peril.

'Well,' said Harker, stroking his beard, 'I suppose that there's no point in advising even more rest. I admire your fighting spirit, Sergeant Keedy. Most patients at the hospital have had it knocked out of them.'

'They have my sympathy.'

'As far as I'm concerned, you can be signed off.'

'That's wonderful. Thank you, Doctor.'

'You've been a model patient.'

'I've been a lucky one and I'm very grateful.'

'When exactly are you getting married?'

'It's at the end of the month,' said Keedy, knotting his tie. 'And I can't wait until the day actually comes.'

Stuart Fryer was seated at his desk when there was a tap on the door of his office, and it opened to allow the manager to pop his head in.

'I'm sorry to disturb you,' said Boucher.

'No apology needed, sir,' said Fryer, rising to his feet.

'I just wanted to thank you for the way that you handled Mr Melrose earlier on.'

'It was a joint effort. Between us, we persuaded him to think again.'

'I only deserve a small amount of praise. The bulk of it is yours. After all, it was your idea to get in touch with Mr Melrose in the first place.'

'Luckily, it was a strategy that worked.'

'You were quite masterly,' said Boucher. 'He came in like a lion and went out like a lamb.'

'I can't promise that my charm will work with every customer.'

'It certainly worked on Melrose. I'm hoping that it will work on Inspector Marmion as well.'

'What do you mean, sir?'

'When I ring him to ask for a progress report, I get fobbed off with excuses. I'm sure that he and his detectives are working hard, but he gives me no details of what they've so far discovered.'

'Leave it to me,' volunteered Fryer, 'I'll ring Scotland Yard at once.'

'It's time they gave us crumbs of comfort.'

'I'll get more than that, sir' promised Fryer. 'We deserve the very latest information. Given the situation, it's our right.'

When he was summoned to the commissioner's office, Claude Chatfield braced himself for more disappointing news from the Western Front. Instead, he found Sir Edward Henry beaming.

'Has something happened?' asked Chatfield.

'It certainly has. I've just been speaking to a friend at the War Office.'

'What's the latest news, Sir Edward?'

'There are good tidings for once. The Spring Offensive – or the *Kaiserschlacht* as the Huns call it – is beginning to falter.'

'Not before time, Sir Edward.'

'The fast-moving stormtrooper units are starting to lose momentum. They can't carry enough food and ammunition to sustain them for long, and their armies can't move in supplies and reinforcements fast enough. Ludendorff's gamble is no longer paying off.'

'What about German casualties?'

'Numbers are steadily mounting.'

'Our armies will get the upper hand in due course.'

'I sincerely hope so,' said the commissioner. 'But let's turn to the Home Front. How is Inspector Marmion getting on with that bank robbery?'

'He's working around the clock, Sir Edward, and believes that he has identified the main suspect. When he has more evidence against the fellow, he will arrest him.'

'What about the stolen money?'

'That's still in the hands of the bank robbers – three deserters from the army.'

'Hunt them down at once.'

'We are endeavouring to do so, Sir Edward.'

'We must show no mercy to them,' said the commissioner. 'And the same goes for any police officer who is listening to the nonsense propagated by that infernal union.'

'I don't think that NUPPO has much support here,' said Chatfield.

'There's bound to be some. That's why I'm determined to

eradicate it. Trade unions are like fires. If you don't stamp them out early on, you'll find yourself in the middle of a real blaze. And that, I promise you, will not happen on my watch.'

Marmion was delighted when Keedy walked into his office and even more pleased to be told that his future son-in-law had been given clearance to return to work. He studied Keedy's face.

'You look so much better, Joe. What has my sister-in-law been feeding you?'

'Lily and Raymond have been marvellous hosts.'

'It was kind of them to take you in,' said Marmion, 'but I daresay they'll heave a sigh of relief when you tell them that you're leaving.'

'I can go back to my own flat now. I'm well enough to look after myself. And I'm ready to start work here again tomorrow.'

'That's music to my ears.'

'How has Cliff Burge been performing?'

'He's been excellent – bright, eager, and ready to tackle anything. He has only one defect.'

'What's that?'

'He's not Detective Sergeant Joe Keedy.'

'Could you really bear to have two of me?'

'Frankly, no.' They shared a laugh. 'Now, I need to bring you up to date.'

'Do you still have the same prime suspect?'

'Yes, we do – Stuart Fryer, the deputy manager.'

'How certain are you that he was involved?'

'Seventy or eighty per cent certain. You've come along at just the right time, Joe.'

'I have?'

'Cliff Burge has followed him twice and learnt something interesting both times. The problem is that Fryer has met him. If he sees Cliff, he'll know he's being tailed. You, however,' said Marmion, 'would be ideal. You're a genius at shadowing a suspect and Fryer has never set eyes on you. Are you up for it, Joe?'

'I'll tail him all day, if you wish.'

'That won't be necessary. You can just watch him going to and from his home. One thing you're certain to see is that he'll be smoking a cigarette.'

'Is that significant?'

'It could be. It's up to you to find out.'

'Do you have a file on him, Harv?'

'No,' said Marmion, opening a drawer in his desk, 'I have two. That's how interested we are in this man.' He lifted two files onto the desk. 'Read both of these and you'll see exactly what we've been doing since that bank was robbed.'

'I'm sure you've been as diligent as ever.'

'That's not what Stuart Fryer thinks.'

'The deputy manager?'

'He phoned me earlier on to complain that I was keeping them in the dark about the progress of the investigation. Fryer was excessively polite, mind you.'

'What makes you think he's in league with the bank robbers?'

Marmion smiled. 'It was those cigarettes of his.'

After moving the new bolts below the trapdoor, Fryer let it fall downwards. He then climbed up into the attic and switched the light on. In less than a minute, he was standing outside in the fresh air, surveying the scene below as he enjoyed his cigarette.

CHAPTER EIGHTEEN

As light began to fall, Hillier took his turn outside in the gloom, keeping his eyes peeled for the approach of any vehicle. His friends were inside the main hut. Sidney Mills took advantage of the fact that he was alone with Gadney to press for details about the man who had hired them.

'Can't you at least tell me his name?' he asked.

'No, I can't,' snapped Gadney.

'It's not fair. You and Terry have met him but I've no idea who he is. Since he employed all three of us, I should at least know his name.'

'He's the person who offered us the chance of a better life. Where would you rather be – still in the army, waiting for the Huns to attack, or enjoying some freedom at last before someone hands you a lot of money?'

'But who is this someone, Max?'

'Never you mind.'

'Terry said you met him by accident.'

'That's true.'

'Where was it?'

'Stop pestering me, will you?'

'Then don't leave me in the dark,' pleaded Mills. 'I risked my life to escape from France with you and Terry. I deserve to know something about the man we worked for. At least tell me how you met him in the first place.'

'It was a pub not far from Paddington Station,' said Gadney, relenting. 'Me and Terry popped in to drown our sorrows. We'd just finished our training and were due to be sent off to France. Before that, we had leave with our families. When we'd had a few pints, we boasted that we were going to France to kill Huns for fun. I was too drunk to notice that someone was watching us.'

'Why was he doing that?'

'We were playing darts. Terry was useless but I was really on form. Almost every dart I threw landed where I wanted it to. I won over a quid off Terry. This man drifted over to us and offered to buy us a drink.'

'What was he like?'

'Quiet, well-dressed, spoke proper. He asked us about our army training.'

'Why?'

'I didn't know at the time,' said Gadney, 'but if I was getting free beer from him, I was ready to tell him whatever he wanted. Terry said how much he'd hated all that marching up and down, but I talked about the bits I really enjoyed.'

'Such as?'

'We were taught how to climb up cliffs then get down the other side by using ropes. Terry was hopeless but I was good at it because I had a head for heights. The bit I loved was abseiling down a cliff, the steeper the better. The man's eyes lit up when I told him that.'

'What happened then?'

'You don't need to know,' warned Gadney. 'All I'll say is that

I got on well with this bloke – very well. When he asked if we were ready to go off to war, I told him the truth. We hated the idea because we had friends who'd come back from the Front with legs or arms blown off. Terry's cousin was shot dead when he had his first taste of action. If it meant staying alive, I told him, we'd be ready to desert. That really interested him. He told me how to get in touch with him if we ever did come back here. He said he'd help us to make a lot of money. That gave us the best reason of all to make a run for it.'

'I was terrified by those German shells,' admitted Mills.

'That's why you agreed to join us, Sid.'

'I jumped at the chance.'

'Aren't you glad?'

'Very glad.'

'Then shut up and think of the money you'll get. You made a good decision. Life on a barge will suit you.'

'That's what I'm hoping.'

'Meanwhile, keep your trap shut, and do what I tell you. Agreed?'

'Yes,' said Mills. 'Agreed.'

Delighted to be back at work again, Joe Keedy arrived by police car near Stuart Fryer's home much earlier than needed. The weather was cold, making him turn up the collar of his raincoat and pull down his hat over his forehead. He kept warm by walking briskly around the block. Having been told what time Fryer was likely to emerge from his house, Keedy was back on the corner from which he had a good view of the building. When the deputy manager came out, he kissed his wife before setting off in the direction of the bank. Fryer then stopped briefly to take out a packet of cigarettes, extract one and light it. He strolled on and left a trail of smoke in his wake. Fryer was one of several people in the area setting off for work, so the pavement was cluttered. Keedy kept close enough to see exactly what he did, yet far enough behind him to ensure that the man was unaware he was being followed. When he was close to the bank, Fryer paused to finish his cigarette then tossed it into the gutter before stamping on it.

Moving on to the bank, he exchanged a few words with a couple of colleagues who were waiting to be let into the building. After unlocking the door, the deputy manager slipped inside to disable the burglar alarm then came out to beckon them in. Keedy stayed long enough to watch other employees arriving then he walked back to the place where he had left the police car. He climbed in beside the driver.

'Scotland Yard,' he said.

After such a long time unable to work, he felt a surge of pleasure. He was back.

As they set off on their beat that morning, Alice passed on the good news to her friend.

'Joe is starting work again this morning,' she said.

'That's wonderful!' exclaimed Iris Goodliffe. 'He's been signed off at last.'

'He was getting so bored with being forced to rest. And much as he liked Uncle Raymond and Auntie Lily, he was dying to move back to his flat. Joe hated to feel he was imposing on them.'

'When will you see him again?'

'When he's good and ready, Iris. You know what he's like. Once he's involved in a case, Joe gives it a hundred per cent of his concentration. I need to be patient.'

'Yes, of course.'

'I'm just glad that he's back doing a job that he loves.'

'There is another side to it, though,' said Iris, worriedly.

'Is there?'

'Yes. I'm delighted that he's fit enough to work again but, in your place, I'd be worried that he'll be dealing with that bank robbery.'

'Why?'

'Well, it's also a murder case.'

'That's true.'

'One policeman was stabbed to death, and another was badly injured. I hope that Joe doesn't come face to face with any of the deserters. Look what happened the last time he confronted a desperate criminal,' said Iris. 'The man shot him in the stomach.'

'Joe will never forget that.'

'It must prey on his mind.'

'He knows that his job involves taking risks,' said Alice. 'And while he'd never been shot before, he has been badly injured a couple of times. In the past, he always shrugged it off and waited until he was fit enough to get back to work. Joe is Joe. Nothing will change him.'

Pleased that Keedy had come back to work, Clifford Burge was worried that he himself would now have to return to being a detective constable. Having been so closely involved in the case, he felt sad that he was about to be replaced by a more experienced detective. Marmion took him aside and assured him that he would remain as an acting detective sergeant until the case was concluded, pointing out that Keedy would need time to absorb all the details of the investigation. Instead of replacing Burge, therefore, Keedy would be working alongside him.

The first thing he needed was to discuss the case in depth.

'How much do you know?' asked Burge.

'Much more than I ought to,' said Keedy with a grin. 'If Chat realised that I'd been kept up to date with every development, he would have had a fit. The inspector singled out Neil Paterson, but my money was on Stuart Fryer from the start. Then I wavered a bit before coming back to the deputy manager. He's my prime suspect. Not that you'd know it to look at him,' he went on. 'When I saw him leave his house this morning, he kissed that pretty wife of his and walked off smoking a cigarette.'

'That's exactly what I saw when I followed him. He was so . . . well, normal.'

'He certainly doesn't look capable of hiring three army deserters to rob his bank. But then, we've learnt not to be deceived by appearances. I once arrested a young curate with the kind of face that would make anyone trust him instantly.'

'What was his crime?'

'Getting too close to young female parishioners,' said Keedy. 'He told me that they threw themselves at him, but the women had a very different story. The bishop was horrified when he realised what the man had been up to.'

'At least we can't accuse Fryer of anything like that. He's a devoted family man.'

'Why was he appointed as deputy manager instead of Neil Paterson?'

'Mr Boucher – he's the manager – told us that Fryer was the better man.'

'It put him in a position where he had charge of security.'

'That's a key factor,' said Burge.

They were alone together in Marmion's office. Having read all the evidence so far gathered, Keedy was now hearing about the role that Burge had played. It was clear that his replacement had been eager and industrious. The only thing he lacked were the insights into criminal behaviour that Keedy had gathered over time.

'What was Neil Paterson like?' he asked.

'I suppose the best way to describe him is that he was very Scottish.'

'Wearing a kilt, you mean?'

'No,' said Burge, 'he didn't go to that extent. He just seemed happier in his home country.'

'Did he have an opinion of Stuart Fryer?'

Burge whispered, 'Let's just say that they didn't get on well together.'

Knocking on the door of the manager's office, Fryer let himself in. Boucher was on the telephone. He waved his visitor to a chair and his deputy sat down. The telephone call soon ended.

'That was Inspector Marmion,' said Boucher, replacing the receiver.

'Have they made any progress?'

'Evidence is still being gathered. That's all he would say. He rang to tell me that he has drafted a new man into his team. Detective Sergeant Keedy is highly experienced and has dealt with bank robberies before.'

'It's rather more than a bank robbery to the inspector.'

'Quite so. That friend of his was murdered as the robbers left the bank.'

'Nothing was going to stop those villains. They were ready to kill.'

'They'll be caught sooner or later,' said Boucher. 'But I'm glad that you're here, Stuart. We've had another customer threatening to move an account elsewhere.'

'Is it anyone of consequence?'

'All customers are valued, however much or little they deposit here.'

'Yes, of course, sir.'

'This letter came from Mrs Lambert,' said the manager, holding it up. 'Since she was widowed, she's taken over the management of her late husband's financial affairs.'

'She's a dear old lady. I remember her well.'

'What's the best way we can change her mind?'

'By telling her that the bank robbers have been caught.'

'But they haven't.'

'It's only a matter of time. Assure her that the police are moving in. When I spoke on the telephone to Inspector Marmion yesterday, I got the impression that he was quietly confident. Now that he has eliminated Neil Paterson from his list of suspects, he has switched his attention elsewhere.'

'It's a pity he didn't say to whom his interest has shifted, but it clearly has.'

'I suggest that we leave the inspector to do his job so that we can do ours. My advice is that you send a message to Mrs Lambert, asking if you might call on her at home to talk about her decision. My memory of her is that she is quite frail and needs a walking stick. It would be unwise to ask that she comes here.'

'I'll write the letter immediately,' said Boucher.

'If nobody is available to deliver it by hand, I'll happily act as your postman.'

'Thank you, Stuart. I may well take advantage of that kind offer.'

When his wife showed him the spare bedroom, Raymond Marmion was impressed. The place was immaculately clean and tidy. Keedy had left it in a far better state than he had found it.

'He did all this before he had an early breakfast,' said Lily. 'Then the police car whisked him off. Joe even took the trouble to put clean sheets on the bed.'

'He can stay here whenever he wants.'

'I hope it won't be necessary.'

'Didn't you enjoy his company?' asked Raymond.

'I enjoyed it very much. What pleased me was how easily he fitted into our routine. Joe was no trouble at all to look after.'

'I keep thinking about that leaflet you found.'

'Yes, he's obviously kept in touch with that union.'

'I daresay that he and my brother have had fierce arguments about it. Harvey doesn't think that policemen should even think about joining a union and he's dead against the idea of a strike. It would bring chaos.'

'Would Joe be part of it?'

'I hope not. He might be kicked out of his job if he did that.'

'That would be terrible. He's like Harvey – dedicated to the Metropolitan Police Force.'

'It doesn't stop him wanting a wage rise, Lily.'

'I know, but think what's at stake.'

'Joe is very much aware of that,' said Raymond. 'He'd hate to be sacked. When he's married, he'll have a mortgage to pay and a wife to support.'

'Also, he's such an asset to Scotland Yard.'

'Harvey reckons that Joe was born to be a detective.'

'What else could he possibly do?' asked Lily.

'We know the answer to that, love.'

'Do we?'

'Yes,' said her husband, grinning. 'Look at what he did in here. Joe obviously has a gift. If he gets the sack at Scotland Yard, he can move into housekeeping full-time.'

Despite its shortcomings, they had quickly adapted to their new home. It was safe, isolated and had better basic amenities than they'd enjoyed when they lived in a deep, muddy, rat-infested trench in France. The irony was that they had a large amount of money in their possession, yet they were living like paupers. When all three were together, Mills came up with a suggestion.

'I've been thinking,' he said.

Gadney snorted. 'That's a change.'

'No, listen to me, Max.'

'You've got nothing worth saying.'

'Yes, I have.'

'Let him talk,' said Hillier. 'Sid's entitled to an opinion.'

'Thanks, Terry. What I've been thinking is this,' said Mills. 'When the money is divided into four parts, we'll all get so much. Agreed? But we'd get even more if it was split between three of us.'

'Does that mean you don't want a share?' teased Gadney.

'Of course, I do.'

'Then who gets cut out?'

'He does, Max – the man who hired us. I know he provided all the information we needed to rob that bank and I know he found places for us to hide for a while. But do we really need him now? Why don't we share out the money then go our separate ways?'

'It's because we owe everything to him,' argued Hillier.

'We're the ones who took part in the robbery, Terry.'

'Without his help, we'd be penniless.'

'Instead of which, we've got thousands of pounds and he's about to take the biggest share of it. I mean, it's not fair, is it? We took the risks.'

'It's what was agreed with him,' said Gadney, 'and it's what's going to happen.'

'But you don't even know his name, Max.'

'I don't need to. He's given us a chance of a new life. I'm very grateful to him.'

'So am I,' added Hillier.

'Well, I think we should take the money and run,' insisted Mills. 'You two have got plans and so have I. What's to stop us going off right now and leaving this dump behind?'

'I'll tell you what stops us,' said Gadney, getting to his feet. 'I gave him my word.'

'So what?'

'I intend to keep it. You're right about one thing, though. When we divide the loot between four of us, we get less than if we share it out between three. But he's not the one who is going to miss out,' warned Gadney. 'It's so much easier if it's you.'

'I earned my share!' protested Mills.

'You were our driver, that's all.'

'Don't forget that boat. You and Terry would never have got here without me.'

'But we don't need a boat any more,' hissed Gadney, 'and Terry is a far better driver than you'll ever be. Do you see what I mean? If anyone is to be dropped, it's got to be you.'

'That's unfair!' wailed Mills. 'I faced dangers.'

'All you did was to steal a car, start a fire at that shop, report it to the fire brigade, then wait outside the bank where Terry and I were opening the safe.'

'Where would you have been without me?'

'Using someone much more reliable.'

'I did everything I was told, Max!'

'Yes, and you complained about it every step of the way.'

'We worked together as a team,' insisted Mills before turning to Hillier. 'You tell him, Terry. I was promised a fair share of whatever was stolen from the bank.'

'That's true,' admitted Hillier.

'Okay,' said Gadney, 'we'll stick to what was agreed. You can have your share of the money right now, then piss off out of here. How far do you think you'll get without the car?'

'Max is right,' said Hillier. 'You look like a tramp, Sid. We all do. What's going to happen when you want to buy some food with a new banknote? Someone will call the police at once.'

'I never thought of that,' confessed Mills.

'The money we've been spending was his,' Gadney emphasised. 'When we got back to the country and got in touch with him, he gave us enough to keep us alive. He also provided us with these old clothes and told us exactly where we could hide after the robbery. He's kept his word, Sid. We must keep ours.'

'I never thought of it like that,' said Mills, sullenly.

When he turned away, he was completely off guard. Gadney acted swiftly. Diving at Mills, he got his forearm around the man's neck and applied as much pressure as he could. Caught unawares, all that Mills could do was to cough, splutter and wriggle madly. He was strong, but Gadney was even stronger, muscles developed by his years in the abattoir. He slowly squeezed the life out of Mills, then broke his neck with one violent twist. He let the lifeless body fall to the floor.

Hillier was shaken. 'There was no need for that.'

'Yes, there was,' said Gadney. 'I'd warned him time and again. We'll toss him into that ditch we found. Sid got what he deserved.'

Seated behind his desk, Marmion scratched his head and heaved a sigh of exasperation.

'Nothing,' he admitted. 'Despite all the publicity about the bank robbery, we've heard nothing at all from the public. Someone must have seen something suspicious. Why haven't they come forward?'

'The robbers have gone to ground,' decided Keedy. 'That's why nobody has spotted them. Whoever planned the robbery – Stuart Fryer, probably – arranged for them to disappear completely.'

'Every constabulary is on the alert, Joe.'

'Yes, but their numbers are limited so the search is not as thorough as it should be.'

'That's true, alas.'

'Do we release the names of the suspects?'

'No, that would be telling the three men that we know who they are. It's much better if they feel safe. That way they'll start to make mistakes.'

'When will Fryer try to get in touch with them?'

'Fairly soon, I'd say. He devised the robbery, after all, and he'll want his share of the money.'

'I'll keep watching him. All the evidence points to Fryer.'

'It does, Joe,' said Marmion 'When you watch him leave the bank this evening, take an umbrella. It's pouring with rain out there.'

'Yes, I noticed.'

'By the way, have you left my brother's house yet?'

'I was picked up early this morning,' replied Keedy, 'and

didn't really have time to say goodbye. Raymond and Lily were in the hostel. They'll have had a nice surprise when they got back to the house.'

'Why is that?'

'I left my room spick and span. They've been so good to me.'

'Sending you there was Ellen's idea,' Marmion recalled. 'It obviously worked.'

They spoilt me, Harv. I'll be sleeping in my own flat from now on so there'll be no more mollycoddling. I'll have to fend for myself.'

'It's a very long time since you did that . . . Oh, there is one thing.'

'What is it?'

'When we do catch up with these men,' said Marmion, 'they are certainly not going to give in without a fight.'

'I'm looking forward to it.'

'They are three trained soldiers who have weathered battles at the Front. I'm going to ask Chat if we can have firearms issued.'

'We'll certainly need more than the truncheons Sam Collard and Harry Lee had.'

'How would you feel about handling a gun again?'

'I'd be delighted, Harv.'

'Are you sure? Think of what happened the last time you did it.'

'When I was shot, I learnt a valuable lesson.'

'What is it?'

'If you face a man with a gun,' said Keedy, 'shoot first.'

It was there again. Ellen was safe and sound in the house, yet she became fearful once more. No matter how active she kept herself, she could not shake off the idea that she was not alone. Someone was either inside the house or watching it from a distance. She checked every room in turn yet found no trace of anyone else. Something was causing her unrelenting apprehension. Ellen did her best to keep calm, looking through windows at the empty street outside. But the fear remained, and it sparked a new sense of panic.

Even when she was completely safe, she felt that she was not. If that were the case, she reasoned, she had another demon to combat. Her mind was no longer her guardian. It was cracking up under the pressure of what had happened. She was forced to do something she had never done before. Ellen started to question her sanity.

When Marmion stepped into the superintendent's office, Chatfield looked up hopefully.

'Good news at last?'

'Not exactly, sir. I came to put in a request.'

'What is it?'

'I think we should be issued with firearms,' said Marmion. 'One thing is certain. The men we're after will put up a fight.'

'We have to find them first.'

'Sergeant Keedy has agreed to carry a weapon.'

'Really?' said Chatfield in surprise. 'In view of what happened last time he did so, I'd have thought the idea would arouse unpleasant memories.'

'He's managed to suppress those, sir.'

'That's to Keedy's credit. How is he settling in?'

'Exactly as you'd expect,' said Marmion. 'He arrived here earlier and went through all the files relating to the bank robbery.'

'Does he agree with your judgement about Fryer?'

'He certainly does. In fact, at this very moment, he's waiting outside the bank for the deputy manager to come out. I've told him to follow the man home.'

Hiding from the rain in a shop doorway, Keedy watched the bank carefully. Various people left the building, but Fryer was not among them. Keedy began to suspect that the man had left before he arrived there. His fears were groundless. Fryer eventually came out and locked the door of the bank behind him. He waited for several minutes until a taxi came along. Moving swiftly, he stepped to the edge of the pavement and flagged the vehicle down. As soon as it moved off with its passenger, Keedy stepped out quickly in search of a taxi himself. The thought of losing track of Fryer made him quake with frustration. Just when he was about to give up, he saw an empty taxi came into view. Keedy waved his arms wildly to attract the driver's attention. When the vehicle pulled up at the kerb, he opened the door, leapt in, and yelled his instruction.

'Drive as fast as you can.'

'Where to, sir?' asked the driver.

'We need to catch up with another taxi on this road.'

'I'll do my best, sir,' said the man, bemused. 'Hold tight.'

The taxi accelerated away from the kerb and began to overtake other vehicles. Paddington Station eventually came into sight. Keedy spotted Fryer, standing beside his taxi as he paid the driver through the open window.

'Pull up at the rank,' he ordered.

His driver brought the taxi to a sudden halt. Jumping out of the vehicle, Keedy paid the driver before running into the

303

station. He wondered which train Fryer was about to catch, only to find that his quarry was not going anywhere by rail. The man instead walked past all the platforms and left the station by another exit. Ignoring the rain, he strode quickly through a couple of streets before stopping outside a house.

Keedy watched him ring a bell then wait to be admitted. After a few minutes, he walked to the house and saw that it consisted of three flats, each one of which had its own bell. There was no need for Keedy to wonder whom Fryer was visiting. He had seen enough.

Having first removed the wallet from his coat, they lugged Mills's body to the ditch and tossed it in. Since they had no shovel, Gadney tore off a branch from a tree and used it to sweep earth over the corpse. When it was completely covered, they stared down at the grave. Hillier was troubled.

'We ought to say something, Max.'

'Why?'

'Well, it's his funeral, isn't it?'

'So?'

'A prayer of some sort is only proper.'

'Then I'll give him one,' said Gadney, cupping his hands. 'Sweet dreams, Sid!' he yelled, then turned to Hillier. 'Will that do?'

'In your position,' said Iris Goodlife, 'I'd be trembling all over.'

'Why?' asked Alice.

'It's only weeks to go before your wedding.'

'You don't need to tell me that.'

'I can't believe how calm you are.'

'I'm grateful, that's all,' explained Alice. 'A month ago, I was still wondering if Joe would be fit enough to make it to the church on the date we'd agreed. He was still poorly. Suddenly, things have changed. Joe is not only out of hospital, he's back at work again.'

Having finished their shift, they were just about to leave the building. Iris had been amazed at the calm way that Alice had behaved all day.

'Don't you get any shivers down your spine?'

'Only when I'm not wearing enough warm clothing,' said Alice.

'You're amazing.'

'No, Iris, I'm just relieved that Joe recovered so well. When I heard that he'd been shot, I thought that I'd lost him. Or – even if I hadn't – that I'd be married to an invalid for the rest of my life. Then there was the other fear, of course.'

'What was that?'

'That we could never have children.'

'Yes, you were brooding about that for ages.'

'It's all in the past now,' said Alice, brightly. 'The only thing we have to worry about is that the wedding may be interrupted in some way.'

'Paul?'

'Either him or that friend of his.'

'They'd never dare to spoil your day, Alice.'

'I can't believe that Paul would, but Garth Price is another matter. He's evil, Iris.'

'What are you going to do?'

'I'm leaving it all to Joe. He'll make sure that nobody is allowed to bother us.'

'That's the advantage of marrying a detective.'

'Security is paramount.'

'I'm sure it is, Alice, and I'm so pleased for you. After all the fears and anxiety, you'll marry a handsome man who will turn out to be a wonderful husband.'

When he first heard the report, Marmion was so surprised that he was speechless. Keedy waited until the inspector found his voice again.

'Are you sure that it was Stuart Fryer?' asked Marmion.

'Completely sure.'

'You might have been mistaken in that driving rain.'

'No,' said Keedy. 'I'd never confuse him with anyone else. He's so distinctive.'

'Yes, I suppose that he is.'

'And I followed him before, remember. When I did it this morning, I tailed a man with a nice house and a pretty wife. At least, that's what I thought. This evening, I discovered that he has a dirty secret. It shocked me, Harv.'

'It's amazed me.'

'I should have noticed the name of the street,' said Keedy, 'because I'd have been warned. I knew that it was notorious for the number of brothels there.'

'It was on Sam Collard's beat. He used to joke about that street.'

'What does that make Stuart Fryer?'

'Well,' said Marmion, 'he's certainly not the happily married man that we thought. He's been leading a double life – both as a husband and as the deputy manager of a bank.'

When he returned home that evening, Fryer had treated his wife with extreme tenderness. He listened to what she had been doing all day then talked about what had happened at the bank. They each had a small glass of sherry before dinner and discussed the future.

'We need a holiday,' he said. 'Somewhere in the country.'

She was thrilled. 'That would be lovely, Stuart! Where shall we go?'

'Wherever you wish.'

'Then I'd prefer to go to somewhere near the sea. I'd like a hotel room overlooking it.'

'Leave it to me.' He squeezed her hand. 'It will be like a second honeymoon.'

Since they had buried Mills in a ditch, Terence Hillier had been very subdued. Gadney clearly had no qualms about what he had done and was determined to cheer his friend up. After pouring beer into two mugs, he put the bottle aside and handed Hillier a mug.

'This will put a smile on your face, Terry,' he said.

'Oh, thanks . . .' muttered the other.

'Is that all you have to say?'

'No, it isn't. The truth is that I don't know if I'll be able to drink it. My stomach is queasy enough as it is. What happened has really upset me.'

'I should have killed him days ago,' said Gadney.

'Why?'

'I got fed up with him whining all day. We saved the bastard's rotten life. If he'd stayed in the army, he'd have been shot to pieces by now. But did he give us any thanks? No, he didn't. He simply complained time and again. It got on my nerves.'

'I remember the good things Sid did.'

'What good things?'

'Well, for a start, he got us safely across the Channel in that boat. I was as sick as a dog.'

'Yes,' conceded the other, 'he was a good sailor, but did he have to keep telling us that he was, twenty times a day? Sid got on my nerves.'

'He was one of us, Max.'

'Then why didn't he show some appreciation?'

'It was wrong to toss him in a ditch like a dead animal.'

'What did you expect – a proper funeral with a hearse pulled by four black horses?'

'There's no need to sneer.'

'Sid asked for it. I warned him time and again.'

'His family will want to know what happened to him.'

'He was killed by an enemy – me.'

Hillier was shocked. 'Do you have no sympathy at all for him?'

'None,' boasted Gadney. 'If he had a proper grave, I'd dance on it.'

'You can be cruel sometimes, Max, and I don't like it.'

'I did us both a favour and you'll soon understand why. Because he's no longer here, we'll have a bigger share of the money. We'll also miss that endless whining of his. Look at those card games. Sid never stopped complaining.'

Hillier got up. 'I fancy a stroll.'

'It's raining out there – and it's dark.'

'That won't stop me,' said Hillier, moving to the door. 'I'd just like to be on my own. I need time to think, that's all. I won't be long.'

Keedy and Marmion were still in the latter's office when Clifford Burge joined them. Marmion passed on the news about Stuart Fryer. Burge was astounded.

'Are you sure about this?' he asked, gaping.

'I was less than twenty yards away,' said Keedy. 'I'd swear on the Bible that I saw Stuart Fryer being let into a brothel not far from Paddington Station.'

'But he has that lovely wife.'

'It's something he chooses to forget from time to time,' said Marmion.

'That's dreadful!'

'It's not for us to sit in judgement on his behaviour. We just need to find conclusive evidence that he conceived the idea of a bank robbery and persuaded three men to put his plan into effect.'

'What's our next step?' asked Burge.

'We remain on the alert,' said Marmion. 'Sooner or later, someone will catch a glimpse of them and report to the police. Then we move in.'

'Equipped with firearms,' added Keedy. 'Chat has given us permission.'

'It sounds like a military operation.'

'That's exactly what it is, Cliff.'

'Yes,' said Marmion. 'We need to beat them at their own game. We must be quick, clinical and decisive. We must attack them before they realise what's happening. When the chance finally comes – and it soon will – we go in hard and frighten the daylights out of them.'

Ellen was so grateful that her daughter had promised to call that evening. As soon as she let her into the house, she grasped her tightly.

'Thank goodness you came, Alice!'

'Why? What's the trouble?'

'I feel so unsafe.'

'But you had that new lock put on the front door.' She stood back and held her mother by the shoulders. 'Has something happened?'

'Yes, I think so.'

'What was it? Did Paul or that friend of his come back?'

'No, they didn't.'

'Then what is all the fuss about?'

Tears came into Ellen's eyes. 'I'm afraid.'

'Afraid of what?'

'Myself.'

Seeing her mother's distress, Alice took her by the arm and led her into the living room so that they could sit side by side on the sofa. She held Ellen's hands in her own.

'You're worrying me, Mummy,' she said.

'I just keep feeling this . . . sense of dread.'

'You're perfectly safe. I'm here and Daddy will join us soon.'

'Neither of you can help me.'

'Of course, we can. We love you. We'll do anything you want us to do.'

'That's the trouble,' said Ellen. 'What I really want is reassurance and neither of you can give me that. I'm on my own.'

'Don't be silly. You have a family.'

'I know and I love them dearly but . . .' She took out a handkerchief to dab at her eyes. 'Earlier on today, I came into the house on my own and thought that someone was here. It made me shake in my shoes, Alice. I knew that I was alone, yet I was terrified. Why? This is the safest place in the world for me. What's making it feel so unsafe?'

'You've been brooding about that money being taken, haven't you?'

'It's worse than that, Alice . . . I feel that my mind is playing tricks on me. This war has gone on for so long and brought so many shocks for us. I thought I was strong enough to bear those shocks but I'm not. Suddenly, I feel frail. I just can't cope.'

Ellen burst into tears. Alice was so alarmed that she flung her arms around her mother and pulled her close, grateful that she was there to offer love and support.

Hillier had gone outside for so long that Gadney began to get worried. Opening the door, he saw that it was still raining. His friend would be soaked. He set off in the direction of the ditch where Mills had been tossed in and covered with earth. When got there, he saw a figure standing in the gloom beside the ditch and gazing down at it. Oblivious to the weather, Hillier was in a world of his own.

Gadney walked over to him and grabbed his shoulder to shake it.

'Leave me be!' cried Hillier.

'Come back inside. You're soaked to the skin.'

'Sid deserves someone to care for him.'

'Well,' said Gadney, 'it certainly won't be me. Now let's get back in the hut to dry off.'

Led away, Hillier made no attempt to resist. He had kept vigil long enough.

Marmion and Keedy were just about to leave Scotland Yard when the superintendent came running after them with a map book in his hand. They had never seen him moving so fast.

'Thank goodness I caught you in time,' said Chatfield, gulping for air.

'Why?' asked Marmion.

'We've finally got a sighting of the bank robbers. I've just had a call from the Oxfordshire Constabulary. They were alerted by a man taking his dog for a walk.'

'What did he see?'

'Earlier today, he saw signs of life in some disused huts on a farm.'

'That's no guarantee that it's the men we're after, sir,' said Keedy. 'They could just be vagrants wanting a bed for a few nights.'

'Vagrants don't have cars, Sergeant.'

'What do you mean?'

'Hidden away behind some trees was a vehicle,' Chatfield told them. 'It matches the description of the car that was stolen on the night of the robbery.'

'It's them,' said Marmion with relief. 'What have the police done?'

'They're keeping the place under observation. Aware of the fact that the men have already killed one victim, they're taking no chances.'

'We need to get there as soon as possible,' said Marmion. 'I can't wait to meet the man who murdered Sam Collard. We'll need our firearms, sir.'

'That's all arranged, Inspector.'

'We need something else as well,' said Keedy. 'Cliff Burge has been working on this case from the start. He deserves to be in at the kill.'

'Pick him up from his digs on the way,' said Chatfield.

'Where exactly is this farm?' asked Marmion.

'It's close to Wheatley in Oxfordshire. I've marked the place on the map.' He opened the book to the correct page and pointed to the cross he had made. 'That's where they're holed up.' He handed the book to Marmion. 'Let's go and sort out the weaponry.'

After a cup of tea and the soothing presence of her daughter, Ellen began to feel much better. She tried to explain how the pressure on her had built up steadily.

'It's the war, Alice,' she explained. 'That's what is behind it all. It's so relentless. I'm starting to believe that it will never end.'

'Of course, it will, Mummy.'

'Well, there's no sign of it. Did I tell you about Mrs Churton?'

'Yes, she's a member of your sewing circle.'

'Not any longer. She can't leave the house.'

'Why not?'

'She just can't, Alice. There's a word for it but I've forgotten what it is. It means you're afraid to go out. Mrs Churton was such a lively person, always ready for a chat if you bumped into her when you were shopping. But she's the complete opposite now,' said Ellen. 'She won't even come to the front door. She only feels safe in her house.'

'It's not a house if she can't leave it, Mummy – it's a prison.'

'I feel so sorry for her. And I'm afraid that I might end up like that.'

'That's a silly idea,' said Alice, sternly. 'Don't even think it. In any case, you haven't been locking yourself away here. It's being in the house that unsettles you.'

'That's true.'

'Think of the advantages of living here. You've got wonderful neighbours like Mrs Horton and you're within easy walking distance of the shops. Also,' said Alice, 'it won't be very long before Joe and I move into the area. We'll only be a few stops on the bus away from you.'

'Yes, you will,' agreed Ellen, smiling.

'I'll be popping around regularly to borrow things from you. The only difference is that I'll have a different name then.'

'That's right, Mrs Keedy.' She hugged her daughter. 'Oh, thank God you came here today.'

Clifford Burge was delighted to be picked up by the police car and given a loaded revolver. The bank robbers would finally be arrested but they would certainly put up a fight beforehand. There was a long drive before that happened, but it seemed to pass very quickly. Burge was curious.

'I thought Chat would want to come with us,' he said.

'I'm glad that he didn't,' said Marmion. 'We've seen him in charge of a siege.'

'Yes,' added Keedy. 'The bit he likes is yelling through a megaphone. That's what he did at the siege where I got shot. And before you ask, the answer is no – I don't feel the least bit afraid. This is a different challenge and I'm ready for it.'

'Gadney is their leader. He'll be dangerous.'

'All three of them will resist arrest, Harv. They know what will happen if they don't.'

'What about the money?' asked Burge. 'Will they have it with them?'

'Where else could it be?' said Marmion. 'They're hanging on to it until they can meet up with Fryer and dole it out. Just think of it. They've got at least a hundred thousand pounds but they're unable to spend a single penny of it. We ought to feel sorry for them.'

They laughed together.

* * *

The banknotes were of identical value and held together in bundles. By the light of some candles, they gave themselves the pleasure of counting it out yet again, wondering how long it would be before they could use it. Gadney was practical.

'I think we should divide Sid's share between us,' he suggested.

'That doesn't seem fair, Max.'

'He took part in the robbery so we should get his reward.'

'That's one way of looking at it, I suppose,' said Hillier. 'Do you think our boss will agree?'

'I'll make him agree, Terry.'

Grinning broadly, he picked up two of the bundles and held them against his cheeks. His pleasure was short-lived. Marmion's voice was amplified by the megaphone he was holding.

'This is the police!' he shouted. 'The hut is surrounded by armed officers. Come out now with your hands up.'

Hillier was aghast. 'How the hell did they find us?' he cried.

'Shut up,' snapped Gadney. 'I need to think.'

'You heard him. They're armed.'

'Well, they're not getting me. We earned this money and I'm keeping some of it.'

Stuffing bundles of banknotes inside his coat, Gadney moved to the window and drew back the curtain very slightly. Hillier followed his example and grabbed some of the money. He also pulled out the cosh he had used during the robbery. Gadney snatched up his bayonet.

'When I give the word,' he said, 'make for the car. It's our only chance.'

'I'm ready, Max.'

Backed by a ring of uniformed policemen, the detectives had taken up their positions. Marmion was in front of the hut with the megaphone in his hand. Keedy and Burge were lurking near the car. There was a long, tense silence. Then an owl hooted in the distance. It was almost as if it were a signal for action. The door was flung open and two figures came hurtling out, racing in the direction of the car. Keedy and Burge stepped out bravely to confront them, pointing their guns in readiness. Gadney kept coming, holding his bayonet aloft.

'That's far enough!' yelled Keedy.

'You're not stopping me,' howled Gadney.

'Oh, yes I am.'

Taking careful aim, Keedy shot him in the leg and produced a howl of pain. As he fell to the ground, Gadney dropped his bayonet so that he could put both hands on the wound. Keedy moved in swiftly to arrest him.

Hillier, meanwhile, had veered away from the car and was running at full pelt across the grass. Burge was on his tail at once, blood racing and weapon at the ready. In the event, there was no need to fire. Hillier was so panic-stricken that he darted blindly into the darkness and stumbled into the ditch where they had left Mills. Before he could get up again, he found Burge standing over him with a pointed gun. Resistance was hopeless. He was caught.

'Where's the third man?' demanded Burge.

'He's dead,' said Hillier.

'Who killed him?'

'Max.'

It was hours before dawn, and he was still fast asleep in bed with his wife. When the doorbell rang, he did not even hear it. Then someone started pounding on the door and the two of them woke up with a start. His wife was alarmed.

'Who on earth can that be?' she asked.

'Leave it to me,' he said, climbing out of bed. 'I'll see who it is.'

Grabbing his dressing gown, he pulled it on and went out onto the landing, switching on the light as he did so. As he descended the stairs, he did up his belt, then strode to the door and pulled back the bolt. When he opened the door, he was facing Marmion and Burge.

'Good morning, sir,' said the inspector, politely. 'I'm sorry to disturb you so early but I'm afraid that you are under arrest.'

'What the devil are you talking about?' he demanded.

'Two men were arrested in the place that you found for them. The third bank robber was already dead. The stolen money has been reclaimed.'

'You surely can't suspect me of being involved in the crime?'

'Yes, I can,' said Marmion, holding up a letter. 'These are the instructions you sent to Max Gadney. By way of a signature, you used the first letter of your Christian name.'

'That's a monstrous claim!' howled the man.

'It won't appear quite so monstrous during your trial,' said Marmion, coldly. 'The game is up. You'll have to come with us, Mr Beale.'

Sir Edward Henry was delighted with the news. He told Chatfield to pass on his congratulations to the detectives involved. They had solved the crime and arrested the two remaining robbers.

'Where is Marmion at the moment?' he asked.

'He's at the bank, Sir Edward, apologising to Mr Fryer for suspecting him of being in league with the three deserters. Also, of course, he handed back the stolen money.'

'And you say that Sergeant Keedy was involved as well?'

'He was responsible for catching Gadney, the leader of the robbers.'

'He had no fears of going into a siege situation again, then?'

'He told me that he enjoyed every second of it.'

'I'll make a point of speaking to him in person– and to Marmion and Burge, of course.'

'They'd appreciate that, Sir Edward. After a few false starts, they finally tracked down the man behind the bank robbery. Marmion never gives up. And there's another cause for celebration. The old Sergeant Keedy is back at last.'

'Excellent!' said the commissioner. 'I'll make a full statement to the press. It's high time they gave us some praise.'

'Martin Beale was clever. He devised a plan that seemed to work perfectly at first. It would have made him a rich man. Thanks to our detectives,' said Chatfield, 'he will now join the two surviving deserters in the queue for the gallows.'

'Marmion, Keedy and Burge deserve congratulations. I'll make a point of speaking to each of them in person. Thank heavens we have men of such quality in our ranks! What they achieved in this investigation has lifted my old heart.'

Edward Marston has written well over a hundred books, including some non-fiction. He is best known for his hugely successful Railway Detective series and he also writes the Bow Street Rivals series featuring twin detectives set during the Regency; the Home Front Detective novels set during the First World War; and the Ocean Liner mysteries.

edwardmarston.com